COFF

REED HAWTHORNE SECURITY

DANIELLE PAYS

Copyright © 2023 by Danielle Pays

All rights reserved.

No part of this book may be reproduced in any form or by any electronic or mechanical means, including information storage and retrieval systems, without written permission from the author, except for the use of brief quotations in a book review.

❋ Created with Vellum

Cover Photography: Furious Fotog/Golden Czermak
Cover Designer: Maria @ Steamy Designs
Editor: Wallflower Edits
Proofreading: ReGina Graham

COFF

CHAPTER 1

Logan "Coff" Folger

"Where the hell is he?" Brian shouts.

I debate grabbing the IV and running into the bathroom to avoid him, but there's no point. This confrontation is going to happen sooner or later.

My brother stomps into my hospital room. "What the hell, Logan?"

I sit up taller and wince from the bullet wound. "Nice to see you, too. I'm doing great, by the way."

Brian shakes his head, then runs his hand through his hair as he walks to the window. "Fourteen years, I followed Rocky Manzia. I was this close." He holds up his thumb and forefinger to show how close. "I had someone ready to flip on him. It took years to get him to agree. And he finally did. We were going to take down the entire Manzia operation. Do you have any idea how big it is?"

I sigh. "No, Brian, I don't. Because you chose never to tell me anything about that family in all these years, including the fact that Rocky might show up while we were in the warehouse."

Brian paces back and forth at the foot of my bed, then stops and stares at me. "It's an ongoing FBI investigation. You know I can't share all the details."

"All the details? You knew seeing that man would throw me off, so maybe sharing his presence was a possibility!" I yell.

"Did you do it on purpose?"

Okay, now he's pissing me off. "Yes, you got me. I purposely got shot so Durango would have to shoot Rocky. It was all part of my big plan before we went into the warehouse. I actually knew Rocky's schedule and that he would be there."

My brother sighs and falls into a chair beside my bed. "This is so fucked up." He buries his face in his hands.

Yeah, he's right about that. Never in a million years did I expect to see that man. Or any of the Manzia family ever again. After my heart was ripped out when his daughter chose her criminal father over me, I swore I'd never think about her again.

Unfortunately, I've thought about her a lot. Too much, despite the fact it's been twelve years since I last saw her.

"Tell me about Delaney," I say.

Brian sits up. "No. No, you don't want to know."

I roll my eyes. "I wouldn't ask if I didn't want to know."

He stares at me for a moment. "All right, but you won't like it. She's married."

His words are a gut punch. Married? I mean, she has every right to be, but the idea that she fell in love again hurts. I've tried to put myself out there, but then I end up comparing everyone to her. Well, the version of her I knew twelve years ago. I need to see her again. Maybe I remember some idealized version of her that isn't realistic. If I see her for who she really is, then I can move on. If she stayed with her family, then she must be a part of it by now.

"Did Delaney stick with her father?" I ask.

Brian nods. "She and her husband live at the family mansion."

She never left him. But now I know where I can find her.

"Don't even think about it," Brian says.

I glance up. "What?"

He leans forward. "Don't go see her. Duke lives there, too. He's ruthless and wouldn't think twice about killing you on sight."

Duke, Delaney's brother, wasn't someone I got to know really well, but the idea he's more ruthless than his father seems unlikely.

"You're saying he's worse than Rocky?"

Brian nods. "But don't ask for details. You know I can't give you any. It may be a messed-up investigation now, but it's still ongoing."

"When's the funeral?"

Brian stands up. "No, not an option."

I shrug and instantly regret it as I wince again.

He steps up to the bed. "Don't even think about going to that funeral."

I tilt my head. "Why are you so hell-bent on my staying away? Is there something you aren't telling me?"

My brother sits on the edge of the bed. "Logan, you think getting one glimpse of her is somehow going to help? It won't. And if the brother of the FBI's lead investigator into their family shows up at their home or at Rocky's funeral, well, I doubt you'd make it out alive."

This man has no idea what I'm capable of, despite using my team and me at Reed Hawthorne Security's services numerous times.

He stands up and walks toward the door but stops and turns back. "I'm glad the bullet didn't hit anything serious. I have to get back to work, but I'll come by again tonight."

"Thanks. I'll see you later."

He leaves, and while I'm happy the bullet didn't hit anything, either, it turns out it was more serious than the initial grazing I thought it was. And that bought me an overnight stay in the hospital.

Sitting in this bed has left me a lot of time to think. Too much time. I grab my phone from the table and search. Of course, Rocky is having a large funeral. In two days. As long as I'm sprung from this place tomorrow, I can make it. I know my brother said not to go, but I'll disguise myself. I just need to see her one more time.

I STARE at the phone in the passenger seat, debating if I should answer it. My brother is calling, and I know why. Today is Rocky Manzia's funeral, and he wants to make sure I'm nowhere near it. And since I'm parked at the cemetery, it's a call I don't want to take.

Everyone is still at the church, but I thought I'd come here early and scope it out. I grab my phone and get out of my rental car. I told my boss, Reed, I needed a couple of days of vacation while here in California, and he okayed it. Of course, I'm supposed to be resting and relaxing on a beach, not stalking the former love of my life.

I pull the hood of my sweatshirt up over my head and make my way toward where there is a tent set up. To my surprise, there are already a handful of people here. Instead of walking into the crowd, I find a grave nearby and kneel. As soon as I see her, I'll leave.

Two black sedans pull up near the tent. A woman steps out of one. It's her. I'd know her anywhere. Delaney. Her head stays down as another man comes around and takes her hand.

It's her husband. I looked him up and found some photos of him. Strangely, she doesn't seem to have any social media accounts or photos that I could find.

They walk toward the tent with another man behind them. Duke. His hair is thinning, and he appears much older than what twelve years would do.

Look up, I urge her. She does but not in my direction. And seeing her again causes all those feelings I'd buried deep inside to rise again. I'm angry at her for choosing her father, but I feel for her and the pain she must be going through.

I squeeze my eyes shut. The meds the doctor gave me must be messing with my head. Then I open my eyes and take another look. The woman is still gorgeous, with her long dark hair flowing down her back. Even with a somber expression, she still captivates me. Now I should leave, but something compels me to stay.

Duke glances in my direction, and I turn away. Shit. If he saw me, he might recognize me. Although I'm not the clean-shaven, clean-cut boy of twenty-one that he used to know.

I turn to walk to my car. Between the sounds of the preacher's words, the wind in the trees, or my own thoughts, I don't hear them coming.

A bag is placed over my head, and what feels like a gun is pressed into my side. Fuck, how did he get the jump on me? No one does that.

"Don't say a word." It's Duke.

He shoves me into the backseat of a car. Without my vision, I don't know what I'm up against, so I choose not to reach for the gun strapped to my right ankle or the knife on my left.

The other backseat door opens, and someone gets in. "Let's go," he says, but I don't recognize his voice.

"What's going on?" I ask.

"You ruined everything!" Duke yells.

"You killed Rocky," the other man says.

"No, I didn't."

"But you know who did," Duke says.

I sigh. "I do."

Duke pushes the gun harder into my side. "Tell me."

"Rocky shot me in the shoulder. He was about to shoot me again when my teammate fired."

They don't say anything for a minute.

"Which shoulder?" Duke asks.

"Left."

The other man yanks down my sweatshirt, ripping it to expose the bandages. He pushes the hoodie back on my shoulder, making sure to apply pressure to the wound, which hurts like hell.

"First, we'll take care of you," the man says. "Then we'll hunt down your teammate."

My mind races to find a way out of this that doesn't result in both of these men dying, and I can't come up with one.

The car stops. We haven't gone far. Duke exits and pulls me out.

"Can I at least see?" I ask.

"Nope," the other man says.

I'm pushed forward.

"Walk," the man says.

I take a breath and plan my move. My hands aren't bound, so I can trip and grab my gun, but I have to move fast.

I take one step and fall. Before I have time to rip the bag off my head, I hit the ground. I yank off the bag and realize I'm in a very deep hole. Then I see it's in the shape of a rectangle. Fuck, it's a grave.

Beep. Beep.

Some type of truck is reversing. What the hell? I stand up and can reach just out of the hole, so I dig my shoe in and try to climb out. Before I can push my body up, a truckload of dirt pours in on me, causing me to fall. It's coming too fast. I can't dig my way out, and it grows heavier and heavier.

Why the hell didn't I listen to my brother? I'm sorry, Brian.

CHAPTER 2

Delaney Manzia

I STARE at the man lying in bed, sleeping next to me. I hate him with every fiber of my being. Now that my father is dead, I hope to end this farce of a marriage.

Tying the robe tightly around my waist, I quietly slip out of the room and down the stairs. As expected, my brother, Duke, is in my dad's office.

The room is dark and dusty. It was a place my dad was proud of and spent most of his time. Seeing it now, though, it seems more like a prison. But then, this entire house feels like a prison to me.

As I enter, he doesn't see me. He's facing the window with his phone to his ear.

"His death does not negate our deal," he whispers.

Why is he whispering?

"Give me time to figure this out," he says.

Then he pulls the phone from his ear and stares at it. "Fuck!" He turns around and spots me. "Delaney? You're up early." He sits down.

I sit in a chair across from him. "Is everything okay?" I nod to his phone.

Despite the fact he won't tell me anything that's going on with him, I want him to know I do care for him.

"Everything's fine. What about you?"

"I want to talk to you before Nelson wakes up." I glance behind me to make sure he didn't follow me down.

Duke frowns. "What's going on?"

"I want a divorce."

Duke's brows nearly jump off his forehead. "Delaney, you can't."

I'd hoped for my brother's support, and I'm surprised by his reaction. I lean forward onto the desk. "Why? The only reason I married the man is because Dad basically forced me to. I don't love him, and he certainly doesn't love me."

Duke scratches the back of his neck. "And would you love anyone? You've said many times love is not for you."

He's right. I've said that ever since my heart was broken all those years ago.

"I'd rather be alone than miserable with him."

My brother stands and walks around the desk, leaning on it in front of me. "I'm sorry, but it isn't that simple. Did Dad tell you why he insisted on your marrying Nelson?"

I shake my head. "I asked, but he wouldn't tell me. He simply said it had to be done for the family."

And being the dutiful daughter, I did what my father

wanted. I always did. Since I had no plans to marry anyway, at least, I thought, perhaps my sacrifice would make my father happy. Although, it didn't change how he was toward me. Until the day he died, he was cold and indifferent.

And what did this sham marriage get me? A life trapped here. Any request to travel or have fun was denied. Happy hour with my best friend, Sam? Gone. A weekend getaway to San Francisco? Nope. Even going to a movie by myself? Nada.

Every time I tried to leave, my dad would simply say it was all too dangerous. Well, screw that.

"Look, you deserve to know the truth and why you can't end your marriage." Duke avoids my gaze. "There was a mix up, and Nelson got it in his head that he had to kill me."

I jump up. "What? That's horrible." As much as I want to know more, I don't ask. He wouldn't tell me anyway.

Duke stares past me. "Somehow, Dad worked out a deal with Nelson's uncle, where Nelson became a part of our family, and we became intertwined with his. Part of the deal meant you two had to get married. Nelson's uncle made it clear if you leave or divorce him, the deal is off."

"What are you saying?"

He turns his gaze to mine. "Nelson's family will come after me and you and take everything we have."

By "come after," I know what he means. They will have us killed. Something I've learned in the last twelve years, along with many other things I wish I had known from the beginning. Because then I would have run off into the sunset with Logan instead of being trapped here.

I break from my brother's gaze. Anytime I think of Logan, tears come to my eyes.

Duke stands and walks back behind the desk. "The funeral is at eleven. The three of us will go in one car."

This is his way of dismissing me after dropping the bombshell he just did. I stand and make my way back up to my bedroom. The shower is running when I walk in. Nelson must have woken while I was gone. I sit on the bed, and my mind goes back to the only time I was in love. Logan stayed here, in the pool house. A place I haven't gone into since he left. I tried once, but all I could think about was him, and it was too painful.

I close my eyes. Why does my mind keep going back to him today? But I don't have to think for long. I know why. I truly believed my dad's death meant I would be able to leave Nelson and this home. And while I have no delusions that Logan is still available or would want anything to do with me, somewhere in my mind, I've relied on that fantasy to keep me going. But apparently, I was wrong about my dad being the warden of my prison. It's Duke, Nelson—all of my family.

Nelson steps out of the bathroom wearing a towel. He's not a bad-looking man, but he's cruel. His words cut, and he rarely has anything nice to say.

"Where were you?" he asks.

I stand up and walk toward the bathroom. "I went to talk to my brother."

Nelson grabs my wrist, wrenching me around toward him.

"Nelson, stop. You're hurting me."

He's been cruel, yes, but never physical.

"Never leave this room again without permission," he says as he releases me.

I take a step back. "What?"

He smacks me. Hard. I fall to the ground. He's never struck me. What's going on?

He bends over me. "Never question me. Do you understand?"

I turn to see the hatred in his eyes. But I do not respond.

He straightens up. "I was kind to you because of your father. But now that he's gone, there's no need for that anymore."

Not hitting me was being kind? "What about Duke?" I ask.

He laughs. "Your brother doesn't scare me. Now get ready. We don't want to be late." He smiles and leaves the room.

I slowly get up, still in a bit of shock about Nelson's behavior change. Even though he left the room, I still lock the bathroom door once inside. After a long, hot shower, I discover his slap left a red mark on my face. I don't like to wear much makeup, but I guess today I have to.

I fight back the tears that threaten as I realize my prison is actually worse without my dad here.

"Delaney?" Duke calls.

I walk out of the bathroom to find my brother struggling with his tie.

"Can you help me with this?" he asks, then glances up. "Hey, what happened to your face?"

I undo the knot he made and retie it. "Nelson hit me. He says that he only didn't before because of Dad."

Duke's hands fist by his sides. "Is that so?"

"He said he's not afraid of you." I finish and pat his chest.

He lifts my chin until I meet his gaze. "I'm sorry. I knew he was a bastard, but I didn't realize he would hurt you."

I turn away before I start to cry. I'm not used to such tenderness from my brother. Nor am I used to fighting off tears. It's been an emotional morning. "This has to nullify whatever deal there was. I won't stay married to that monster."

He closes his eyes. "I'm sorry. But that doesn't change anything as far as his family is concerned. Our lives would be in danger."

I let the tears fall. It's one thing to live with a man I don't love but to endure whatever hell he has in store…I don't think I can do it.

"There must be something we can do," I say.

"Duke, there you are. Can I have a word?" Nelson asks from the door.

I walk to the bathroom. "I need to finish getting ready." I close the door. Footsteps make their way down the hall, so I know I'm alone.

Fortunately, makeup can hide a lot. Once I'm presentable, I meet my brother and Nelson downstairs. We go to the church, and I'm still the dutiful daughter saying and doing all the right things. I know he was my father, and I should be sad, but after I learned who he really was, I could no longer view him as my dad. In my mind, the dad I loved died years ago.

We ride in silence from the service to the cemetery. There's already a crowd building. I wonder if the man who shot my dad is here. Duke assured me he'd take care of the situation and not to worry. But I worry. Anyone outside of our family assumes I'm just as much a part of everything. I'm not. My dad never wanted me to know anything. And now Duke is fine having all the control.

We get out of the car, and Nelson takes my hand in his, leading me to the crowd. But I stop. I feel him.

Logan.

I haven't felt him in twelve years, but right now, right here, I feel him. Is it possible he's here? I scan the faces at the tent. No, why would he be here? Although my dad's death did make the news.

Movement to my side catches my attention. A man in a hoodie is walking away from a grave toward a car. The way he walks, could it be him? *Turn around,* I will him. He doesn't.

I sigh. I'm so desperate for any way out of my situation that I'm imagining Logan showing up after twelve years to save me. Now that is a fantasy.

"Stay here," Nelson says.

Duke and Nelson follow the man in the hoodie. Then Duke puts a bag over his head. I glance back at the crowd. No one notices. How can no one notice? Are all these people so used to looking the other way? But why did Duke have a bag on him? Hell, maybe his pockets are full of torture devices.

I glance back as they all get into a car. I step in their direction, hoping to stop them, but someone grabs my wrist.

"Delaney, I'm so sorry," one of my dad's friends says. He drops my wrist, and I nod but don't reply.

Thankfully, no one expects me to speak, as they are all certain I'm grief ridden. Another one of my dad's friends leads me to the front of the crowd, in front of the casket. As I stare down at it, I'm angry. Angry for the position he put me in. For the one that Duke now says I must stay in, being married to Nelson.

My brother and husband return to the crowd quickly. Maybe they just drove the man out of the cemetery. Duke steps up beside me. As much as I want to ask about the guy, I know this is not the place.

We stand there, appearing sad through the rest of the service. Once it's over, we return to the car that brought us here. Now that we have privacy, I turn to both men.

"Who was that?"

Duke shakes his head. "No one."

"Was it Logan?" I haven't said his name in all these years.

Nelson turns to me, rage in his eyes. "Who the fuck is Logan?"

Duke's eyes widen. "The boy you dated while you were in college?"

"Are you in contact with him?" Nelson asks.

Duke glares at him. "Leave her alone." Then he turns his eyes back to me. "It wasn't him. Now drop it."

And I do. But now that I've felt Logan's presence again, I can't stop thinking about him. I want to know if he is near. I need to know.

CHAPTER 3

Logan

"Hurry!" a muffled voice yells.

"Get in there!" someone else yells.

Something touches my back. "I found him!"

The pile of dirt on me slowly becomes lighter and lighter. When it first came in, I thought quickly and hunched over, attempting to keep the area around my nose and throat clear. But the oxygen was running out fast. Thank God they were right here.

"You get that arm, and I'll pull this one," a man says.

They lift me, and within seconds, I'm free of the grave. I'm released on the grass, where I cough and sputter, trying to get in air and get the dust and dirt out.

"What the fuck? I told you not to come here!" Brian yells at me.

"Thanks for the save," I get out between coughs.

"If it weren't for me following your ass, you'd be dead. Dammit, Logan! I knew you'd come despite my order."

I wipe as much of the dirt off as I can. "I saw you near Rocky's grave. But I will admit, I wasn't sure if you followed me or were already here." I continue to cough.

"Take him to the hospital," Brian tells a man.

I'd argue, but my lungs feel like I've inhaled thousands of mini razors, so I probably should get checked out.

"Hey, I'm Larkin. Nice to meet you finally. My car is this way," the man says.

As I follow him to a black sedan, I notice he's covered in dirt. He saved me.

"Thanks," I say.

We both get in the car but before he starts it, he turns and stares at me.

"What?" I ask.

The man chuckles. "The way your brother talks about you. He's clearly very proud of you, but he says you're an idiot, too."

I grin. "That about sums up our relationship."

Larkin starts the car and drives slowly until we are out of the cemetery. "I don't have any siblings, but it must be nice to have that automatic best friend."

"Automatic best friend? I wouldn't call Brian that."

The man shrugs. "I mean, someone you know has your back. That's all."

Larkin pulls up in front of the emergency doors.

"I'm not sure if this is necessary," I say.

He doesn't respond but gets out of the driver's side, so I get out of the car, too. He's right there, leading me inside.

Well, I'm trying to follow. He's walking really fast for some reason.

I'm halfway to the front desk, and darkness threatens at the edges of my eyes. "Larkin? Something isn't right."

I feel myself sway, but I can't stop it.

"Let's get him back here now," someone yells.

I fall against something or someone.

"Hold on, Logan," Larkin says.

Hold on to what? I wonder.

"WE NEED to keep him for a couple of days to rule out infection," a deep voice says.

"But he's out of the woods, right?" Brian asks.

I struggle to open my eyes but can't.

"He's made it this far, which is a good thing. Now we have to wait and see," the deep voice says.

Footsteps move away from my bed. Is Brian leaving? I need my damn eyes to open. I grunt in frustration.

"Logan? Are you awake?" Brian asks, taking my hand in his.

Finally, I'm able to blink. My chest hurts like hell, as does my throat. "What's going on?" I croak out in a voice I don't recognize.

Brian glances past me, and I follow his gaze. The door to my room is open. He stands and closes it, then returns to the chair beside me. "Do you remember being buried alive?"

I shift in the bed, trying to get more comfortable. "I remember a little bit of dirt. I wasn't buried."

Brian frowns but doesn't argue, which tells me this situation is serious. "Well, some of the dirt got into your lungs. You passed out once you arrived here. The doctor had you on a ventilator for a couple of days while your lungs cleared out."

A couple of days? "Has Duke tried coming after me again?"

Brian shakes his head. "I've got someone on the inside who said Nelson is bragging about burying you alive. They didn't see us dig you out."

"Did he know it was me?"

Brian nods.

Huh, I thought I looked different, but Duke must have recognized me and told Nelson who I was. It has been twelve years. An itch in my chest sets off a coughing spell. Brian hands me some water. I take a sip.

"I thought you said my lungs were cleared out."

He shakes his head. "I thought they were supposed to be, but I spoke to the doctor before you woke up. He wants to keep you here for a couple more days. Apparently, you need to cough up as much as you can. There's a chance you could get a nasty infection."

I sit up more. "Then why was I on a ventilator?"

The moment my brother's eyes turn glassy, I know I'm not going to like his answer. "When you collapsed, you stopped breathing."

"Did you call Mom and Dad?"

Brian shakes his head. "I was ordered not to tell anyone about your condition."

I let that sink in. Duke and Nelson really must believe I'm dead. That's a good thing. Maybe I can get close to Delaney now.

"Stop," Brian says.

I turn to him. "What?"

He's shaking his head. "This is not an opportunity to try to see her again. Next time, I won't be there to save your ass."

Save my ass? I don't bother to remind him I'm a trained Navy SEAL. I can save my own ass. Although even I have to admit I needed help in that hole.

My brother stands up. "You will be here for a couple of days, then you are to undergo a psychological evaluation. Once you pass that, you are on the next flight back to New York."

"Psych eval? What are you talking about?"

He glances toward the door again, then back at me. "Logan, you were buried alive. And considering by whom, Reed and I decided you need to talk to someone. If that person clears you, you will be free to go."

I sit up farther, which hurts like hell and causes me to start coughing. Brian waits till I'm done. "What do you mean, *free*? Is this an in-patient thing?"

He frowns. "No. But you will stay at my place after you are discharged here."

I guess I can't complain. I haven't seen his new place since he moved to California. But then again, I don't recall getting an invite. "You're actually going to let me see your place?"

He frowns. "You've been waiting for an invitation to see it?"

I shrug. "You're not exactly a fan of people popping by."

A smile tugs at his lips. "Yeah, well, that was when I was with Sara."

His ex, Sara, was more of a free spirit. And while it seemed good for Brian's stick-up-the-ass, inflexible ways, her open-door policy for friends finally was too much for him.

"Sorry about you two. I really thought she was the one for you."

He laughs. "I did, too, until we lived together. It never would have worked. But the good news is that now I have the space for you."

"Okay, but only for a few days," I say.

"Reed okayed a week."

Of course he did.

My brother bends down and unplugs something, then hands me my phone. "Here, he said he sent you a text."

My phone is covered in some kind of dusty film, and there is dirt all around the edges of the cover. I hold it up. "Wasn't this in my pocket? Why the hell is it so dirty?"

"Your pockets were filled with dirt. It probably happened when we pulled you out of there," he says. "I've got your wallet at my place. It's in pretty bad shape, too."

I guess I am going to my brother's house. At the very least, I need my wallet. After checking my messages and confirming that Reed has indeed given me a week to heal and get my head on straight, as he put it, I set down my phone.

"I have to go to the office. Listen to the doctors and get better," Brian says as he walks to the door.

"I will," I say. And for the most part, I plan to. But maybe not the psychologist. Damn, the last thing I want to do is talk to someone about my feelings.

Feelings. Funny how that word has my mind jumping to thoughts of Delaney. All these years, I've tried not to think about her, but it's been impossible. Anytime I saw a woman with long dark hair, I'd think of her.

After we broke up, I told myself I wasn't in love. It was just infatuation. It had to be. I was young, and although we were together for over six months, most of that time was long distance. It was easy at first to believe I fell in love with the idea of her but not her.

I almost had myself fooled until I met Kate. By all accounts, she was perfect for me. But every time I kissed her, all I could see in my mind was Delaney. Then I started to compare the two, and Kate fell short every time. It became clear what I was doing wasn't fair to Kate. After two months of dating, I ended it. She cried because she thought everything was fine.

It was then that I realized I couldn't do that to another woman. Relationships weren't for me. Not unless I could get Delaney out of my system.

Twelve years later, she's still haunting me. And the reason we couldn't be together, her father, is dead. But what can I do about it? She's married. And she probably forgot about me a long time ago.

I lay there with my thoughts, and while I know I should let it go, I can't. Maybe if I see for myself that she's happy, I could move on. All it would take is one afternoon of watching her, then I could let her go. Now that I'll have free time here, I decide that's what I will do.

With a plan in place, I let myself fall asleep. There's nothing I can do but get better and then get out of here.

CHAPTER 4

Delaney

"Good morning!" Doris says, causing me to jump. "Oh, sorry, dear! I didn't mean to scare you."

I smile. "It's fine. I'm just a bit jumpy today."

Doris grows concerned. "Is everything all right? You're here early."

I stand and stretch. "Yes, everything is fine. I had a little extra time and thought I'd relax in the office. It's always so quiet in here." It's a lie, but Doris doesn't question it.

"Oh, I'll let you relax then." She puts her purse in a desk drawer and her jacket on a chair before leaving the room.

Once a week, I volunteer at the local library, helping with whatever they need. It was my dad's suggestion a few years ago that I should try to connect more with the community. He figured if the community liked me, they would leave our family alone. He was right, for the most part.

I gladly accepted the role because it got me away from that mansion, the business, and most importantly, Nelson. And today, I'm thankful because after tossing and turning all night, only thinking about one thing, I knew I had to search for Logan.

Since I'm not sure if Nelson monitors my phone, I decided searching on the public library computers was my best option. Not that I can't search for whatever or whoever I want to. Who the hell am I kidding? Nelson would probably hit me, take my phone, and go after Logan just to hurt me further.

How the hell did I get into this mess? There was a time I was independent, right? My mind goes to the nights I spent with Logan after we first met. Aside from that week I spent with him, I was following my dad's orders.

I need to focus because there isn't much time before the rest of the library employees arrive. Opening a browser window, I search for Logan Folger. The only hits that come up are of his running times back in high school.

Sighing, I lean back. Then I remember that he mentioned his brother, Brian. Or was it Bryan with a *Y*? I search for both and get a hit.

Brian Folger is a special agent with the FBI working in the San Diego office. FBI? Could that be his brother? There's only one way to find out. I'll need to go in person. If I call and it is his brother, he'll tell Logan.

But how would I explain to Nelson why I was gone all day? Maybe I could ask Samantha to say I'm with her. No. I blow out a breath. I'm not going to visit an FBI agent just because he might be Logan's brother.

Instead, I search Brian's name on various social media sites. Nothing. The more I search and find nothing, the more frustrated I become. Why the hell isn't there anything about him out there?

Voices outside the door alert me that I'm out of time. I copy Brian's work phone number just in case I change my mind and then close the browser.

I turn my attention to the pile of books on my left just as the door to the office opens.

"Delaney? You're early."

I glance up to see Janet staring at me. Janet is a nice but strict woman who must be in her sixties. While she appears elegant, wearing designer clothes, and her hair is always pulled back without one out of place, her damning stare is anything but. Rumor has it, she runs the library because her family funded it many years ago. I don't know if that is true. But I do know her reputation for not tolerating anything she doesn't deem appropriate is well known in our town. And that is the only reason Nelson didn't throw a fit when I said I wanted to volunteer at the library.

My dad was all for it, viewing it as a great way for me to become involved in the community in a way that didn't conflict with his business.

I tried to volunteer with the senior center working on various projects, such as knitting and painting with the residents. It's not the design work I dreamed of, but at least it let me use my creative side. My dad said no, it was not a good use of my time.

What he meant was he wanted me working around someone who would benefit us in some way. And that is how I ended up at the library. Janet's brother is the mayor of our town.

My mission was to make sure Janet and her brother both saw me as an honest woman willing to do anything to help my town. The moment Janet heard my last name, it was clear that wasn't going to happen.

"Have you been in here alone?" Janet asks.

Right there is the problem. She doesn't trust me because of who my father is. Or was. But seriously, what sort of crime does she think I might commit at the library? Perhaps I shoved a book into my purse and plan to run off with it.

"No, I've been in here with her," Doris says, standing behind Janet.

Janet turns to Doris, her hands on her hips. "You weren't just now."

Doris smiles. "Just a quick trip to the bathroom. I'm back now." Doris winks at me, and I bite my lip to hide my smile.

While I want to tell Janet off, I don't. My need to have a place to escape overrides my need to put her in her place.

The woman clearly isn't going to let up. "Why are you here early?" she asks, standing over me.

I put down the pen I'm holding and look up at her. While I can't directly tell her off, I can certainly make her look bad in front of Doris.

"I'm sorry. It's just I haven't been able to sleep since my

dad was killed. I can't believe he's gone." I glance away and sniffle.

Doris is by my side in an instant, rubbing my shoulders. "You poor thing. I can't imagine. And what your mother must be going through, too."

My mother has been in her bedroom since my dad died and skipped out on attending his funeral. For one moment, I thought about asking her for advice on how to get out of my marriage to Nelson. But she stayed with my dad all these years, and I can't say I saw any affection between them. Did she ever love him? Was she trapped like I am? It's a conversation I'm not ready to have.

"She's struggling," I tell Doris.

Janet hangs her coat on a rack near the door. "Enough chitchat. We have a delivery today, and I need you two to get them entered into the system and out on the shelves." She walks to the door. "Try to have that done before you leave, please." Then she walks out of the office.

This isn't the type of work I volunteered for, but as long as it keeps me busy, I'll do it. And if I can spend an entire Saturday here, even better. Nelson is sometimes home on the weekends. In the past, we simply stayed out of each other's way, but after the other night, I'm not so sure he's going to uphold his end of the bargain.

"Well, it sounds like we have a full day ahead. Do you mind helping me with the delivery?" Doris asks. She is well aware of what I volunteered to do here.

"Of course not."

She smiles as Janet pops her head into the office. "Delaney, your husband is here. Please deal with it quietly."

By "deal with it," she means get him out of here.

I step out and try to view Nelson objectively. He's an intimidating man to anyone he meets. He's six four and all muscle. Tattoos peek out of his suit jacket, hinting at the sleeves he has underneath. Once upon a time, I found him physically attractive. It was the only way I got through the marriage and our so-called honeymoon. But as those dark eyes pierce me when I step into his view, I'm reminded why I don't want to be around him now.

"Nelson, what are you doing here?" I ask.

He glares at me. "Why did you leave the house early?"

I frown. "I came here to volunteer like I usually do on Saturdays."

He steps closer, and I wince. His lip curls up. Dammit, he knows I'm scared of him.

"You didn't answer my question. Why did you leave earlier than normal? Did you meet someone?"

The man doesn't want me, but he doesn't want anyone else to have me, either. I'm property to him. "No, I came straight here. I couldn't sleep, so I thought I would make use of my time here."

He grips my shoulder hard.

"Nelson, stop. You're hurting me."

He grips harder. "Prove to me that you came straight here."

I nod, and he lets go. Doris walks out of the office. As much as I don't want to advertise my marital problems, Nelson isn't giving me a choice.

"Doris, can you check the time I punched in the door code?"

Doris frowns, then glances at Nelson, then at me. "Okay. Let me pull that up." She walks to the computer on the counter and types something in.

"It was seven eighteen this morning."

I turn back to Nelson, biting back a smile, as that would only make him angrier.

He stares at me for a beat. "All right. But I want you home by two. Got it?"

"Yes," I say. While I want to tell him I need to stay longer, I can tell by his demeanor this is not the time to disagree with him.

When I turn back, I avoid Doris's gaze. This isn't something I want to share with anyone, much less here, my one escape.

"Delaney, I know it's none of my business, but if you ever need help to get away from that man, I'm here for you."

Doris never asks me about my family or marriage. Something I've always appreciated. So, this offer comes as a surprise.

"Get away?" If only I could, I would have long ago.

She sighs. "Look, you don't have to say anything, but I've known men like him. They are controlling, and I'd put money on him being the cause of that bruise on your cheek."

My hand goes to my cheek. Since I rushed out this morning, I forgot to cover it with makeup. Something I regretted the moment I saw myself in the mirror here. All I want is to forget he slapped me and hope like hell it doesn't happen again. But I know it will.

"Thank you. I'll keep that in mind," I tell her. I'm not going to tell her she's wrong about my husband. She's not. And hell, I would love help getting away. But he'd kill Duke, then hunt me down.

No, I need to find another way out of this mess.

And I want to know why I sensed Logan here. After the search turned up nothing, I think maybe I should visit Brian Folger at the FBI. Monday morning, I'll find an excuse to leave the office. If Logan is in town, his brother will know.

CHAPTER 5

Logan

"Don't forget to take your antibiotics," my brother says as he puts on his jacket. "I'll be back after five with dinner. Any requests?"

I sit up and cough. Apparently, this cough might stick around for a while. "Anything without avocado would be great."

Brian laughs. "I'll try."

That's one thing that drives me nuts about this place. Or maybe it's just what Brian is bringing home, but I swear every meal here includes avocado. I like a lot of things, but avocado is not on that list.

He grabs his keys, then turns back. "Are you sure you're okay getting to your appointment?"

I laugh. "Yes, I'm a grown man. I'll be fine."

With a nod, he turns. "All right. See you later."

Once he's gone, I call a cab to take me to the closest car rental place. I need my own car for the plans I have. Plans I cannot share with my brother. After I was discharged from the hospital yesterday, I asked him to take me to a car rental place. He refused. According to him, I need to rest, see the psychologist, and then get more rest. That's how he envisions my week here with him.

Sorry, Brian, but sitting around doing nothing won't work for me. During my downtime in the hospital, I asked Trip, our tech guy who can find anything for us, to find what he could on Delaney Manzia.

All these years later, she lives in the same house and works at the same construction company. Part of me wonders if she is happy despite never pursuing the design work she really wanted to do. And that part of me needs to see her, to see for myself if she's happy.

And if she's not? Well, hell, I haven't thought that far ahead yet. I can't. She might not even be the same woman I knew twelve years ago. Likely she isn't. For all I know, she has kids with this husband of hers. That's not something I will get in the middle of, no matter how much I miss her.

The cab I called pulls up to the curb, and I get in. After I tell him where to go, I sit back. What exactly am I hoping to get out of watching Delaney? At first, I told myself closure. I thought seeing her at the funeral would be enough. But it wasn't. It was like getting a taste of catnip, and now I need more.

Fuck, I'm not some damn cat. No, but I'm something when it comes to her.

I get a rental car and make it to my appointment just in

time. My brother will be happy. I know he'll check to make sure I'm here.

As I sit in the waiting room, I take in the few magazines on the table. One about home improvement and another about cars. My eyes move to the television that's on and tuned to a home renovation show. Maybe handy people are more likely to see a psychologist?

"Logan Folger?" An older woman is standing outside an open door.

I stand up. "Yes."

"Follow me."

She leads me to a small room with a desk, two chairs, and a couch. "Sit wherever you're most comfortable."

Is this a test? I stare at the two chairs and the couch. Finally, I choose to sit on the couch. She closes the door and sits in the chair on the other side of the desk.

"What brings you in today?" she asks.

"My brother." It's honest.

She claps her hands in front of her on the desk, then leans forward. "What is going on with him?"

I stare for a moment, then realize she misunderstood. "No, my brother insisted I see you."

She waits, and I don't say more. Then she responds. "Why?"

I cross one leg over the other knee. "Something happened to me, and he thinks I need to talk to someone about it."

Again, she waits. Silence doesn't seem to faze her, since she doesn't rush to fill it.

"And I told him I would so he would stop bothering me."

"What happened to you?"

As much as I don't want to discuss it, I have to talk about something, so I tell her about getting tossed into the grave and then the dirt pouring in.

"That must have been scary," she says.

I shrug. "I've been in worse situations."

She leans back in the chair. "You have?"

I nod.

"Military?" she asks.

I nod again.

"Do you want to talk about what happened there?"

I laugh. "Sorry, it's just not something most people would understand."

"I would."

I uncross my legs. "You serve?"

She nods. "Eight years until I lost my leg. Now I work with others in the military."

"Ah, I bet my brother knew that but didn't tell me."

"You know now. Tell me, are you having nightmares? Reliving being buried alive?"

Leaning forward, I meet her gaze. For two seconds, I debate bringing this up, but then I realize, why not? She's objective and probably the only person I can talk to about it. "No, nothing like that. What's bothering me is something else. Something I'm not sure how to deal with."

She waits for me to say what it is.

"A long time ago, I dated someone. Well, more than dated. I fell in love with her. But I had to leave, and I asked her to come with me. She said no. We were over before we could really begin."

I stand up and walk to the only window in the room. "I've never forgotten about her. I've tried, and I can't. Recently, I saw her again."

"How did you feel when you saw her?"

I turn to her. "Hurt, happy, angry, confused. A lot of things. She's married. I've tried to date, but I can't stop comparing everyone to her. It's driving me crazy."

"Now that she's married, can you let her go?"

I should be able to, but that's just it; I can't. And it's worse now. "No. Seeing her brought back all those old feelings. I don't know how to let them go."

"Maybe letting them go isn't the solution. Maybe you need to learn to live with them."

I blink a few times. Learn to live with them? Well, that's shit advice. "No. I don't want to. I've tried for twelve years. It doesn't work."

Her eyes widen. "Twelve years? That is a long time, but when it comes to love, you don't always get a choice of who you love or when."

Great, she sounds like a damn fortune cookie. I sit back on the couch.

"It sounds like seeing her again triggered you. And discovering she is married... Sometimes it helps to surround yourself with friends at times like these. Instead of focusing on her, focus on others."

Although my plans for the rest of the day might paint a different picture, I really have tried to focus on anything else. I spoke with Piper, Davenport, and Ozzie from the hospital. Reed checked in on me, too. Thunder, Lightning, and Axel are on assignment; otherwise, they would be calling, as well.

"Based on that frown, I'm guessing you've tried that already. Let me ask you this: have you thought about her more since you were buried alive?"

"Yes." I leave out that I was buried by her brother and another man, and it was after crashing her dad's funeral.

She smiles. "You went through a traumatic event. And instead of dealing with the fact you were almost killed, your mind is focusing on a different traumatic event. Maybe one that you have already been dealing with. Something your brain believes it can handle."

I blink. No, that's not it at all, but based on the knowing look on her face, she's convinced it is.

"I'm supposed to see you each day for the next four days," she says.

"You are?" I guess I hadn't asked how many sessions Brian had scheduled.

"Yes, and now that we know you are displacing your fears, we can discuss more tomorrow about how to notice whenever you do that and what to do instead."

Yeah, I'm not doing that.

"I think if you make enough progress in the next couple of days, I should be able to sign off on your back-to-work plans."

"Back-to-work plans?"

She tilts her head. "Didn't your boss," she turns to her computer and stares at the screen for a moment, "Reed, tell you?"

I shake my head, not sure I want to hear whatever she's about to say.

"He said you are to keep seeing me until I find you fit to go back to work."

That doesn't sound like Reed. But it does sound like my brother. And I'm guessing he didn't tell me about this because he knows I'll be pissed. But since I want her to sign the papers, I simply smile. "I wasn't aware."

She stands. "Don't worry about it. I think we're on the right track. I'll see you tomorrow at the same time."

I guess that's our time. I stand and head straight to my brother's office. He's not expecting me, nor will he be expecting me to accuse him of impersonating Reed to my therapist. But I know that's what happened.

I step off the elevator onto his floor as a woman steps on. She's staring down at her phone, but it hits me instantly. I spin to face her.

"Delaney?"

She glances up from her phone with wide eyes. "Logan?"

I'm frozen, staring at her. She looks the same, and my body wants to pull her into my arms like no time has passed. Before we say another word, the elevator doors close. I slam the button to call the elevator back, but it's too late. Knowing she is likely going to the lobby, I find the stairs and run down them. But when I get to the lobby, she isn't there. Maybe she went back up. To avoid missing her again, I wait in the lobby, but after ten minutes, I must admit to myself that she's not coming back.

She saw me and ran. Or maybe her husband was

waiting for her and she left with him. Wait, did I want her to wait for me? I squeeze my eyes shut, trying to push out the thoughts before I drive myself crazy.

I get back in the elevator and head to my brother's floor. When the elevator doors open, I step out and look around. The FBI uses this entire floor. Why was Delaney meeting with someone here?

It's none of my business. I take a deep breath and enter the small lobby area, then ask for Brian. He steps into the lobby.

"Logan, I'm surprised to see you. I'm afraid I don't have time—"

I hold up my hand. "Time isn't necessary. I know you impersonated Reed to get those appointments with the psychologist. I came here to yell at you about it, but now I've run out of steam. Just don't do it again."

I spin on my heel and leave. Once outside, I soak up the Californian sun while I debate my next step. Without any reason not to go, I drive to where Delaney should be working.

The address for Manzia Construction had changed from all those years ago, and when I pull up, I see why. This building is much larger and nicer. Looks like business has been good for them over the years.

I park across the street and stare at the building. Is she in there, or did she take the day off? It's not like I can walk in and risk Delaney or Duke seeing me.

Before I figure out my plan, I spot her. Delaney walks out of the building with another woman. The other woman is talking animatedly while Delaney simply nods.

Her usual sunny disposition is missing. There's a sadness to her. It could be she's still grieving her father. Just because I hated the guy, I need to remember she loved him.

She stops walking and glances around. Does she sense I'm watching her? Her friend puts her hand on her arm. Delaney nods, then they walk down the block and into a coffee shop. Several people go in and out, indicating it's busy inside. I put on a hat and my sunglasses, then get out of the car. As I walk to the door of the coffee shop, I spot Delaney with her back to the window, sitting at a table for two.

Perfect.

I step inside and spot an empty chair near their table. I grab it and sit down. Many people are sitting in here without drinks, presumably waiting for their coffee to be ready, so hopefully, I blend in.

"What's wrong?" the other woman asks her. "Why are you looking around? Are you expecting someone?"

Delaney sighs. "I saw him."

"Him who?"

"*Him*," Delaney draws out.

"Oh shit, you saw Logan?"

Wait, if she knows from just that, then that means Delaney has likely mentioned me over the years. Maybe I'm not alone in this obsession. But my good mood quickly fades as I realize she saw me. Did she see me parked across the street?

"I swear I felt him at my dad's funeral, and then today, I saw him as I stepped onto an elevator."

Relief washes over me. She has no idea I'm here now.

The other woman takes a deep breath. "Oh, Delaney, I think your mind is playing tricks on you. Remember, he lives in Virginia."

Delaney leans back. "Yeah, maybe. But let's drop it. I have something else we need to talk about."

"Okay, what's this other thing?" the other woman asks.

Delaney is silent for a moment, and I wonder if she's whispering, but then she speaks. "Sam, do not tell anyone."

Wait, that's Sam? As in her best friend, Samantha, who was at the bar with her the night we met. It's been years, but that woman doesn't look the same. Regardless, she might recognize me, so I move so my back is to both of them.

"Nelson hit me."

When I hear her words, I clench my fists. To hear that he laid a hand on her, I want to pummel the guy.

"What?" Samantha asks.

"The morning of my dad's funeral. He said now that my dad was gone, he can hit me. I fucking hate him so much."

Then why are you married to him?

"Divorce him. Then move out of that house. Delaney, you always told me you did what you did to please your dad. But he's gone. It's time to start living for you," the woman says.

Delaney laughs. "Oh, I wish it was that simple."

"It is!"

"Samantha!" a barista calls out.

I turn my head a little and spot the woman walking up to the counter to grab two coffees. As much as I want to steal a glance at Delaney, I don't dare.

"Here," the woman says to Delaney as she sits down. "Now, I know a great divorce attorney. Did you sign a prenup?"

"Samantha, if I divorce him, he will kill my brother."

"Kill Duke? Are you serious? He never mentioned anything about that."

There is silence for a moment.

"Why would Duke tell you?" Delaney asks.

"You know how he complains about things. Figure that's something he would have complained about to you when I was around." She takes a sip of her drink. "Oh wait, does Duke know? Maybe he can take out Nelson first."

Actually, that's not a bad idea. Maybe someone needs to clue Duke in.

"Not an option. This isn't just about Nelson. It has to do with two families coming together. It's why I married him in the first place. And now, I'm trapped." Delaney sniffles.

My first instinct is to comfort her, but I remain still.

"Don't think that way. We'll come up with a plan. Okay?" Samantha says.

"I love your optimism, but I'm afraid there are no options here. I'm just thankful he doesn't want to have sex with me. At least I don't have to endure that."

"That is good, but it sucks that you are missing out on enjoying your prime years without someone you want to be with," Sam says. "Oh! I have an idea."

"No. I know you and your ideas. No."

"No, you'll love this one. I know how we are going to end your marriage."

Delaney stands directly behind me. "No. I'm not risking Duke's life. I've got to get back to work. Walk with me?"

Samantha's chair squeaks. "Fine. But when you're ready, just know I have a plan."

I stare down at the table as they walk past. Once I'm back in my car, her words go through my head over and over. She hates her husband and has a sexless marriage. She feels trapped. Well, fuck. I hated the idea she could just move on from me, but now, knowing she's trapped and miserable, I don't think I can walk away.

CHAPTER 6

Delaney

I LOVE SAMANTHA, but when she thinks she has a great plan, well, she doesn't. I finally broke down and asked her what she was thinking as we walked back to the office.

Her grand idea was to figure out who hates Nelson and pit the two against each other. Basically, she's suggesting murder but keeping our hands clean. I told her she listens to too many true crime podcasts and said goodbye.

Now my mind is racing. If Nelson wants to divorce me, then that would solve our problems. How can I convince him to do that? If he fell in love with someone else, perhaps? But I don't think he's capable of love. No, I need another way.

Speak of the devil, Nelson walks in the front door wearing a fitted suit. The first time I saw him, I was a teenager, and I remember thinking he was hot. That was before I got to know him. Now all I notice is the strong angles of his face and how he's always angry.

"I have an important delivery coming in tomorrow, and I need to make sure the Miller warehouse is clear," he says.

No, hello, how are you? Not that I care to have small talk with the man, but he's never even tried to make this a real marriage.

Duke once told me all the threats and the marriage were all with one goal in mind: Nelson wanted access to our resources for himself. Now that I know Nelson agreed to the marriage in exchange for not killing Duke, I have to agree. It certainly wasn't me he was after.

And boy, did he get access. He lives in our house and works for our company. The only thing he doesn't have access to is the safe. Only my dad and Duke ever knew that combination.

"I'll make sure no one uses the warehouse tomorrow," I assure him. "Do you need anything else?"

He shakes his head.

"What is being delivered?" I ask before I think it through.

His gaze whips to mine. I never ask for details. As soon as we married, he made it clear to never ask questions.

"Sorry, I didn't mean to ask."

His hand strikes my cheek before I see it coming. "It's none of your business."

Shit, that hurt. He struck the same place as before but much harder this time. No doubt it will leave an obvious mark. I turn away, holding my cheek, hoping he will leave.

"Look at me when I'm talking to you!" he shouts.

Slowly I turn back to him, but before he can hit me again, glass shatters outside. Then a car alarm goes off.

"My car!" he yells as he runs outside.

I breathe a sigh of relief as I walk to the window to see what's going on. Nelson's precious Porsche has a shattered back window, and the alarm is blaring. Movement to the left catches my eye. A man in a hat is walking away from the area. The hairs on the back of my neck go up. The way he moves is familiar. And then I feel him again.

Logan.

Nelson is cursing as he gets into his car and drives off. This is my chance to find out if that is Logan. I leave the office and walk in the direction the man went. As I approach the next block, I spot him ducking into a car. He pulls out from the road before I can get close.

My head falls back as I look at the sky. Am I losing my mind, or do I just really want it to be Logan? If he is back and watching me, could he save me? Getting lost in fantasy land is the last thing I have time for now. He can't save me without putting Duke at risk. No, I got myself into this mess, and I will get myself out.

When I get back into the office, my phone is ringing. "Hello?"

"I got the perfect plan!" Samantha says.

"What?" I ask.

"Become a nun. That gets you out of the marriage and that house."

I fall back into my chair and rub my eyes with my free hand. "Samantha, I'm not Catholic or a virgin or whatever their requirements are."

Even if I were, there is no way Nelson would let me run off and join some church like that. I know too much now. I'd be a liability. Maybe that's why I want Logan to be here. When we were together, I had no idea what my family did. I wish that was still the case.

"Well, look into it. I think it would really work," she says.

"Okay, I will." No, I won't. "I have to go. Talk to you later." I end the call before she comes up with more ideas like that one.

Duke walks in, scowling. Usually, I wouldn't talk to him when he's in a mood, but today I need to.

"Duke, Nelson requested that the Miller warehouse be empty tomorrow for some delivery. Do you know about it?"

Duke spins on his heel to face me. "Miller? No, I don't. That's our biggest space. Did he tell you what's coming in?"

My hand goes to my cheek. "No, when I asked, he smacked me."

Duke winces. "Fuck, Delaney. I'll make him pay for all of this; I swear."

I nod. "Trust me, I understand. I want him out of our lives, but I can't think of a way."

Duke steps closer. "Listen to me. Don't do anything. I know you want him gone, but it isn't that easy. Even if something happened to him, his brother or his uncle would step in, and you might not believe this, but they're worse. Leave it to me, all right?"

I nod to appease my brother. I know despite all the shit that has been put on him, he really does look out for me.

Right now, the last thing he needs to worry about is his sister. If I do come up with anything, I'll leave him in the dark. For his sake.

"If anyone calls, take a message, would you?" Duke asks as he walks backward toward his office.

Once my dad passed away, Duke took over the main office and, with it, all the business dealings. Despite working the front desk and the finances, I still don't know everything my dad was involved in. Based on how smooth everything seems to appear to be running, I'm guessing Duke did.

I sit up front until the end of the day, but my mind is on anything but work. No, I need to know if Logan is back in town. He seems to be where I am, so perhaps he's watching me. If that's true, then it might not be so hard to meet up with him.

When I leave the office, I bypass my car and instead walk toward the pier. It's not too far, and once I'm there, I stare out at the ocean.

The hairs on the back of my neck stand up. He's near; I can feel him. I turn around and take in everyone I can see. Of course, he'd keep himself out of sight.

"I know you're here!" I shout. "Show yourself."

One couple furrows their brows as they walk by. Another man picks up his pace. But Logan doesn't emerge from the shadows.

"Logan!" I shout in case he has any doubt I'm referring to him.

But he doesn't appear from thin air. I turn back to the ocean, wondering if I'm losing my mind. Hell, maybe

Nelson has someone following me. If that's true and I said another man's name, tonight might be hell.

"Don't turn or acknowledge me. Keep your eyes on the ocean," a deep voice says near me. A voice I'll always recognize.

"Logan," I say quietly. My heart is pounding, and I want to turn and not only look at him but touch him to make sure he's real.

"Yes," he confirmed.

My eyes well with tears at being this close to him once again. So many emotions I never dealt with because soon after he left, I was forced to marry Nelson.

"Why are you here?" I ask.

"I'm visiting my brother, and I couldn't stop myself from tracking you down."

I let the tears fall down my cheeks as his words sink in. He couldn't stop himself. All these years and he still feels the pull I feel. Maybe there is hope for us.

"Why can't I acknowledge you?"

"You're married," he says, his tone harsh.

"Not by choice," I say.

"What the hell does that mean?" he asks.

I take a deep breath and decide to give him the short version. "Nelson's family was going to kill my brother. My dad somehow worked out a deal where if I married Nelson, it would solve whatever the issue was, and we would be one big happy family."

He's silent for a moment, and I dare a quick glance. He's wearing a hoodie and is turned away from me so I can't see his face.

"You're father forced you to marry?"

"Yes." My voice quivers, and I swallow back the sobs that want to follow. Everything about that day is something I've tried to forget. The only reason I didn't fight it harder was that I'd given up on love. Logan's leaving hurt me deeply. I should be angry with him, but after all these years of missing him, I can't be.

"Your dad is gone. Divorce him now."

I laugh. "I thought I could, but my brother informed me the threat is still there, which means I have to stay married to that monster forever."

His shoes shuffle on the wooden pier, and in my peripheral, I note he is facing me now.

"Monster? Does he hit you often?"

I hide my gasp. "How did you know?"

"I was at your office when he slapped you. It took everything not to march in and hit him back."

I turn and stare into his eyes. The deep-blue eyes that I've only seen in my dreams for the past twelve years. His gaze is full of concern, and I wish I could go back in time and make different choices. I'd pick him every time. Knowing I chose the wrong path tears me up. Tears fall, and I don't try to stop them.

His gaze is a mix of concern and anger. Then he turns back to the water. "We shouldn't be seen together." Then he takes a few steps away.

"Wait!" I say.

He stops but keeps his back to me.

"Will I see you again?"

His head drops, but he doesn't turn around. "Take care

of yourself, Delaney." And then, he walks several blocks and turns out of sight.

Take care? What the hell? Why has he been following me if he's just going to leave again? He can't deny the emotions he's feeling. They were there in his eyes.

I slump against the pier. But why would he want to take on my mess? One wrong move and he could be killed. He probably followed me long enough to see I have too much baggage.

Why did I let myself get my hopes up that maybe somehow he was here to save me? Oh yeah, because I have no idea how to save myself. But I better figure it out fast because relying on the men in my life has only given me grief.

CHAPTER 7

Logan

Knowing Delaney's husband hurts her is all I can think about. I had to force myself to get in my car and drive away before I did something foolish, like whisking her away somewhere. No, she needs to get away from that situation, but there needs to be a plan in place. Otherwise, her husband or brother will search for her.

Imagining Nelson and what he might have done filled me with rage yesterday. I tried to go for a run, but my lungs said no. I ended up getting a guest pass at my brother's gym and lifting weights for an hour.

It helped until this morning when I woke up with all of it front and center in my mind again. When I saw Nelson slap her, I threw the rock at his car to stop him from going further. But knowing he'll do it again. I have to find a way to stop him.

And that's why I'm following Nelson today. After watching Delaney for two days, I've discovered her movement is limited. She works, gets coffee, goes home. Three places. That's it.

Well, except for her visit to the FBI offices.

It's like she's in a prison with little freedom. It's hard to make sense of that and the Delaney I knew. She was spontaneous and said what was on her mind. Her dad did this to her. The dad she wasn't willing to leave behind.

I shake those thoughts from my head. Right now, I need to stay focused. But as I wait for Nelson to leave the restaurant, my mind keeps drifting back to Delaney. When we talked all those years ago about her college courses, she was upset that she couldn't pursue what she wanted. She loved design, but her dad insisted she pursue business. Whenever her dad asked something of her, she did it without question. But now that he's gone, can't she see she is free? I don't know why Duke has her believing he's in danger if she divorces. One thing I know about Duke Manzia is he can take care of himself.

My phone rings. Brian. If I don't answer it, he'll keep calling.

"Hello?"

"Where are you? Your appointment ended hours ago, and you're not at my place."

I check the time, and it's barely after lunch. "Are you home?"

"No."

I scratch my forehead. "Then how do you know I'm not?"

He laughs. "How do you think?"

Of course. I should have known. I lean my head back. "Security cameras."

"Where the hell are you?"

Now, I could tell him the truth, but I know that will get me a lecture or two. Instead, I lie. Not something I usually do with my brother. "I decided to walk around and clear my head." Well, I did walk around, so it's not entirely untrue.

"Uh-huh." He's not buying my bullshit. "You aren't too far from the therapist's office, then? Give me the cross streets, and I'll pick you up."

And he called me on it.

"No need. I rented a car. I can drive myself back."

"Fuck, Logan, you went to find her, didn't you?" He doesn't need to say who he's referring to; we both know. "Don't deny it," he says.

Nelson walks out of the restaurant and gets into his car. The window is still out, but now he has clear plastic taped up over the gaping hole. I turn the phone on speaker and toss it into the passenger seat so I can follow this man wherever he goes.

"Logan, you're losing your touch."

I laugh to myself. "Why do you say that?"

Nelson pulls out onto the road. I wait a beat, then follow.

"Because Delaney came to my office to see me."

She went to see my brother? "Why?"

"She wanted to know if you're in town. She said she thought she saw you."

So that's why she was there. Maybe I wasn't as discreet as I thought I'd been. Wait, how the hell would Delaney know who Brian is or where he works? Nelson gets on the highway, and I follow a couple of cars back.

"Brian, have you been talking to her all these years?"

Nelson exits the highway, and I do the same.

A door clicks shut through the phone. "What? No."

"Then how did she know who you were or how to find you?"

While I'm trying to focus on where Nelson is going, my focus is on whether my brother has been hiding something from me all these years. "Is she one of your informants?"

Finally, Nelson pulls into a parking lot of a large warehouse. I keep driving down the road, then turn around about a block later.

"No, she's not. She said you mentioned you had a brother, Brian, years ago, and the first thing she did was confirm I have a brother named Logan. It's the first time I've ever spoken to her."

She remembered something I said all those years ago. It shouldn't matter, but it makes me smile.

I spot the man's car in the front row. He's no longer in it. I park in the back of the lot and keep my eyes on the building.

"If she saw you, then that means you are doing a shit job of stalking her," he says.

"I'm not stalking her." Because I'm stalking her husband now.

"Uh-huh. I don't believe that. What is going on? All these years, you were fine, and then you see Rocky Manzia once, and now you have to get close to her? It's too dangerous. You need to leave it alone."

Not going to happen. I know she's miserable, and that tugs at me. I can't leave it alone now.

"What did you tell her?"

He sighs. "I told her I haven't seen you in months. Then she left."

And that's when I saw her.

Another car pulls into the lot and parks in the front. Three men get out of the vehicle, and based on the way they are scanning the area, I'm going to bet they will go in the same door as Nelson.

"Just go back to my place. We'll talk when I get home, all right?"

"Okay." I need to end this call, and agreeing with my brother is the only way.

"I'll grab dinner. See you then." He ends the call.

The men go in the same door as I slowly get out of my vehicle. There are many cars in this lot, so I can't be certain how many people are inside. I walk toward another door farther up that is propped open. Casually, I walk past it and glance inside. The interior is one big room and not sectioned off as I suspected it would be. Leaning against the wall behind the door, I focus on the voices inside. They echo and carry far enough that I can make out what is being said.

"He'll be here. Stop worrying," a man says.

"He's late. That's unacceptable." I know that second voice. Nelson.

"Nelson, relax. He probably got stuck in traffic."

The cock of a gun puts me on high alert. "Never tell me to relax."

"Okay!" the first man says. "I'm sorry. It won't happen again."

Metal hits metal. If I were a betting man, I'd guess Nelson tossed his gun onto a tabletop of some kind.

"The area is ready," a third man says.

"Good," Nelson says.

Damn, I need to see inside to know what's going on.

Another car pulls into the lot, and I shove my hands into my pockets and walk parallel to the warehouse. Fortunately, I'm near the end of the building.

Two car doors close behind me, but I know better than to glance back. Once I get to the end of the warehouse, I cross the street. If I'm being watched, hopefully, they'll think I walked by the warehouse only as a shortcut.

On this side of the street is an apartment building. I step into the parking lot, then turn back to the warehouse and spot the two men going in.

"Duke!" one yells.

Duke? I didn't see him go in there. I run back to the warehouse and step up next to the propped-open door.

"Where's Duke?" one of the men asks.

"You're dealing with me today," Nelson says.

"We have the money. Where's our stuff?"

"Over here," Nelson says.

The men are silent for a moment.

"Looks good. Here's your payment," a man says.

The sound of a zipper opening carries outside. A duffle bag, likely.

"Nice doing business with you," Nelson says. "Come on, guys, let's go."

Footsteps grow louder as I realize they are coming toward the door I'm standing behind. I run to the end of the building. When I peek around the corner, Nelson and another man are getting into one car, and the three men I saw arrive earlier get back into their car. The man with Nelson must have already been here.

Okay, although I didn't see anything, I feel certain Nelson just did some kind of major drug deal. If only I could get a look at what he sold the other guys. Maybe they will carry it out in the open. Not the smartest thing, but I can hope.

While it's clear, I make my way back to my car. I notice a large sign near the entrance to the lot stating it's a park and ride. Odd place for one, but it explains why there are so many vehicles here.

After I get back into my rental, I position my phone camera to snap some photos of whatever they carry out of that warehouse. At the very least, I'll have photos of the men that my brother might find helpful.

As I'm waiting, an explosion rocks the building, shattering the windows on the second level and blowing off two of the doors. I duck down as debris flies from the building and lands on several cars, causing two car alarms to activate.

Slowly, I sit up. My car seems fine, which is good since I didn't opt for any extra insurance. But the building is not fine. The warehouse is on fire and going up fast. Is this what the guy meant when he said it was ready? Did Nelson take their money and then kill them?

Of course, he did. None of this should surprise me. I know what kind of man Rocky Manzia was, and anyone associated with him will be just as bad, if not worse.

But what about Duke? A man called his name in the building. If he was inside I doubt he survived. Did Nelson just take him out, too?

Several people run across the street from the apartments into the parking lot. Sirens grow louder, and I need to get out of here. I pull out of the parking spot and make my way to the back exit. As I approach, a black car blocks it. Then Brian steps out and aims his gun at my car.

"Get out of the car, now!" he shouts.

I open my door and put my hands out first so he can see I'm unarmed. Then I slowly stand up until I'm looking into the eyes of my brother.

"You've got to be fucking kidding me," he says as he lowers his gun.

I shrug. Really, what else can I do?

"Did you do this?" He nods to the building.

I bite back a smile. Call me crazy, but it makes me happy that my brother knows I'm capable of blowing up a building. "No, but I know who did."

"Unbelievable," he says.

"How the hell did you get here so quick? I heard your office door close on our phone call," I ask.

Brian frowns. "You heard my car door. I had a tip I was racing to."

"A tip? From whom?"

He shakes his head. "Can't tell you, you know that. Now follow me back to my office." He gets into his car, and I follow him.

While he thinks he's going to be questioning me, I'm not leaving his office until I know who gave him that tip.

CHAPTER 8

Delaney

Fortunately, Nelson didn't come home last night. I noticed because I was tossing and turning, thinking about my run-in with Logan. It's been years, but now the idea of never seeing him again really bothers me. I think it was because I always held out hope that we would find our way back to each other. I've wanted to be able to tell him he was right about my father and that I had been too naïve to believe it.

He doesn't want to see me again. Hell, he's probably married with a family. And that was the thought that kept me up most of the night. But it shouldn't. I made peace years ago with the fact he was making me choose him over my family. He knew I couldn't do that.

By the time I make it to the office, I'm grumpy and

exhausted. I make a pot of coffee and am sipping on my first cup when Duke walks in.

"Good morning," he says.

I set down my cup. "You're cheery this morning. Did you get good news?"

He stops at my desk. "No, just in a good mood."

Nelson walks in wearing the same clothes as yesterday, but now they are crumpled.

"You didn't come back to the house last night," Duke says as he crosses his arms.

Nelson gives him a smile. "No, I stayed with a friend. A flexible friend." He winks at Duke.

Duke stalks up to him. "You will not disrespect my sister like that. If I hear you are stepping out on her again, I'll—"

"Duke, stop," I say as I stand up. "Nelson and I have an arrangement. It's fine."

Duke's brows shoot up as he glances at me and then back at Nelson. "It's fine that he's not only stepping out on your marriage but apparently is brazen about it? How the hell is she going to get the respect of this community with you as her husband?"

Nelson crosses his arms. "I'm respectable, and no one cares what bed I'm in. All they care about is if this family upholds its promises. Which, by the way, you're welcome."

Duke's eyes narrow. "You're welcome for what?"

Nelson grins as he walks past Duke to the coffeemaker. He slowly pours himself a cup without answering. This is Nelson. He wants you to hang on his every word. Duke knows him well enough not to react. Likely that irritates Nelson even more.

Finally, the man turns around and takes a sip of coffee. He lowers the mug and grins at my brother. "We were having trouble with a supplier. I dealt with them."

Duke closes his eyes. "What did you do?"

"You have insurance on the Miller warehouse, right?"

My brother rubs his temples as I watch this back-and-forth match. Nelson has taken matters into his own hands on many occasions, and Duke ends up cleaning up the mess. Every time Duke threatens him if he does it again, Nelson reminds him of who his family is and what will happen if even a hair is out of place on his body.

"Do we still have a warehouse?" Duke asks.

Nelson shrugs. "I didn't stick around. Hopefully, the fire department saved some of it. But really, they should have contacted you by now."

The warehouse isn't in either of our names. It's owned by a corporation that will be hard to track down because Duke made sure of it. We also don't have any insurance on that building, and Nelson knows it. The last thing we needed was someone requesting an inspection at the wrong time.

Damn, I'm not sure what bothers me more, the fact I know all of this or the fact that I'm upset about losing the warehouse. I shouldn't care. But even I know it's the source of most of our revenue.

Revenue. More like dirty money, and while Duke opened an account for me years ago that has grown larger than I can even fathom, I don't want it. I only take what I need to survive. I refuse to enjoy their drug money.

My stomach rolls the more I think about everything these two men and my father have done. If I could find a way out, I would run and never look back. I used to stay for my father. But once I found out what he really was, I was trapped because of Nelson.

One time I tried to talk to my mother. All she told me was that I couldn't escape. But she did. A few days after my dad's funeral, she flew off to Barcelona. And I haven't heard from her since.

"You destroyed the warehouse?" Duke asks. He doesn't try to hide the anger in his voice. "You know that's where most of our business comes in."

Nelson smiles. "Oh, is it? Oops."

The vein in Duke's forehead is popping out, and based on the smirk Nelson is wearing, that was his goal.

"I need to take care of a few things," Duke says as he grabs his jacket and leaves.

Realizing I'm alone with Nelson and what happened the last time he was here, I focus my attention on my work.

"Hey," he says.

I glance up.

"Thanks for saying what you did. The last thing I need is shit from your brother."

I nod but say nothing. He finishes his coffee and sets his empty cup on my desk.

"I have business to deal with, too. See you later." He walks out, and I breathe a sigh of relief.

With each passing day, it isn't a matter of should I try to leave Nelson. It's a matter of I have to.

An hour later, the door slams.

"Fuck!" Duke yells.

I stand up and walk to him. "Are you all right?"

He shakes his head. "I found out what Nelson was up to, and it isn't good. The warehouse has been destroyed, and people are saying I ordered the hit."

I frown. "The hit?"

Duke squeezes his eyes shut. "Delaney, I know you know more about this family, so please don't act all innocent now."

I cross my arms. "I found out the hard way Dad dealt drugs. But the hit? Are you saying you kill people, Duke?"

He glares at me. "Sometimes I don't know what is going on in your head. But right now, we need to leave."

"Leave?"

Duke goes into the back office, and I follow. He opens the safe, and I'm shocked at how much cash is in there.

Duke shoves the money into a grocery bag he got from somewhere. "Yes, leave. Nelson wasn't fixing some problem he had. He was creating one for us. Two of Ruiz's men died in that explosion. One survived, and apparently, he's told anyone who will listen that I set them up. We need to get out of town now." He grabs my hand. "Let's go."

We walk out of the office, not bothering to lock it. I get into his car, and before I even have time to put on my seat belt, he's tearing out of the parking lot.

"Where are we going?" I ask.

Duke stares in the rearview mirror, then back at the

road. "I'm not sure. There isn't time to grab our passports. I have to think where they won't find us."

"Go east," I say.

He glances at me. "Why?"

"Well, if someone were running from San Diego, my first thought would be they would go south to Tijuana. If not there, then north along the coast toward Los Angeles. Both provide crowded places we could hide in."

He shakes his head. "Crowded places sound like a good idea. Why would we go east and try to lose them in the desert?"

"Duke, do you look like someone who would go to the desert over a city?"

He glances down at himself in his designer suit and shoes. The man is always polished. He grins. "You're right. I hate the fucking desert. East it is."

As we drive, Duke brings up memories from our childhood back when we were innocent and had no idea what the hell we would be left with. A few hours later, we enter Yuma.

"Duke, who is Ruiz?"

He clenches his jaw, then glances at me. "Someone you don't fuck with. Nelson knows that. He did this on purpose."

"Why would he do that?"

Duke barks out a laugh. "Well, with one move, he destroyed our main revenue source and now there is a hit out on both of us."

I sit up taller. "Why me?"

"Because you're my sister. That's the only reason they need."

Someone wants to kill both of us.

"We need to stop for gas and a bathroom," he says. "We should grab some lunch and snacks, too."

I offer to gas up the car while he goes into the store for supplies. Once he is out of sight, I call Brian. When his assistant offers to take a message, I make it clear this is an emergency.

"Delaney? What's going on?" Brian asks once he gets on the phone.

I tell him all about what Nelson did and how someone is coming after Duke and me, but I have no idea who other than the name Ruiz.

"I know who that is. One of my informants said several people are looking for your brother to make him pay."

"It wasn't him. We're on the run now, but I'm afraid of what will happen if anyone catches up with us."

Brian sighs. "Talk to your brother. If you two are willing to turn on Nelson and his family, I think I can offer you both protection."

Duke steps up to the counter inside and then glances out.

I turn so he doesn't see the phone. "I'll ask and get back to you."

I end the call and pocket my phone just as the tank fills up. By the time Duke gets outside, I'm in the car.

He tosses a bag into the back seat, then hands a wrapped sandwich to me. "Lunch."

"Thanks."

"Who were you talking to?" he asks as he gets into the car and starts it.

There is no way he is going to be okay with this idea, but it might be the only way to stay alive. I think through how to approach this with him as I unwrap the sandwich and take a bite.

"Hey, are you ignoring me?" he asks.

I shake my head and point at my mouth as I chew. He rolls his eyes and then turns onto the highway.

Finally, I swallow. "You aren't going to like this, but I do have a way for us to stay alive."

Duke stares straight ahead and doesn't say anything. About a mile later, he turns off onto another highway. Finally, he turns to me. "Tell me."

I explain how I called Brian and what his offer entails. Duke sighs several times.

"Are you serious? You called the fucking FBI? Have you been talking to him?"

"No!"

Duke turns his gaze to me for a moment. "Okay, then, why is his number on your phone?"

And as much as I don't want to tell him about Logan, I don't have a choice. "I thought I sensed Logan around me a couple of times, so I went to his brother, Brian, to find out if he was in town."

Duke's eyes nearly pop out of his head. "You saw Logan?"

I stare ahead. "No, I just thought I did," I lie. "That's why I have Brian's number on my phone."

My brother has made it clear he despises Logan for

how he left me all those years ago. No need to tell him Logan was here. Although I'm still unsure if that was Logan at my father's funeral. But I asked Duke, and clearly, he isn't going to tell me the truth on that one.

"So, your suggestion is that we turn ourselves over to the FBI and tell them everything we know?"

It sounds simple when he puts it like that. "Yes, then they can put Nelson and his family away and we can be free."

Duke laughs. Then he laughs harder. "Delaney, you naïve fuck. I love you, but damn, you don't get it. We wouldn't go free. Once people find out we turned on a family, we'd have targets on our backs. The fact you think anyone would let us walk around free, wow. I don't know what to say."

I turn in my seat to face him. "Why not? It's only Nelson's family we have issues with."

He shakes his head. "No, it's not. It's Ruiz now, too, and he is someone you don't want to mess with. I know a lot about a lot of people in our town. And if we turned on a few, why should they believe we wouldn't turn on them, too?" He glances at me. "I'll save you the time to think it through. They wouldn't believe it. That would make us a threat. And there is one way they deal with threats."

He doesn't need to say it. I know what he means.

"Give me your phone," he demands.

I hand it to him, and he throws it out the window.

"Why did you do that?"

"Because we are not going to the FBI for anything. And

since they have your number and know what's going on, I guarantee you they will be tracing that phone."

"If we don't rely on the FBI, what are we going to do?" I ask.

"Rely on each other. We'll figure this out."

He sounds confident, but I'm not so sure.

CHAPTER 9

Logan

I leave the psychologist's office with a smile. Three sessions in and I believe I have her convinced I'm fine. Not that I have to convince her. I am fine. But I need her to tell my brother that to get him off my back.

But then I remember what Brian told me, and I'm angry all over again. Nelson called in the tip about the warehouse, claiming Duke had set a trap, killing those men inside. He also confirmed what I was certain of. Duke wasn't in that warehouse. Since I'd been watching the place, I knew Nelson's tip was a lie. Which apparently makes me a potential witness and has amped up my brother's concern about me.

If it weren't for Delaney, I would never have stuck around for the counseling sessions, and I'd already be back in New York. Delaney. Why the fuck am I even staying for her? She's married. What we had was in the past. Clearly, I must be obsessed, which is another reason to get myself back home.

But dammit, she didn't marry for love. But she's still married. But she shouldn't be. God, I'm going to drive myself crazy.

I climb into my car and toss my phone onto the passenger seat. It instantly vibrates with a call. My brother, probably checking up on me.

"Hey, Brian. Yes, I just got done with another session."

"This isn't about that. Do you still have eyes on Delaney Manzia?"

I sit up taller. "No, why?"

"Shit." His shoes click on the floor as he walks fast. "My informant told me there's a hit out for Duke and his entire family for what happened at the warehouse. She called me, and she sounded scared."

She called him? "I'll find her." I toss the phone back onto the seat, then pull out of the parking lot.

Her car is in the lot of the Manzia building. I run into the office, but no one is there. I check each room and find the safe in the back office open and empty. Maybe Duke left in a hurry and took his sister with him.

It's unlikely he'd go back to their house, but I go there to check, just in case. When I knock on the door, I hear laughter. Finally, the door opens, and Nelson stands there in only underwear. There are two women in the room behind him, also only in underwear.

He grins and points at me. "I recognize you. You were at the cemetery. Hey, how did you get out of that grave?"

"Where are Delaney and Duke?"

His smile drops. "Don't know. Don't care." Then he slams the door in my face.

My instinct is to break it down and ruin his day, but the odds of Delaney or Duke being here are low.

My phone buzzes with a text from my brother. I scan it as I get back into my car.

Delaney's number. She's ignoring Brian, but he thinks she might respond to me.

I stare at it, debating whether to call or text. Since I have no idea if she is in danger at the moment, I send a text not to further jeopardize her.

Me: *It's Logan. Looking for you.*

I lean back, racking my brain about how to let her know I know she's in danger without coming out and saying it. Then it comes to me.

Me: *I got your favorite pizza and am heading over. Pepperoni and onions.*

Hopefully, she remembers that conversation we had years ago and will know it's me. How can anyone hate onions on a pizza? The memory of her nose shriveling up when I suggested that pizza has me smiling.

I drive up and down all the streets around her house and her work, but I don't find her. And she doesn't respond to my text.

I'm out of ideas when my phone buzzes again. When I see it's not Delaney, I'm disappointed. But then I read the message.

Brian: *We got a hit on Delaney's phone outside Yuma, Arizona. I'll send you the location.*

Shit. That's three hours away. Why the hell is she there? I can speculate all day, but what I need are answers.

Me: *I'm on my way.*

As I'm driving, it hits me. My brother asked for my help with this case. I ruminate on that for a while but finally conclude he knows I'll protect Delaney better than anyone else. And he also knows that if anything happens to her, I'll… I'll what? I'll be heartbroken? Never love again. Well, hell, all that's already come true. But the need to keep her safe is too strong for me to ignore.

When I reach the location Brian sent me, I pull over on the shoulder. The highway is four lanes and cuts through farmland.

Brian also sent her number, so I call it, and sure enough, I hear it ring. I follow the sound until I locate her phone on the side of the road. Dammit.

Me: *Found her phone on the side of the road. No sign of her.*

My brother responds right away.

Brian: *Duke's phone also pinged there last, too. They are together. When you find them, protect both of them.*

I stare at the message. First, I need to determine if anyone else is with them. Second, my brother wants me to protect Duke, too? I'll have to ask about that later. I made good time, but they are at least two and a half hours ahead of me. I leave the phones in the ditch. If my brother can trace them here, so can someone else. And not someone I want to lead right to them.

Me: *I'm going to keep driving up this highway. Any idea what car they are in?*

He sends me the make and model of Duke's car. I need

more information than my brother can legally provide, and I know who to call to get it.

"Pizza Haven, how can I help you?" Trip answers.

I laugh. Only this guy could get me to laugh despite my shitty current mood. "Didn't that place really exist?"

"Yeah, they all existed at one point."

Trip is our go-to guy for anything we need traced or searched. I don't know how he does it, and I know better than to ask. He often answers the phone as a fast-food joint. He claims he did it to Cowboy from Morgan Thompson Security as a joke, but he's kept it up for years, and now a few of us at Reed Hawthorne Security get the same treatment.

"What's up?" he asks.

I explain what is going on, and he knows exactly what I need.

"I'll see if there are any hits on their credit cards, and do you happen to have the license plate number for Duke's car?"

I sigh. "I don't."

"No worries, I can get it. It will just take a little time. I'll see if there are any hits on any highway cameras or if there are any toll booths out that way."

I knew I could count on Trip. "Thank you. I really appreciate this."

"No problem. But you should probably tell Reed what's going on. Last I heard, he thinks you're on vacation."

Vacation? Huh, I guess that's easier to say than the truth. Besides, I shouldn't be surprised. For the most part, Reed keeps our confidence. Unless it's about Lightning and involves costumes. Damn, I still can't believe Reed sent him, of all people, on an assignment where he had to dress up like a fox.

"Coff? You still there?"

My mind is wandering. I need to stay focused. "Yeah, I'm here. Thanks for your help."

"I'll call you once I have something. Talk to you later." He ends the call, and I toss my phone onto the passenger seat.

For the next two hours, I drive north as my mind wanders back to the past. A place I closed off years ago. When I met Delaney in a bar, I figured it would just be a one-night stand. But as we talked, something clicked. It was as if I'd known her for years. Then the sex that night. I smile, thinking back. It was amazing. All these years later, no one has compared to her, which really sucks for me.

I'm not sure how, but that one night became a one-week stand. We were together every day and night of my leave. And when I had to go back to Virginia, neither one of us wanted it to end. Despite only being together a week, we made a long-distance relationship work until I was able to return just over six months later.

But that was when everything went wrong. Fortunately, my phone rings because that's not part of our story I like to think about.

I answer the call, and Trip's voice comes through the speakers.

"Hey, Duke used his credit card at a motel in Henderson."

Henderson? "Do you think they're headed for Vegas?"

"Not sure, but figured if he's there for the night, you can catch up to them. How far are you from there now?"

"At least two hours away."

"Okay, I'll send you the motel details so you can pull up the address when you get closer. Also, the car registered to the room matches Duke's. What I don't know is how many people are in that room."

That's the problem. I don't know if anyone else is with them, forcing them to drive. I'm also curious how Trip was able to tap into the motel's records, but I don't ask him for details. When Reed hired me, he made it clear Trip can find just about anything you need, but never ask him how he does it. He won't tell you anyway.

"Thank you. I really appreciate this."

"Anytime. Let me know if you need anything else."

"Will do."

I end the call and settle in. Hopefully, in a couple more hours, I'll find them, and then Brian can put them in protective custody. Although the idea of Duke going along with that seems unlikely.

CHAPTER 10

Delaney

DUKE OPENS the car door and leans in. "I got us a room. Let's go."

We step inside, and I want to step back out. But unfortunately, we are stuck here.

There are two beds, thankfully, but the covers are orange, and the carpet is a shade of brown that I'd bet is from the eighties. There is a faint smell of cigarette smoke mixed with mildew and bleach.

"It's just for the night."

"Did this use up all your cash?" I ask sarcastically. While I know he grabbed whatever was in the safe, I have no idea how much that was. But based on what I saw, it was a lot.

When he went to rent the room, I counted what I had on me, and it's only twenty dollars. I'm not used to carrying much cash.

"No, I used the credit card." He walks into the bathroom and shuts the door.

The credit card? What the hell? "Duke!" I yell to him. "You tossed our phones because they can be traced, but you used a credit card here?"

He pops out of the bathroom. "Nelson's family can trace our phones. They don't have a way to trace credit cards."

My brother is not this naïve, is he? I glance out the window. At least his car isn't near this room.

He comes out of the bathroom and flops onto one of the beds. I turn to face him. "Nelson might have paid off a cop to run a search on your credit card."

Duke smiles. "He might, but he won't get the results for a few days. Trust me. I know how it works."

I don't trust him, but I don't have much of a choice right now. Considering we have no clothes other than what we are wearing and no toothbrush, I get as ready as I can for bed.

When I crawl into bed, I notice the bleach aroma is stronger. Fortunately, I'm too tired to care.

"I set the alarm to wake us in exactly five hours, so try to get some sleep," he says.

"Only five?"

He shrugs. "Better to be safe and get out of here alive."

"You're right. Goodnight," I say.

He nods and turns off the lamp between us. Despite our circumstances, I drift off to sleep.

"Rise and Shine!" Duke yells.

I cover my head. "Not until morning!"

"Sorry, but we have to go."

I sit up, remembering where I am and why I'm here. The room is dark except for the lamp he turned on. "What time is it?"

"Three in the morning." He walks by and ruffles up my hair.

I flop back down. "That's not morning. That's cruelty."

He laughs. "Well, we need to get going in case Nelson was able to have someone track us here."

I get up and stretch my arms above my head. "Go where? We are running but where to? Don't you have connections back home that can fix whatever is going on?"

Duke sighs as he sits on his bed. "I tried. I have to hand it to Nelson; he knew exactly who to lure into that warehouse to get a hit on me." He shakes his head. "He knew too much about me and our business. Dad said once you two were married to treat him like family, but that was a mistake."

"Why do you say that?" I mean, I think marrying him was a mistake for many reasons, but I'm not privy to most of the business to know what went wrong there.

"Get ready to go. We can talk when we're on the road."

My first stop is to the desk, but there is no coffee maker. I spin around. "Where's the coffee maker?"

Duke laughs. "They don't have one. Don't worry. We'll find some drive-through place and get you one."

Ten minutes later, we are walking toward Duke's car when a man gets out of the car next to it. Duke stops and grabs my arm, stopping me as well. It's dark, so I can't make out who it is. He steps toward us with his hands in the air. Duke's hand reflexively goes to the back of his pants, where he carries his gun.

"It's Logan. I'm here to protect both of you on order of the FBI."

Logan? He steps closer to the light. It's him.

I glance at Duke, who is frowning. "How the hell?"

Logan nods to the motel. "Traced your credit card."

I elbow Duke. "Told you."

Duke frowns at me, but then turns his attention back to Logan.

"No, I mean, how are you alive?"

Logan glances at me, then at Duke.

I hit Duke in the arm, hard. "That was Logan at the funeral, wasn't it?"

"He was there," Duke says. He doesn't add more, so I know this can't be good.

"And what did you do to him?"

Duke doesn't answer, but Logan steps closer and fills me in.

"He and your husband buried me alive in a grave."

I shriek and then cover my mouth, hoping I didn't wake anyone. Then I turn to Duke. Tears fall from my eyes, and I don't try to hide them. "You tried to kill him? Why would you do that?"

Duke's brow shoots up. "You're kidding, right?" He points at Logan. "This asshole ripped out your heart and killed our father," Duke says. "I wanted to do a hell of a lot more to him."

Logan's hands go up again. "I told you; my teammate

shot your father. He had no choice. Your father was going to shoot me again."

Ignoring the first part of what Duke said, I focus on the second. "You were there when my dad died?"

Logan nods. "He wasn't supposed to be there. Then he recognized me and…"

"Tried to kill you."

Logan nods.

I step away from Duke. "My dad recognized you after all these years." I process that and what Duke did to Logan. I spin back to my brother. "What the hell? Both you and Dad tried to kill him?"

Duke throws his hands into the air. "Because of this asshole, you swore off ever loving anyone again. That made Dad think he could marry you off in convenience to Nelson. If it weren't for him," Duke points to Logan, "we wouldn't be in this situation right now."

Oh, that's rich. I'm not going to let my brother go on thinking he's blameless in all this. I press my finger into his chest. "I married Nelson to save your life. If you hadn't fucked with his business or whatever the hell you did, it never would have been an issue. We are in this mess because of you, not Logan!"

Logan steps into our space. "I hate to interrupt, but we need to keep it down and not draw attention."

He's right. It's just after five in the morning, and we are probably waking people up. People who will call and complain.

"We should go," Logan says, then turns to Duke. "Because of what you've done, I want to leave your ass here, but my brother asked me not to, so I guess it's your lucky day."

"Your brother?"

Logan sigh. "You know exactly who my brother is. Isn't that part of the reason you wanted me dead?"

Duke frowns but quickly turns it to a glare. But I caught it, and Logan likely did, too. What are you hiding now, brother?

"What you did to Delaney is enough reason for me to want you dead."

Logan grabs his phone. "I'll let my brother know you've declined his protection."

"Stop," Duke says. He grumbles something that sounds like asshole, but I can't be sure. "FBI protection, you say?"

Logan nods.

"It's better than us blindly running," I tell him. "Can you stop hating Logan long enough for us to get out of this mess Nelson put us in?"

Duke nods. "For you, I can do that." Then he leans in to give me a hug, but I push him away.

"You just told me you tried to kill Logan. No hugs. I'm too mad at you."

Logan grins, but he turns quickly enough that Duke didn't notice. We follow him to his car.

Before Duke ducks his head into the back seat, he stares down Logan over the roof of the car. "I'm going along with this for her. But I'll warn you now, if I sense you even so much as glancing or flirting in her direction, I'll break both your arms."

Logan leans his arms onto the roof of the car and smiles. "I'd love to see you try that."

"Stop!" I say, probably too loudly. "You two," I point at both of them, "are going to get along. If you can't, then shut up. I've had enough damn drama lately." I get into the passenger seat and shut my door.

Once they both get in, Logan drives onto the highway, heading south. Duke notices, too.

"What the hell are you doing? We should be driving away from the men who want to kill us!" he says.

Logan shakes his head. "That's what they'll expect. Once they find your car, they'll assume you got a new one and drove north."

Logan's phone rings, and he answers.

"Did you find her?" a man asks over the speakers.

"I did. She and her brother are in the car with me now. Want to say hi?"

"Duke Manzia?"

Duke leans forward. "Who the fuck is that?"

"Special Agent Brian Folger with the FBI."

Duke falls back against the seat. "The damn FBI."

Brian responds. "We need to get you both into protective custody."

I turn to Duke, and he's frowning. "Just get us out of this area, and we will be fine on our own."

"No, you won't," Brian says.

Duke laughs. "Do we have a choice?"

"No. Logan, keep me apprised of your location. I'll call if anything new turns up."

"Sounds good," Logan says.

We drive for a couple of hours in silence. Duke snores in the back seat. How the hell he can fall asleep is beyond me. The throbbing of my head reminds me I need caffeine.

"Can we stop for coffee?" I ask.

Logan doesn't respond.

"A drive-through is fine. Please."

He sighs. "I'll find a place. I should gas up, too."

Twenty minutes later, he pulls up at a mini mart. "Hope you aren't too much of a coffee snob. They should have something in there, though."

"It works. Want one?"

"Sure."

I glance back at Duke, and he's still sleeping. Once inside the mini mart, I find the bathroom, then buy three black coffees. When he wakes up, Duke will want one. I manage to get them back to the car without dropping any.

Logan finishes gassing up the car and then gets in. I take the opportunity to really study him. When I saw him the other day, we were standing side by side, and I didn't get a chance to really look him over. He has a beard now, and his hair is longer. But also, his demeanor has changed. I can't put my finger on it, but he's more serious now. Well, of course, he would be.

"You're staring," he says.

"You're different," I say.

He nods. "Been through a lot since we were kids."

I wince. We were kids, but somehow, his saying that diminishes what we were to each other. "Is that all we were? Kids? With some crush?" I ask.

He turns to me and licks his lips. "It was more than a crush for me."

I nod. "Me too."

I want to ask more, but he made it clear the other day that he didn't want to see me again. He's only here because his brother asked him to be. That much, I'm sure of. So, I don't ask. Sometimes you don't want to know the answers.

CHAPTER 11

Logan

I'm surprised when my brother calls back so soon. Hopefully, he has a solid plan.

"Hey, you're on speakerphone again," I answer.

"Good. You all should hear this. I've talked to Reed, and this is now officially your assignment."

I frown. "Okay, not sure why everyone needed to hear that."

Brian laughs. "There's more, dumbass. Reed and I worked out a plan. The three of you will be flying out of Phoenix tonight to New York City. Reed is arranging a place for the three of you to stay."

I rub my eyes. I've been awake for over twenty-four hours, driving for most of them. The idea of driving all the way to Phoenix, well, it isn't my first choice.

"Logan?"

"Yeah, I'm here."

"I'll send you the flight information. I gotta go. Call me if you have any questions."

I reach for the coffee Delaney got me, only to discover it's empty. The moment we hit the road again, I'd downed it.

"Here," she says, handing me hers. "I only drank half."

"Thanks." I take it and down it, too.

Duke snores in the backseat.

"You two not get much sleep last night?" I ask.

She scoffs. "We got five hours, but he's always been like this. It's why he always has to set an alarm. He could sleep all day."

I glance back at Duke lying across the back seat as best he can fit. "That doesn't sound healthy."

She shrugs. "It's not like he keeps great hours."

The only sound in the car is Duke's snoring for the next thirty miles. So many questions run through my mind, and finally, my curiosity wins out. I need to know what she knows.

"You and Duke were running."

She turns to me but doesn't respond.

"Do you know what you were running from?"

"Duke said Nelson framed him, and some guys put out a hit on him and his family, which means me."

I nod. "Not your mom?"

"She's out of the country."

Well, good for her. I bet once Rocky died, she finally had a taste of freedom.

"Do you know who it is coming after you or how Nelson set your brother up?"

She reclines her seat a bit. "No. He wouldn't tell me. He never tells me anything about the business. All I know is what I'm told to work with at the office."

I glance over, and she's staring down at her hands in her lap.

"Really? You just do what you're told?"

She looks up and arches a brow. "Yes, is that hard to believe?"

I blink a few times. "Well, yeah. If I had told you what to do, you would have told me to leave."

"That's what I did, isn't it?" She turns away.

We both know she's referring to the night I asked her to run away with me. I'd discovered her father was being investigated by my brother, and he told me I had to get out of there. When I told her about her dad, she didn't believe me and refused to leave her family.

"I should have listened to you." Her words are so faint I wonder if I heard her correctly.

"Where are we?" Duke sits up in the back seat.

"On our way to Phoenix," Delaney says.

He looks out all the windows. "I need to take a piss. Is this coffee for me?"

"Yes, but it's cold now," she says.

He chugs it. "Still coffee, but why the hell is the cup so small?" Then he removes the lid, and the sound of his pants unzipping catches my attention.

"What are you doing?" I glance back, and to my horror, the man is relieving himself into the cup.

"You better not spill any of that," I warn.

"I'm not worried," Duke says.

The stream of piss sounds too strong for that small cup, and moments later, my fear is confirmed.

"Oh shit, the cup is almost full."

Delaney grabs her cup and pulls off the lid. "Here, use this."

"I don't have enough hands. Take this first!" he yells.

She leans forward. "I'm not grabbing your piss cup!"

"Take it! Fast! It's going to overflow!" He's panicking as I take the next exit.

I pull off the side of the exit and turn in my seat. The cup is filled to the rim. I grab it and hand him the empty cup.

Then I realize I'm holding a cup of piss. This is not what I signed up for. It's yellow and stinks. I do the only thing I can. I open my window and throw out the cup. Now I'm not a litterer, but I'll be damned if I'm holding another man's piss that was seconds from ending up on me.

"Ah, that feels so much better!" Duke leans past me, his new fresh cup of pee coming way too close to my face.

"Get that the hell away from me!"

He tosses the cup out my window as well.

Okay, this is too much. "Sit back down!" I yell. "If you have to pee again, we will stop. If you whip your dick out in my car again, I will punch it. Do you understand?"

Duke winces as he leans back and zips up his pants. "Ouch. You don't have to be so hostile."

Hostile? I blow out a breath. If this is how he's going to

be, I'm going to need someone to help in New York. Ah, yes, this would be a good way to get back at Lightning for all the crap he's pulled on me over the years. The thought of it makes me smile. I'll make sure to let Reed know I will need his help.

The rest of the drive is less eventful. Duke asks to stop at a restroom once before we arrive in Phoenix, which gives me a chance to read the details of our flight that Brian sent. We're almost to the rental car drop-off when Reed calls.

"Reed, you're on speakerphone, and Duke and Delaney are in the car with me."

"Coff, glad I caught you before your flight. We had to change your tickets. The flight leaves thirty minutes earlier. Can you make that?"

I glance at the time. "Yes, we are close to the airport now."

"Good. You will also be flying into JFK instead. Somehow, someone found out about your flights to Newark, and that location has been compromised."

How the hell did someone find out about our flights? "Understood. I'll check in once we land in case it happens again."

"Sounds good. Have a safe flight."

I end the call.

"Did he call you Cough? Like *cough* *cough*?" Duke coughs to make his point clear.

"Something like that. It's a nickname." I really don't want to explain it to Duke. I told Delaney the story years ago. I doubt she still remembers it.

"What kind of a name is that?" Duke continues.

Delaney turns around. "It's because his last name is Folger. Someone said he's Coffee, and then people started calling him Coff for short.

I glance at her, surprised. "You remember?"

She shrugs. "I remember everything about you."

Her words crack something inside my heart because I remember everything about her, too. Is that normal for young love? I've always thought my feelings for her should have faded over the years, but they never did.

Everyone is silent as I return the rental. When Delaney uses the bathroom, I convince Duke to toss his gun into a trashcan. It would never make it through airport security.

Right before we step into the security line at the airport, I stop them. "You heard Reed on the phone. Someone knows we are flying to New York, and they might have learned our flights were changed. Don't let down your guard. Got it?"

They both nod. Fortunately, they have their driver's licenses on them, so that won't be an issue. I am concerned about the bag Duke has been clutching.

"What's in there?"

He clears his throat. "Money," he says quietly.

Shit. That could get us flagged. "How much?"

Duke glances at Delaney, then back to me. "About ten thousand."

I sigh. "About?"

He shrugs.

I glance around and make sure no one can hear us talking. "Anything more than ten thousand and you have to declare it. But frankly, that much cash is going to get you noticed and probably questioned."

"Let's split it up," Delaney suggests.

Duke's eyes widen. "No."

Delaney shakes her head. "Don't be an idiot. We'll give it back when we land."

I nod to confirm.

His grip grows tighter on the bag as he mulls over what to do. Finally, he hands the bag to Delaney. "Fine."

We stand close enough that no one can see what we are doing. Delaney places a wad of cash into her purse. I hold out my hand, and Duke glares at me.

"We're good," he says.

Fine with me, but if he gets pulled aside, we're not waiting for him.

As we approach security, Delaney grips her purse tightly as she glances around. Duke stares straight ahead as if he doesn't have a care in the world.

If I had any doubts as to what Delaney knew about the business, I don't now. It's clear Duke is used to hiding things, and Delaney is scared to get caught.

Fortunately, we all make it through security with no issues. We make it to our gate as the last group is boarding. I scan everyone, and no one appears suspicious. We board, and since the tickets were purchased last minute, we are all sitting apart from each other. That's probably for the best because, frankly, I need some sleep.

The moment I'm buckled in, I lean my head back and I'm out.

"Sir. Excuse me, Sir."

I blink a few times, wondering why someone is being so loud.

"Sir. Sorry to wake you."

I open my eyes, and one of the attendants is staring at me. "The man back there ordered a drink and said you would pay for it."

I turn in my seat and spot Duke smiling at me. He gives me a little wave. On the one hand, I could be a dick and refuse. But maybe this will keep him happy. I doubt he'll sleep at all after he slept all day in the car.

"Sure," I say. "And also, anything the woman in twenty-three b wants as well."

I hand her my credit card. "Thank you. I'll be right back."

A moment later, she returns with my card and hands it to me.

"How long have we been in the air?" I ask.

"About an hour," she says. "Would you like anything to drink? You were asleep when we went past."

I shake my head. "No, thank you." All I want is sleep because I need to be alert once we land.

CHAPTER 12

Delaney

My first time on a plane and it's while on the run from some men who want to kill Duke and me. Not what I imagined. But then, I never would have imagined Logan being the man tasked with keeping us safe, especially after what he said the other day. Is that why he was in town? He knew something might happen to us?

And what does his keeping us safe mean? Will he be staying in the same hotel room or apartment with us? Or will we be locked away in New York until someone says it's safe?

New York City. I've never been there but always wanted to go. Is that where Logan lives? I still don't know anything about him or what has happened to him over the years. It's not like I can ask much with Duke here.

Dammit, my mind is going a mile a minute. I take several deep breaths.

"I'm a nervous flyer, too," the man next to me says. Before I can correct him, he continues. "I have to take something before each flight." He reaches into his pocket. "Would you like one?" He holds out a prescription bottle.

"No, thank you." Yeah, that's the last thing I need is to take some random pills from some guy on the airplane.

"A glass of wine might work, too," he offers.

"I'm fine."

He turns away, and I'm thankful for the peace. If I had my phone, I would at least have something to do. What I should do is sleep, since I have no idea what will happen once we land.

I close my eyes, and images of Logan from twelve years ago fill my mind. The first time I saw him, I thought he was out of my league, but Sam pushed me to talk to him. When he smiled, I was a goner. That week we spent together was magical, and despite all the hurt he caused, I wouldn't take it back. Those memories are the only thing that has gotten me through these last few years.

I'm jolted awake by the plane touching down.

"You slept well," the guy next to me says. "And now we've landed."

I blink at him a few times and bite back the comment I want to make. I'm sure he's a nice guy and I'm just in a crap mood. Once we stop at our gate, everyone unbuckles their seat belts, and suddenly Logan is next to my aisle.

"I'll meet you at the gate," he says.

I nod. He can't move forward any farther because most

of those in the aisle seats are now standing. I glance back and spot Duke near the back of the plane.

Logan is standing tall with his eyes focused on the front of the aircraft. I want to ask him if he received any warning messages, but I can't do that here. Not in front of everyone.

Finally, the crowd moves, and we get off the plane. Logan is waiting for us, as he said he would.

"Stay close to me at all times. There is a car waiting for us," he says.

As we follow him, he is glancing in all directions, scanning everyone. My heart is pounding so hard that it's all I can hear. We finally make it outside, and he leads us to a large black SUV.

"Get in," he says.

The three of us get into the back seat, and the car immediately pulls out.

"Good to see you, Coff," the driver says.

"You too, Ozzie. Will you be staying with us?"

The driver shakes his head. "I'm just delivering you."

As we make our way out of the airport, my attention is focused on the sights. Or lack of them.

"Where's the Statue of Liberty?" I ask.

"You won't see it on the route we're taking," Ozzie says.

Even though we are running for our lives, I'm disappointed that I won't get to see a famous landmark. Perhaps I'm in denial about my situation.

"Coff, have you heard about Stacy's latest move?"

My ears perk up. Who's Stacy? Is she an ex of Coff's?

"No, did she get out or something?"

Ozzie shakes his head. "Thankfully, no. She's suing Reed and Stormy."

Coff leans forward. "For what?"

Ozzie takes an exit that puts us on a new highway. "She's claiming she was pressured into selling Hawthorne's share of the business and that Reed and Stormy gave her fraudulent information."

Coff leans back. "That's bullshit."

I glance at Duke, who shrugs. "Who's Stacy?"

Ozzie glances back at us in the rearview mirror but doesn't answer. Coff doesn't, either, and I wonder why they are ignoring my question. But then Coff turns toward Duke and me.

"She was our former boss's wife. He died, and she agreed to sell his share of the company to another man. It was all legitimate. But what we didn't know at the time is that this woman conspired to have her husband killed, then tried to kill her stepdaughter in order to get more money, and all around, she's a nasty person we all wish would go away. She's in prison now for all she did."

Wow, that's a lot. "I'm sorry about your boss. That sounds horrible."

"What does she want? The business back?" Coff asks.

Ozzie laughs. "What she always wants. Money. Apparently, Reed and Stormy signed a high-profile client, and Stacy filed her lawsuit a week later. Part of her claim is they knew this deal was in the works, and they pressured her to sell her share fast."

Coff stares out the window. "Is there anything we can do to help?"

Ozzie shakes his head. "No, Reed's dad is handling it for them."

Everyone is silent for the next hour as I stare out the window. It becomes clear we aren't going into the city. The lights become fewer and farther between as we drive. Finally, we pull onto a gravel driveway.

"The place is fully stocked. There's a phone charger on the counter. Reed will be in touch soon. In the meantime, he says you need to stay inside," Ozzie says.

"I really appreciate this, Oz," Coff says.

"Just stay safe. You haven't paid next month's rent yet."

Coff laughs. "Got it."

Rent? Is this his roommate? If it is, that might mean Logan is single. For a moment, there are butterflies in my stomach at the possibility of us again. But then I remember, I'm not single. No, I'm married to a man I hate. A man who is doing his damndest to get us killed.

Oz hands Logan a piece of paper. "The code."

He turns back to us. "Let's go."

We follow him to the door. He punches in the numbers, and we all walk in. The place is nicer than I expected. After a quick tour, we discover three bedrooms and the kitchen is fully stocked. Duke pulls out several items.

"Delaney, you want a sandwich?"

"Yes, please. I'm starving."

He nods and gets to work. I go back into the bedrooms and check out the closets and dressers. Empty.

"You looking for something?" Logan asks.

I spin to find him standing close. "I was hoping there might be an extra T-shirt or something."

He nods. "I'll ask if we can get some clothes. If we are only here for the night, then likely not."

One night? This seems like a lot of effort for one night. But maybe they use this place all the time.

We eat sandwiches, then Duke goes into his bedroom to sleep. Logan sits on the couch.

"Are you going to sleep?" I ask.

He nods. "I'll be fine here."

The man is over six feet tall, and the couch is not that long.

"Why would you sleep on the couch when there is a bed down the hall?"

He nods to the door. "If anyone comes in, I want them to see me first."

I shiver at the thought of someone finding us here. "There's no way anyone can find us."

He tilts his head. "I found you."

"Yes, but you said that was because Duke used his credit card."

He stands up. "And your real names were used for your airline tickets. Someone could have seen us get into the car at the airport."

I wrap my arms around myself. "You think we were followed?"

"No, but there are many ways people have of finding someone. I want to be ready, just in case."

The idea of someone bursting in here when we are in the middle of nowhere scares me. At least Duke has his gun. Wait, he can't; otherwise, he wouldn't have gotten on the plane.

"Duke had a gun but—"

Logan stares at me. "I made him get rid of it when you were in the bathroom at the rental car place."

I swallow as I stare back at him. "Do you have a gun?"

He shakes his head.

They have a stocked house but they don't keep a gun here? Wait, if no one has a weapon…a tear escapes. "What if someone breaks in with a gun?"

"Hey," he says. "I don't need a gun to protect us. Trust me, all right?"

I nod, but I'm still scared.

"Come here," he says as he pulls me into his arms.

My hands are plastered against his chest, and I don't move. He rubs his hand up and down my back, and with just that movement, I'm transported to all those years ago when being in his arms felt so natural. I relax and move my hands down and around his back. It doesn't go unnoticed that he is solid muscle under his shirt. He's filled out since I knew him. And despite the fact I was scared a minute ago, all I can think of now is what he might look like without his shirt on.

"What the hell is going on?" Duke asks.

We break apart. "He was just comforting me."

Duke crosses his arms. "Was he now? Or is he taking advantage of you?"

Logan walks over to Duke. "It was only a hug. Now we should all get some sleep."

"He's right. Come on, Delaney, I'll walk you to your bedroom." He glares at Logan.

I'm too tired to deal with Duke right now, so I go.

Once inside, Duke leans down. "You should lock your door."

I check, and sure enough, the door does have a lock. I nod, and as soon as it's closed, I lock it to appease him.

The bedroom has a bathroom attached, and in there is a toothbrush and toothpaste. I brush my teeth, then climb into bed.

Duke was right to interrupt. Even if Logan was only comforting me, my thoughts were starting to go somewhere else. Somewhere they can't go. Not as long as I'm married. Even if it isn't a marriage of love, I have to be free from Nelson before I even consider anything with Logan.

What the hell am I even thinking? The man comforted me; he didn't hit on me. I take a deep breath. If I don't get out of my own head, I will drive myself crazy. I might not have my phone, but I can do the bedtime meditation from memory. And that's what I force myself to do, even though it's a struggle to keep thoughts of what Coff would look like without a shirt on out of my head.

CHAPTER 13

Logan

Once Delaney and Duke are in their bedrooms, I fall back onto the sofa, wondering what the hell I just did. Why did I pull her into my arms? She was upset, and the urge to hold her was too strong to deny. And once she relaxed, it felt right.

Maybe I'm not the right person to be protecting her. Can I even be objective? Throughout the drive today, I found my mind wandering back to the past. That's not something I can afford to have happen again. I must stay focused.

Maybe I'll ask Reed in the morning if someone else can take over. Who's not out on assignment? I quickly scan the messages from the guys. We have an official text chain that includes our boss, Reed. But then there is another one that doesn't, and it's basically the guys cracking jokes.

Durango and Axel are in town. Ozzie is, too, and he's my first choice because I'm fully aware he's hung up on someone, which means he wouldn't look twice at Delaney. But the other two are the other single guys in the group. The idea of one of them being there for Delaney when she cries or needs help doesn't sit right. Dammit. I need to suck up how I'm feeling and stay here with them.

I close my eyes and drift off to sleep.

Glass breaks, and I jump up and look around.

"Sorry," Duke says. "I dropped a glass."

My eyes scan the door and all the windows. Everything is closed. But it's light out.

Duke opens several cabinets. I hope he's looking for a broom and dustpan. I check my phone. Seven in the morning. No messages from Reed or any of the guys.

"Heard anything yet?" Duke asks as he cleans up the shards.

"No."

Duke opens the fridge and stares. Then he grabs several items. I watch as he cracks a dozen eggs into a bowl, cuts up some onion, bell pepper, and spinach. He glances up. "I'm making a scramble for us. Figure we need to fill up since we don't know what the day holds."

I nod. "Good idea. I'm going to grab a shower."

Despite the fact I'll be putting the same clothes back on, I need a shower to help me wake up. By the time I come out, the place smells like freshly brewed coffee and eggs. Delaney is sitting at the kitchen table, sipping from a mug.

"Good morning," I say.

"Good morning," she replies.

My phone rings on the counter where I left it charging.

I grab it. "Hey, Reed." I'm happy to hear from him and hoping he has good news for us.

"I have bad news," he says.

I walk toward the back door. Even though I want to go out and let off some of the steam built up being this close to Delaney, I can't. Anyone could be watching.

"What's going on?"

Reed's chair squeaks as it does when he sits in it. "Duke is being charged with murder and destruction of property in San Diego. I've spoken with Brian, and the police have agreed to hold off their search to give Brian time to work a deal."

I frown. "A deal? What do you mean? He knows Duke didn't do it."

"Yeah, not that kind of deal."

Of course, my brother is thinking about his own case and career. He's been working on taking down Rocky Manzia for fourteen years.

"For now, you all need to stay at that house. Stay hidden," Reed continues.

I take a breath, knowing there is no point in discussing my brother's priorities with Reed. No, I will take that up with him directly.

"We need clothes."

"Come in," Reed says to someone else. "Yes, I'll have some delivered today. Send me the sizes you need."

"Thank you. I will." I take another deep breath, but this one sends me into a coughing fit. Damn, my lungs still aren't fully healed yet.

"How are you doing?" Reed asks. "Sounds like maybe you need to get checked out again."

"No, I'm fine. The doctor gave me something to use if it gets too bad. I should be back to normal soon." It's not a lie. The doctor did give me some kind of inhaler. Unfortunately, I left it back at my brother's place. Although, to be honest, I never intended to use it anyway.

"Okay. There's one more thing."

Reed hesitates, and that tells me whatever it is, I won't like it. "Brian told me about your history with Delaney Manzia. Do you think you can be objective, or should I send Axel to replace you?"

I close my eyes. Axel. The man is some kind of woman magnet. I don't get it, but some woman is always hitting on him.

"No," I grit out. "I'll be fine."

"Uh-huh. You don't sound fine."

"I am. I'm just a bit sore from the coughing." That could explain the roughness in my voice, although we both know it's not the reason for it.

"Okay, I'm sending Axel with the clothes. If you change your mind, he'll be ready to take over. Talk to you later."

He ends the call, but I keep the phone to my ear as I stare outside to give myself a minute before Delaney and Duke descend with their questions.

Finally, I pocket my phone and turn around. Duke is now sitting at the kitchen table, eating breakfast. There's a fresh plate for me. I sit down.

"Thank you for cooking."

He nods. "You got bad news."

"I did. You've been charged with murder and destruction of property in San Diego. But the good news is they've agreed to hold off searching for you until Brian has a chance to talk to you."

He swallows his bite. "The FBI?"

"Yes."

Delaney hasn't touched her food. Her gaze moves from the eggs to me. "They can't prove he did it because he didn't do it."

"I know," I say.

Duke's head jerks in my direction. "You believe me?"

I lean back. "I was there. In the parking lot. You weren't. Nelson was responsible for all of it."

Duke's eyes widen. "You're a witness? Holy shit! This is great. Call the cops in San Diego and tell them."

I stand up and pour myself a cup of coffee. "Brian is aware of all of this. As soon as the police become aware of this, Nelson might find out and grow more desperate to get me out of the picture. If he starts hunting for me, New York is the first place he'll look."

"Why?" Delaney asks.

I sit back down and taste a bit of the egg scramble. It's actually pretty good. "Mmm, you can cook," I say to Duke.

"The secret ingredient is butter. It makes everything taste better," he says.

I turn my attention to Delaney. "I live and work in the city."

"Are you married?" she asks. Then her hand shoots to her mouth. "I'm sorry. That's none of my business."

I take another bite. After I swallow, I lean back. "Never married and no kids."

She blinks a few times, then returns her attention to her food. We eat in silence, everyone lost in their own thoughts.

"I'll clean up," Delaney says as she stands up.

That reminds me. I need to send Reed their clothing sizes. "What size do you wear?" I ask her.

Duke glares at me.

Delaney's mouth falls open. "What?"

"My boss is having someone pick up some clothes for us and bring them by. I need to tell him what sizes you both wear."

"Oh. Medium." She takes her plate and Duke's to the sink.

"Extra-large," Duke says. "On top. Medium or size thirty-four waist for the bottom."

I send Reed a message with their information and mine, then carry my plate over. I notice the counter and stovetop are clean. Duke is not only a decent cook but a clean one at that. That is not something I would have expected.

"Can I talk to you?" Duke asks me.

"Sure."

He nods his head down the hall, indicating he wants to be away from his sister. I follow him into the bedroom where he slept.

"Your brother is going to ask me to give up Nelson and his entire family, isn't he?"

I lean against the wall. "I really don't know what he

wants from you." It's the truth. I could speculate, but there's no point.

"Can you call him? I want to know so I have time to think about it." Duke sits on the bed, but his bouncing leg tells me he's not comfortable with this situation.

I grab my phone from my pocket and call my brother.

"Logan, what's up?"

"Duke wants to know what you want from him. He's right here. Ready to talk?"

My brother sighs. "Sure, put him on."

Instead of handing the phone to him, I turn on the speakerphone. I need to know what Brian is requesting because I also need to know if he has a plan to get us out of this mess any time soon.

"Hey," Duke says.

"Duke? Am I on speakerphone?"

"Yes."

My brother is silent for a moment. "Glad to talk to you. Has Logan told you about the charges pending against you back home?"

Duke nods, then realizes Brian can't hear him. "Yes, he did."

"I can get you out of those charges, but you'd have to make a deal with the FBI."

Duke runs his hand through his hair. "What kind of deal?"

"I need to know everything about Nelson and his family. By everything, I mean their business associates, where they pick up their product, and anything else you can tell me."

Going after Nelson's family now. Interesting. "Are you offering him and Delaney protection in exchange for this information?" I ask.

"Maybe. If that is something they are interested in, I can see if that's a possibility."

Duke frowns. "I told you I can't turn on Nelson." Duke's brow shoots up. "I mean, I told your brother, Logan."

I watch the man. He's clearly lying. Has my brother approached him before about Nelson's family? I guess I shouldn't be surprised. With Rocky out of the picture, Nelson's family would probably win Brian more praise to take down at this point.

Duke clears his throat. "Protection? Would it be for life because friends of Nelson's family would never stop coming for me?"

Delaney walks into the room but doesn't say anything.

"No, but we can keep you protected until all the big players are in prison."

Duke laughs. "You think them being in prison will keep me safe? Jesus."

"You're not safe now," Brian says.

Duke jumps up and walks out of the room.

"He left the room," I say.

Brian sighs. "Tell him I need to know his answer by tomorrow." My brother ends the call.

Delaney shakes her head. "He won't do it. It would be a death sentence."

She's right. We all know it.

"Then I guess we need to find another way to deal with the men coming after you two."

CHAPTER 14

Delaney

Find another way to deal with the men who want to kill us. Other than killing them first, I don't see another way.

This isn't me or how I think. Yet this is what my life has become.

"Maybe I can talk to Nelson and get him to call off whoever is looking for Duke." Even as the words leave my mouth, I realize Nelson would never agree to it. But what else can I do?

Logan types something on his phone.

"What are you doing?" I ask.

"Requesting a burner phone be delivered with the clothes. I doubt Nelson will give you what you want, but maybe we can at least find out who is coming after you and Duke."

"That's actually a good idea. Any information is better than what we have now."

For the rest of the day, we all stay in our own areas. Fortunately, there are some mystery books here; otherwise, I'd be bored out of my mind. Duke found a crossword puzzle book; that's keeping him occupied. Logan goes back and forth between walking around, staring out windows, to checking his phone.

It's almost dinnertime when Logan jumps up. "Our clothes are here," he says as he walks to the door.

He opens it and in walks a very large man. I thought Logan had muscles. This guy has muscles on his muscles.

Logan clears his throat. When I glance at him, he arches a brow, and I realize I was staring at the new man.

"Hey, here are the clothes," the man hands Logan a bag. "And here is the burner phone." He hands him a box.

"Thanks." Logan takes the items as the man turns to me.

He smiles at me. "Hey, I'm Axel."

"Delaney," I say.

"Okay, that's all we need. Thank you," Logan says as he practically pushes Axel out the door.

The man laughs. "Okay, I get it. Call if you need anything else."

"Will do."

Logan locks the door, then empties the bag on the table and separates everything into three piles.

I'm still wondering why he rushed the guy out, but I'm also happy to have fresh clothes. "I'm going to shower," I say as I grab my pile.

On the way to the bathroom, I stop in Duke's room. He's lying across the bed. "Fresh clothes just arrived."

He glances up. "Okay, thanks."

By the time I emerge from the shower, the place smells good. Someone cooked something.

"Whatever you cooked, I'm all in," I say as I walk into the kitchen.

Duke laughs. "Don't get too excited. I found some frozen meals and heated them in the microwave." The microwave dings. "And yours is now ready."

I join Logan at the table, and Duke follows right behind me.

"Here is the burner phone," Logan says. "After dinner, you can make that call."

Duke freezes with his fork halfway to his mouth. "What call?"

"I'm going to call Nelson to see if I can find out anything."

Duke shoves the food into his mouth, then leans back. Once he swallows, he shakes his head. "He won't tell you anything. But I guess it doesn't hurt to try."

We eat the rest of our meal in silence. It's been silent all day, and it's driving me nuts.

"After I make this call, maybe we can turn on some music or something."

Logan grunts. "Sorry, but we need to be able to hear anyone coming. That's one reason that driveway is gravel."

Oh, I hadn't thought of that. I guess it makes sense.

"Hey," Duke says. "Ask Nelson why he set me up. That's

something I can't make sense of. He had access to more supply with me around."

I nod. "I guess I should make the call." The idea of talking to my husband makes me nervous. I never was before, but since my father's death, the true Nelson has been coming out more and more. He's worse than I thought he was.

I step into the living room and turn on the speakerphone before I make the call.

"Hello?" he answers.

I wasn't sure if he'd answer an unknown number. "Hey, it's Delaney."

"Wow. I didn't think I'd hear from you."

Of course, he didn't. He was hoping I was dead.

"Surprise, your goons haven't killed me yet." There's an edge to my voice, but dammit, he deserves it.

He laughs. The man has the gall to laugh.

"This isn't funny," I say. "Why did you frame Duke?"

He takes a deep breath and calms his laughter. "Sorry. My goons, as you call them, are not who is coming after you two. It's Ruiz's men."

"Who's Ruiz?"

He sighs. "Jesus, how can you be around all this for so long and still be so clueless? Ask your brother. Is he there with you?"

"No," I lie and glance at my brother, who nods. "Why did you frame him?"

The sound of fabric against leather fills the air, and I know exactly where he is. He's sitting in my dad's leather office chair, probably drinking his good scotch and going through drawers he shouldn't. But I bite back the anger at how comfortable Nelson has made himself in our family. I need answers.

"Why do you think? Why the hell do you think I married you? My family is taking over all of Manzia's business."

I turn to Duke as I process what he said. "What do you mean all of Manzia's business?"

He mumbles something into the phone. "Look, I don't have time to school Daddy's sheltered little girl. The short version is your dad had a lucrative business. Now that he's gone, it belongs to my family. I'm sorry about framing Duke, but it was the only way."

Okay, I may not know a lot about what my dad did, but I do know he had legitimate businesses. Ones which I thought were all he participated in once upon a time. And those are both mine and Duke's.

"Framing Duke doesn't give you anything. It means it would all go to me. Is that why you want me dead?"

He laughs again. I swear if I ever see him in person, I'll smack that smile off his face. The man towers over me, so the likelihood of that happening is slim. But it's an image I need to focus on to get through this call.

"Delaney, I really don't want you dead. You're a gorgeous woman, and it would be a shame for you to die over something you really don't know much about. I have a proposal for you."

I sit on the couch to brace myself. "What proposal?"

"A divorce."

My ears perk up. He knows that's exactly what I want.

"What's the catch?"

He swallows a few times, which confirms my belief he is indeed drinking my dad's scotch.

"You give me everything. Well, all the businesses. You can keep this house and whatever you have in any bank account. But the construction business and everything else will be signed over to me."

I lean back as Logan and Duke stare at the phone I'm holding. Duke shakes his head. He would never give up the business. But what choice will he have if he's in prison? I don't care about any of it, but I'm not letting Nelson have it that easy.

"Duke needs to be cleared before I'll consider your offer," I say.

He doesn't reply.

"Nelson?"

"I'm here. I don't think you're understanding. This isn't a negotiation. If you don't take this offer, I won't stop the hit that's out on you. And frankly, if you die, I'll get everything. So maybe I'll just let everything play out."

Duke jumps up and walks to the other room. Logan shakes his head and presses his finger into his hand, indicating I should end the call.

"I'll think about it and get back to you," I say, then end the call. Then I stare at the phone. "Can he trace this?"

Logan scratches his head. "No."

"That son of a bitch!" Duke yells. "Everything he said was bullshit. I knew the moment he laid a hand on you that he was a lying sack of shit!"

Logan jumps up. "How many times had he hit you before that day in the office?"

"Once," I say.

Duke steps back into the room and right up to Logan. "You were there that day in the office? And you didn't stop him?"

I step between the two men. "He did stop him. He threw a rock and broke the back window of his car," I say.

Duke grins. "Really? You hurt his car? Okay, maybe I do like you after all. Sorry about the grave thing."

Logan clenches his fists, and it's clear he does not accept the apology, but there is nothing he can do about it now. He takes a deep breath, then sits down. "Delaney, do not agree to the divorce deal. It's a setup. Like he said, he gains more if you're dead."

I hate hearing his words, but he's right. Nelson would probably lure me somewhere to sign documents, and bam, I'm dead.

"As for you," Logan says to Duke. "We wait for the investigation to finish. Hopefully, there will be more evidence to clear you than just what I witnessed."

"Won't that be enough to clear him?" I ask.

Logan shakes his head. "The prosecution will dig, and if they find out we have a history or that we all hid out together, they'll say I'm lying."

Duke falls back onto the couch, rubbing his eyes. "The only way out of this is if Nelson is dead."

I turn to him. "How does that help clear you or stop Ruiz's men from coming for you? And who is Ruiz?"

Duke stares at the ceiling. "Ruiz is a man I hope you

will never meet. If you do, promise me you'll run." His stare is intense, and I know he's worried about me.

"Promise," I say.

Duke leans back again. "As for clearing my name, whether Nelson is alive or dead won't matter. But I'm going to make sure that asshole doesn't end up with any of our family's things."

CHAPTER 15

LOGAN

THE NEXT MORNING, I wake up with an uneasy feeling. I jump out of bed and check on Delaney. She's sleeping. I then check on Duke, but his room is empty. He's not in the kitchen. I search every inch of the place and can't find him. I call out his name.

Delaney appears in the hall, her hair messed up and her eyes barely open. "What's going on?"

My eyes take her in. She's only wearing a T-shirt that clings to her body, leaving nothing to the imagination. Not that it would need to because I remember every inch of her.

"Logan?"

I cough, giving myself a minute to refocus. I can't keep letting thoughts of her distract me like this. "I can't find Duke."

Her eyes widen, and she helps me search. I go to the garage, hoping I'm wrong. But I'm not. There is always a car in this garage for anyone who needs it. I've used this place as a hideout before, so I'm well aware of what should be here.

Delaney finds me. "What's going on?"

"The car is gone. How the hell would he have started it without keys?"

When we arrived, I placed the keys in my pocket for safekeeping, and they are still there.

"You're kidding, right?" she asks.

Then I realize, I forgot who I was talking to. Of course, he knows how to get a car going without keys.

But how did I not hear him leave last night? I stare at the gravel. He must have driven very slowly over that.

Once I get back inside, I grab my phone.

"Reed Hawthorne Security," Piper answers.

"Hey, it's Coff. Can you connect me to Reed?"

"Sure can."

That's one thing I'm grateful about Piper. She knows when to skip the small talk and just connect me.

"Coff, what's going on?"

"Duke took the car and is gone. The last thing he said was he'd be better off with Nelson dead."

"You think he is going after Nelson?" Reed asks.

"I do. But I'm also concerned he may have compromised our location."

Delaney steps into the living room to join me. Thankfully, she's fully clothed now. She hugs herself, and I want to comfort her, but I have to keep her at a distance so I can remain focused.

"I'll send someone to pick you two up. You'll come back here until we figure out plan B."

"Sounds good. We'll be ready."

I end the call. "We should eat. One of my coworkers will be picking us up in about an hour.

Tears well in her eyes. "Duke is going after Nelson, isn't he?"

"I think so."

"Dammit. He's going to get himself killed." She sniffles, and that's my undoing.

I wrap my arms around her, and she sinks into my body. As she sobs, I rub her back. "We'll find him. But in the meantime, we're going to go back to my office until we can find a new safe place."

She nods against my chest. A memory from years ago flashes through my mind. We'd spent the entire day in bed and had gotten up to get something to eat. But even then, we couldn't not hold each other for more than a few minutes. Damn, that week with her was the best of my life. I always wondered what would have happened if I hadn't discovered what her dad did when I visited her. Would we have stayed together? Married?

Hell, Brian would have ruined that dream before it could have happened. Once he heard her father's name, he would have told me that was who he was investigating.

I squeeze her, then let her go. "We better get going before we run out of time." And if I keep holding her, I'm going to want to do more than simply comfort her.

She nods and walks to the kitchen. I take a quick cold shower because I don't want to leave her alone for very long. Afterward, I pack up some of the snack food in case we don't get another chance to eat for a while.

Ozzie: *I'll be your ride today. I'm about three minutes from your door.*

"Okay, he's almost here."

Sure enough, he arrives in exactly three minutes. I climb into the back seat with Delaney.

Ozzie arches a brow at me in the rearview mirror. "Guess I really am a taxi service."

"If we need to duck, it's better I'm back here," I tell him.

He grins at me in the mirror. He's not buying it, and I don't blame him. There was no reason I couldn't sit in the front seat except I have this strong desire to keep touching Delaney.

Ozzie pulls out on the road. "Reed had second thoughts and decided we shouldn't go back to the office."

That makes sense.

"Do you have any idea who is after you?" Ozzie asks.

"Nelson said Ruiz's men. I don't know who Ruiz is, though."

Ozzie nods. "We'll find out. In the meantime, Delaney, we need to get you somewhere safe. Then Coff and I will go find Duke."

Wait, leave Delaney with who? Damn, when did I turn into such a jealous prick?

Delaney meets my eyes. "No. I'm going with you. He's my brother. And if anyone can find him, it's me. You need me."

Ozzie glances back at me.

"She does have a point. She'd know where to look for him. But Delaney, you aren't trained for this sort of thing."

She leans away from me. "I know how to use a gun, and I'm trained in Krav Maga."

I blink a few times. "What?" I can't imagine Nelson would have been okay with her learning any of that. That man is controlling.

She grins. "My dad insisted I know how to use a gun. And a few years ago, Duke hired someone to come to the office a couple times a week to teach me Krav Maga."

Well, damn. I'm almost starting to like Duke. At least I know he looks out for her when he can.

"Hey, that's great, but I'm afraid that makes you more dangerous," Ozzie says. "Because now you are confident and still not trained enough."

She crosses her arms and stares at Ozzie in the rearview mirror. "I'm not going to run into a room and challenge someone to a fight. I'll simply show you where he could be."

I don't like her coming with us, but then again, I don't think keeping her cooped up with Axel is a great idea, either. And yes, I'm sure it would be Axel since he's already met her.

I lean back. Damn, my emotions are taking control, and I can't let them.

"Fine," Ozzie says, surprising me. "You can come, but you have to wait in the car."

She rolls her eyes. "Yes, Dad."

Ozzie laughs.

Well, if he thinks it's okay, then I'll go with it. But if I don't want her with Axel, I need to analyze that. Actually, I don't. I know what's going on. The idea of her with anyone feels wrong. But she is with someone, Nelson. Although, since he's trying to kill her, I think we can assume the marriage is over.

"Where do you think Duke went?" Ozzie asks.

She stares out the window. "His first stop is probably the house. When Nelson was on the phone, it sounded like he was in my dad's office drinking his scotch. I'm sure Duke picked up on that, too."

Huh, she was paying more attention to detail than I realized. "Okay, that's a good start, but that's in California. How do you think he's going to get there with no money?"

That's right, no money. I hid his bag of cash, thinking it would persuade him not to leave.

She turns in her seat and stares at me. "No money? He has his credit cards. If he is on his way to find Nelson, he won't care who tracks him."

Shit. She's right. And that is what could get him killed. I pull out my phone and call Trip.

"Trip, hey, I need a favor." I explain that we need to find Duke, and he likely booked a commercial flight.

"Okay, I'll call you back once I have something," he says, then ends the call.

"Who's Trip?" Delaney asks.

"He's the guy you call when you need to find out where someone is or anything about them," I say.

Ozzie chuckles. "He's a mysterious one, for sure. But he's helped us out of many jams."

A few minutes later, Trip calls back and confirms Duke booked a commercial flight to San Diego that lands in about six hours.

"That doesn't give us much time," Ozzie says.

Delaney shakes her head. "We'll never make it in time. Dammit, Duke."

I call Brian and explain everything going on. "If you want us to stop this, then we'll need a private plane."

Delaney's brows shoot up as she watches me on the phone.

"I need to make a few phone calls, but I think I can make that happen," Brian says. "I'll call you back."

I stare at my phone, imagining how this could go, and in every scenario, Delaney is in danger. "Delaney, I think you should consider staying here. We are likely walking into a shooting match," I say.

She sighs. "I'll wait in the car. But like I said, I can defend myself."

"Did you use any of the moves you learned on Nelson when he hurt you?" It's a low question but one I have to ask.

She flinches. "No. I was too shocked by what he'd done."

I nod. "And if someone comes at you with a gun, you will likely be too shocked again. You aren't trained for this, Delaney. We are."

Without even looking at me, she smiles and says evenly, "I'm going with you. End of story."

I glance at Ozzie in the rearview mirror, and the asshole is trying not to laugh. While I will admit I need her to show us where her brother could be, I'm not comfortable with her going into any building with us. I did say she had to stay in the car. I'll make sure she knows that's her only option. But as I replay her words in my head, I bite back my smile. It's the Delaney I knew. The one who wouldn't take shit from anyone. I'm happy to see her reemerging.

Ten minutes later, Reed calls. A plane is set up for us at an airport outside the city.

"That was really fast," I say.

Reed laughs. "Apparently, your brother has some pull. Good luck out there."

Part of me wants to know exactly what my brother told Reed to have him okay with Ozzie and me going to California and putting ourselves in the middle of the Manzia mess. Perhaps Brian didn't fully fill Reed in on that family's history.

Hell, I haven't been fully filled in myself. Going in blind is not how I like to operate. But as I watch Delaney nervously chew on her bottom lip, I know this is something I need to do, save her brother. And if her asshole husband suffers in the process, well, I won't be upset about that.

CHAPTER 16

Delaney

TWO FIRSTS THIS WEEK. My first flight out of state was when I went to New York. And now, my first flight on a private jet. I wish it was under better circumstances where I could enjoy a glass of champagne and not have my stomach in knots. At least we were able to eat on the flight.

As the plane lands, I check the time. Logan assured me we would arrive before Duke, since his flight is not direct.

Before we get off the plane, Logan takes my hand. "From the moment we exit this plane, you need to stay very close to me. Understand?"

I nod.

We follow Ozzie off the plane, and despite this not being their home airport, they navigate it like it is. Logan holds my hand the entire time until we get into a rental car. In my mind, I imagine the worst as we drive to my house. Please, Duke, let us beat you there. Logan glances back at me several times from the passenger seat. Yes, he sat up front for this ride. Between his hand holding warmth and then him distancing himself like now, it's confusing me. Not that I should be confused. The man is here to protect me because his brother asked him to. And I can't expect more. I'm married. Even though it isn't a real marriage, it still is one, and I respect Logan too much to ask him to break any sort of rules. I lean my head back. What the hell am I even thinking? Oh yeah, that I still care more deeply for this man than I have for anyone else in my life. And being near him makes me wish for the things we once had. But that doesn't mean he feels the same. No, he's here for a job, and then he'll go back to New York.

Once we can ensure that Duke is safe, maybe I should consider Nelson's offer, especially if it would include Duke. I really don't know what to do.

Fortunately, I don't have to think about any of that right now because my house is in view. We pull up, and no cars are in front.

"Nelson isn't here," I say. "Pull around back over there." I point, and Ozzie parks the rental car beside the house. It isn't visible to anyone pulling up.

I get out of the car, but before I take a step, Logan grabs my hand again.

"You are to stay in the car," he says.

"There's a panic room inside. I'll be safer in there." It's actually true, although I don't intend to go in it.

Logan nods, and we walk to the front door. I punch in the code.

Ozzie enters first with a gun drawn. Logan releases my hand and goes next. I follow. Ozzie goes upstairs while I follow Logan as he checks out every room downstairs.

"All clear," Ozzie says as he walks back down the stairs. But then he stops mid-step. "Someone's coming. It's a red Porsche." From the stairs, he can see the entire driveway from the upper window.

"It's Nelson. We can hide upstairs," I say. "Nelson will likely stay in the office down here."

"Sounds good," Ozzie says as he runs back up the stairs.

"No. Where's the panic room?" Logan asks.

"Downstairs. There's no time," I say, then run up the steps before Logan can stop me.

I lead them to my mom's room. When I open the door, I stop, and the guys run into me. The room is bare of anything that was my mom's. She really did leave. For good, based on the fact that she took everything.

"Sorry." I step to the side to allow room for them just as the front door opens, then slams shut.

Footsteps walk past the entry and around to my dad's office. I was right. One thing about Nelson, he's predictable.

"Duke's here," Ozzie says from the window.

"I thought we'd have more lead time," Logan says.

I run over in time to spot my brother exiting a car with a gun in his hand.

"We have to stop him!" I run to the door, and Logan catches me before I can exit the room.

"Is someone here?" Nelson shouts, then begins walking up the stairs.

We stand still, but we don't have time to be quiet now.

"Oh shit," Ozzie says quietly. "We have company."

I go back to the window and see another car pull up. Three men jump out.

"Duke Manzia! Just the man we are looking for!" A tall man aims a gun and fires.

Duke dives into a bush as Nelson runs downstairs toward the back of the house.

Logan takes my hand. "Where is the nearest bathroom?"

I point to a closed door near the window. He leads me in there and points. "Get in the bathtub and stay there."

I frown. "Why?"

"I'm trying to keep you from getting shot by a stray bullet. Now get in there," he orders.

There's something in his tone that I decide it's best to just listen and not argue right now. Or maybe it's the fact that between those men and my brother, a lot of shots are being fired.

I lie down in the tub, and then glass breaks. I sit up enough to spot Ozzie aiming his gun out the window. He fires several shots. I sink back into the tub and hope Duke isn't caught in the crossfire.

"Those three men are down," Ozzie announces.

I climb out of the tub.

"Get back in there!" Logan shouts at me. "Nelson is still out there somewhere."

"Nelson! You asshole, where are you?" Duke shouts from inside the house.

"Stay here!" Logan orders.

He and Ozzie run out of the room. I appreciate his

wanting to keep me safe, but there is no way I can sit here. My dad keeps a gun in the office. I need to get to it before Nelson finds Duke.

I run down the back stairs. I'd always thought it was dumb to have two staircases, but right now, I'm grateful for them.

They lead me to the kitchen, which is empty. Slowly, I round a corner on my way to the office. I'm certain I'll find Nelson waiting there for Duke. But I am wrong. As I round that corner, someone grabs me and puts their hand over my mouth. His grip is tight.

"Hello, wifey. Glad you could stop by."

I go limp. Nelson.

"Wouldn't it be funny if your brother accidentally killed you? Oh, I'm not sure he could live with that. Let's find out!" Nelson drags me to the middle of the hallway. "Duke, I'm over here," he yells.

No, that is not how this is going down. I take this opportunity to catch Nelson off guard as I use his body weight to flip him until he's onto his back.

"You bitch!" He grabs my ankle, and I go down hard.

He climbs over me and has a fistful of hair. I try to get out of his grasp, but the way he's holding my hair, every time I move, it pulls harder.

"Let her go!" Duke yells.

The next moment happens so fast. Nelson releases me and reaches for a pistol in his waistband as he turns toward Duke.

"He has a gun!" I shout.

A shot rings through the air, and I swear time stands

still. Nelson freezes. From what I can see of Duke, he freezes.

Then Nelson drops his gun and collapses onto his side next to me. "Who the fuck are you?" Nelson grits out.

I look to see who Nelson is talking to. Ozzie is standing next to us. He kicks Nelson's gun away. I scramble to stand up.

"Her protection," Ozzie says, nodding to me.

"I called Brian, and he's sending an ambulance," Logan says, "and other support."

I have no idea what other support is, and right now, I don't care. "Duke?"

"Over here," he says.

I run to him. He's leaning against the wall, breathing hard. Then I notice the blood. "Did you get shot?"

He nods as he lifts his shirt to reveal a bullet wound in his side.

"He's been shot!" I shout to the guys. That's when I realize they are focused on Nelson.

"Who's coming after Duke?" Logan asks.

Nelson laughs, then coughs. "Everyone."

"No!" Logan says. "Wake up!" He shakes Nelson.

Ozzie pulls him back. "He's gone."

They both stand up, and Nelson's lifeless body lies there.

"He's dead?" I ask.

"Yes," Ozzie says.

While I should feel bad that a man died, I don't. I hated Nelson. Instead, I feel lighter. Freer.

Car doors slam outside. Ozzie goes to check it out. He runs back. "Paramedics are here."

He leads them to Duke.

"Ma'am, we need you to step back," one of the paramedics says.

Logan grabs me by the waist and half leads, half carries me out of the hallway.

"I need to go with him," I say.

Logan holds me tight. "He's going to need surgery. I'll make sure you're there when he gets out."

Surgery. The reality of the situation hits me, and I turn in Logan's arms. "Is he going to die?"

He pushes some of my hair behind my shoulder. "I'm not a doctor. I can't say."

I break out of Logan's grasp and run to my brother. "Duke, don't die on me. I need you." Tears fall from my eyes.

Duke holds out his hand toward me from the stretcher as they wheel him out of the house. "I'll try not to," he says.

I've had a love/hate relationship with my brother for years. But when it comes down to it, he's really the only family I have left. And the only one who understands all I went through. Hell, I married a monster for him. The least he can do is survive now.

"Let's go," Logan says as he leads me to the rental car.

Ozzie is already behind the wheel. He helps me into the passenger seat.

"You'll keep your eyes on her at all times?" he asks Ozzie.

"I will."

He closes the door, and I roll down the window.

"Wait. That's it?"

He turns back and shakes his head. "No, I'll find you when I can." Then he spins around and walks away.

Despite his words, something about this feels final. Is this how it ends? Neither one of us can say goodbye again, so he just walks away?

CHAPTER 17

Logan

"What the hell happened?" Brian yells as he gets out of his car.

"I told you Duke was on his way to confront Nelson."

Brian stands in front of me, waiting for me to say more. Finally, he sighs and waves his arms toward the other car. "Then who the fuck are all those dead men?"

I shrug. "They appeared to be after Duke, so perhaps Ruiz's men?"

Brian takes a step back. "You know who Ruiz is?"

Well, I must be on the right track. "No, but Nelson told Delaney that it was Ruiz's men who wanted Duke dead. When the men got out of the car, they yelled for Duke. Who the hell is Ruiz?"

"Folger, over here!" Larkin calls out.

Brian runs over, and I follow. "What do you have?"

Then Brian stops at one of the bodies. "Why the hell was he here?"

I glance at the man but don't recognize him.

"Dammit!" Brian shouts, then storms away.

"Who is it?" I ask Larkin.

He shoves his hands in his pockets as he stares sadly at the man. "An informant. A very important one."

Now I'm confused. "I thought you had an informant in Rocky Manzia's organization."

The agent frowns. "You did?"

I nod. "I'm working with Brian on this."

Larkin stares off after Brian, then turns back to me. "Well, I'm not sure how privy you are to what's going on, but if you have questions, you'll need to ask him."

Is it possible my brother lied to me about having an informant ready to take down Manzia? But for what purpose?

"I will," I tell Larkin. Then I turn and go searching for my brother.

He's down the driveway with his phone to his ear. The wind rustles the trees covering my steps. The man doesn't even glance behind him. I need to talk to him about his lack of awareness.

"Why the hell did you send Murray?" he yells into the phone.

Whoever is on the other line must be yelling cause I can hear a voice, but I can't make out what they are saying.

"Yeah, well, he's dead. Which means we no longer have a contact the cartel trusts."

Cartel? This sounds like it goes well beyond the Manzia family.

"Ruiz, you fucked up," Brian says.

I take a step back. Ruiz? Why is my brother talking to Ruiz?

"No, they didn't take out the target. Your men are all dead."

The target? They said they were after Duke. My brother was in on this? Then why the hell did he ask me to keep them safe? Maybe because he knew Delaney would insist her brother was protected too.

My stomach lurches as I realize my brother knew Duke was coming to this house because I told him. I walk back to the front of the house before my brother notices I'm there.

I must have misunderstood. There's no way my brother would turn dirty. But if he did, he's the one who had Duke taken away in an ambulance. Shit, I need to find Duke now.

I run to Brian's car. Sure enough, he left the keys in the ignition. I've chastised him more times than I can count for doing that, but right now, I'm thankful.

As I pull down the driveway, he spots me. "Hey! You can't take my car."

I roll down the window. "Something came up, sorry!"

At the first stoplight I come to, I grab my phone and punch in the name of the hospital Brian had told Ozzie. I follow the phone's directions, breaking a few speeding laws and pull right up to the emergency room. I jump out and run inside. Ozzie is in the waiting room.

"Is he here?" I ask.

Ozzie frowns. "Who?"

"Duke."

Ozzie nods. "Yes, we followed the ambulance, and they took him right back. He's in surgery."

I collapse into a chair.

"What's going on?" Ozzie asks.

I glance around. "Where's Delaney?"

Ozzie nods toward the front desk where she's sitting. "Filling out paperwork." He looks me up and down. "What's going on?"

I close my eyes, not sure how to say the words. "I overheard my brother on the phone. He was talking to Ruiz, and it sounded like he might have tipped those men off about Duke's being there."

Ozzie's brows shoot up. "You think your brother is working with the other side?"

I shrug. "I don't know for sure. But what I overheard shook me."

"Want to talk about it?"

I glance around at the crowded waiting room. "I do, but not here. And not in front of Delaney. It will have to wait."

He nods. Delaney walks back, her eyes red rimmed and glassy. "They said the surgery could take hours."

I push all my thoughts of my brother aside so I can be here for this woman. She takes the empty seat next to me.

Ozzie stands up. "I'm going to check in with Reed."

I nod, letting him know I'll stay here with her.

Delaney meets my gaze. "I didn't think I'd see you again. I've been feeling that way a lot these last few days."

I want to reach out and touch her, especially when she's

hurting. But I force myself not to. "It's been a crazy few days," I say.

An image of Delaney flipping Nelson takes over. I have to say I was impressed because the man is twice her size. Or was. I turn to her. "The way you flipped Nelson was impressive."

She pulls her feet up onto the chair so her knees are bent. She rests her head on her knees. "I told you that I've been taking some Krav Maga classes."

I hadn't realized how effective that would be for her. "I'm happy your brother did that for you. Was your Dad okay with you taking those classes?" Then I wince. That's a low thing to say. "Sorry, I didn't mean it like that."

She sighs. "He didn't know. Only Duke. I didn't even tell my best friend, Samantha."

"Why not?"

She shrugs. "It was something I did for me. I didn't want to share it."

I wonder how she kept that from her father. The man seemed to keep close tabs on his daughter. "How long have you been taking classes?"

She turns to stare straight ahead. "A little over three years."

Wow, that's longer than I expected. But then I have a feeling I know why she chose to do this. "How long have you been married to Nelson?"

She turns her gaze back to mine. "Almost four years."

"Did Duke set up those classes because of Nelson?"

She shrugs again. "He never said. I figured it was just him being a protective older brother." She takes my hand in hers. "Nelson didn't hit me until after my father passed away. Before that, he really didn't pay any attention to me."

There's so much more I want to ask her about Nelson, but it really isn't my business. Nor do I want to open old wounds.

Ozzie returns, and we all sit there, waiting until a doctor comes out in scrubs.

"Duke Manzia's family?" he asks.

Delaney stands up. "Yes." Her legs are shaking, so I stand up and put my arm around her waist to hold her steady.

"Duke's going to be fine. We were able to get the bullet out, and no major organs were damaged."

Delaney goes limp, and I catch her. "Thank you!"

"He'll need to stay here for a few days to make sure he's healing and has no infection."

"Can I see him?" she asks.

"The nurse will let you know when you can. He's still groggy from surgery, so it will be about thirty minutes or so."

Ozzie steps forward. "He needs security outside his door since this was an attempt on his life. What room is he in?"

The doctor nods. "Follow me."

Once they're gone, Delaney throws her arms around me. "Thank you for being here."

I hug her back, and I'm transported to all those years ago when holding her was second nature. Back when I thought she was my future. Hell, I still have the ring I bought for her. One time I tried to pawn it, but it felt wrong, so I packed it away instead.

Seeing Delaney again has stirred a lot of memories and feelings that I thought I'd buried. But right now, they are right at the surface.

"Did you love him? Nelson?" I ask. Damn, I guess I can't let my questions go.

She stiffens in my arms, then pulls back. "No. Never. Marrying him was the last thing I ever wanted."

I shake my head. "Then why did you?"

She said she was forced to, but I have to know if there was anything more to it.

She steps back out of my arms. "I told you. My dad forced me to. He said it was the only way to save Duke's life. Apparently, he'd done something, and the only way to fix it was for our families to merge."

I clench my fists as anger bubbles up inside me. "Did your father know Nelson was an asshole?"

She wraps her arms around herself. "He knew his whole family was, so he probably figured Nelson was, too."

I clench my jaw as I take a steadying breath. "I don't understand how your father could do that."

While I have never liked her father, I at least thought he would protect her.

"I told you; we had no choice. If we didn't marry, they would have killed Duke."

I take a few steps away. He sacrificed one child for another. I turn back. "And how long were you supposed to stay married?"

She shrugs. "There was no end date."

"Did you have kids?"

She shakes her head. "He wanted them, but I stayed on the pill. I lied and told him I had stopped. He decided I'm infertile, which is good because he went elsewhere for sex."

Ah, her marriage wasn't sexless at first. The thought of that asshole touching her is too much. I take several steps away. I need to get control of myself. It's not like I've been some kind of celibate saint all these years.

"I didn't like having sex with him," she says.

I whirl back to her. I'm going to lose it if I hear anything more. "Stop. I can't hear anymore."

She nods. "Sorry."

"No, don't apologize. I asked. Just no more. Not now."

She nods again.

"Ms. Manzia? Your brother is asking for you," a nurse says.

I follow her and the nurse to the room, then stop outside next to Ozzie.

"Do you have a plan?" he asks.

"Not yet."

"They're sitting ducks here," Ozzie says.

"I know." Somehow, we have to get both of them out of here and somewhere safe until we can figure out what is going on.

And I also have to deal with my brother. I need to figure out which side of the law he is actually on. If it's not the right side, I'm not sure what I'll do. But if he is working with the man trying to kill Delaney, he's going to have to answer to me.

CHAPTER 18

Delaney

THE HOTEL ROOM door slams shut, and I sit straight up, looking for Logan.

"I got us coffee," he says as he sets two cups on the table. "Did you sleep well?"

I stretch and get out of bed. Logan rented us a room for the night with two beds so we could get some sleep.

"I did. Thank you. How about you?"

He shrugs. "Not too great, but I'll catch up later." He smiles, but it doesn't reach his eyes.

"Is there something more you're not telling me?" I ask.

He sits on his bed. "No, I just keep going over everything that happened, trying to make sense of it." His eyes meet mine. "How did those men know Duke would be at the house? They showed up and called to him."

I hadn't thought of that. "Maybe Nelson knew he was on a plane? Or that he rented a car?"

Although, how would Nelson know that?

"Doubtful. And even if he did know, how would he know Duke was going to the house?"

I get up and grab the coffee from the table. "The only people who knew Duke was likely going to the house were you, me, and Ozzie." I take a sip as I think of anyone else. Then I turn to him. "And your brother. Maybe he accidentally told the pilot or rental car company."

I shake my head. "He wouldn't have."

"Okay, but he had to tell his boss in order to get the approval for everything, right?"

Logan takes another drink of his coffee and stares straight ahead. "Maybe."

I sit across from him on my bed. "But that would mean someone in the FBI is working with Ruiz's men." Damn, why have I never heard that name before? Who the hell are they? Did my dad work with them?

Logan grabs his phone off the nightstand and makes a call. "Hey, Trip, can you do me a favor?" He pauses and stares at me. "I need you to look into the finances for Brian Folger."

I frown. Does he suspect his own brother?

"Yes, he's my brother. And I'm not sure who his boss is, but I need a report on him, too, if you can."

If he is digging into his brother, I guess they aren't close.

"Thanks." He ends the call.

"You think your brother sold us out?"

He finishes his coffee and stands up. "I don't want to think that, but until I have all the facts, I need to treat everyone as a suspect."

I follow him to the window. "But your brother is the one who called the ambulance for my brother. If he wanted him dead, why have him taken to a hospital?"

"I've wondered the same thing. Maybe because others were around at that point in time." He turns to me. "We should get to the hospital and see when Duke can be released."

"I'll get ready." I shower and dress quickly while Logan makes a few more calls.

When we get to the hospital, Logan punches in a different floor on the elevator. "Your brother has been moved to a different room."

As we get off the elevator, we are approached by a man I don't recognize. His hair is light brown and cut short. When his eyes turn to mine, I'm struck by their color. Gray. I can't say I've ever seen anyone with eyes that color.

"Delaney, this is Fox. He works with a security firm in Seattle. He's good."

The man holds out his hand, and I shake it. It's then that I notice his T-shirt is snug and he's all muscle. Why is it that everyone Logan knows is so built?

"Fox, this is Delaney, Duke's sister."

"Nice to meet you."

"You too."

"He took over for Ozzie last night so Ozzie could get some sleep," Logan explains.

Fox glances over his shoulder. "Your brother has a

visitor who just got here. Someone named Sam. He said she was cool."

"Yeah, she is," I say. "Which room?"

"Four twelve," he says.

I march ahead, eager to see both my brother and friend. Logan walks up next to me. The door to the room is ajar, and I'm about to push it open when I hear Sam.

"Why the hell did you leave Delaney with him?"

I stop and glance at Logan, who is frowning.

"Hello, I got shot. Not like I had a lot of options," Duke says.

"She's going to fall for him again," Sam says.

Heat creeps up my neck to my cheeks. This isn't what I want him overhearing. Maybe I should walk in.

"It's your fault for putting them together in the first place," Duke says.

What is he talking about? I continue to listen.

"My fault?" Sam asks. "You told me to make sure she flirted with him that night. You were the one who told me where to take her. If I'd known it would have broken her heart, I wouldn't have done it."

I take a step back, numb. Is she talking about the night I met Logan?

"Yes, you would have. You would do anything for me, remember? Come here," Duke says.

Wet smacking comes through the open door. Are they kissing? Then my brother moans. "God, I've missed you," Duke says.

Duke and Sam are together? Since when? She's always told me she can't stand him and that he's an asshole.

"I'm serious, Duke. It's not a good idea for her to be with him."

Duke sighs. "I know, but she's safe with him. Hopefully, she won't get caught up by him again like last time."

"God, what a mistake that was."

"Yeah, she got hurt, and for nothing. It didn't stop his brother from pursuing my family."

I can't be hearing this right. Bile rises in my throat, and I run down the hall to the restroom. Logan is right behind me. I throw open the door, and he comes in, too. I make it to the toilet just as the coffee I had comes back up.

When I finish, Logan hands me a wet paper towel. Fortunately, the bathroom is a single, so no one else will walk in.

"I heard wrong, didn't I?" I ask.

Logan leans against the door. "It sounds like your brother and friend somehow planned for us to meet that night in the bar."

I turn to him. "But why? And how would they have known who you were? Or that I would go up to you? I never do that. You were the only time."

Memories flood my mind. Sam bought drinks that night and kept insisting we do shots. That was not something she normally did, but she said we needed to enjoy the night. Then she was the one who pointed out Logan.

"See that guy?" she said. "I dare you to go talk to him."

She pointed me in his direction and gave me a little push. I walked up to him but then started to chicken out. Until he turned around. The moment his eyes locked on mine, I was done.

"She pointed you out to me and kept buying me shots," I say.

"Look, I have no idea how she found out who my brother is or how I would be there on leave. But everything that happened between us was real. Maybe she did give you a push for all the wrong reasons. Just don't lose sight of the fact that what we had was good."

I glance up, and he's staring at me so intensely that it brings me back to that time. "It was good, wasn't it?" I ask.

He nods. "The best."

I toss the paper towel into the garbage. "But that doesn't change the fact that my brother and best friend used me to try to… What was your brother doing that they wanted stopped?"

He sighs. "I found out when I came to see you that winter that my brother had been investigating your father for a couple of years. He said I had to get out of there, or it would jeopardize everything. That was why I asked you to run away with me right then."

I turn away from him as the tears come. "They put us in an impossible situation. Either you betray your brother, or I lose my family."

"Yeah, that's about right."

I turn around to face him. "And we both chose our family."

He steps closer. "No. Even if my brother hadn't been investigating your dad, I still couldn't have stayed once I found out what your dad was doing. I couldn't stand by and do nothing."

"So, you had to go."

"Yes."

I want to tell him how his leaving crushed me. How I never wanted to get close to another man again. But Duke kind of already did in the parking lot of that hotel. And right now, I'm too raw with everything that's happened. I need time to process. But first, I need some answers.

I storm out of the bathroom to my brother's room. Sam is kissing Duke, and she jumps back.

"Delaney? I-I was just checking on Duke." She narrows her eyes as she focused behind me. "Logan. It's been a while."

"Save it. I overheard you two talking. Why did you set Logan and me up to meet all those years ago? What was in it for you?"

I glare at Sam, then at Duke. Both are wide-eyed, and they exchange glances.

"Delaney, I'm sorry. I never meant for you to get hurt," Sam says. She walks to me and reaches out, but I back up.

My eyes are on my brother. "Answer me."

He licks his lips. "I'm sorry, Delaney. Dad told me the FBI was monitoring him, and he had a private investigator look into the main agent."

I glance at Logan, and his jaw clenches.

"Dad found out the agent had a brother who was on leave. Dad ordered me to get you on a date with the brother."

"All we needed were photos or you two kissing or something," Sam says.

"Sam was with me when I got the call from Dad that I had to get you to the bar. I asked Sam to help me."

I sit in a chair as I remember. "That's why you rushed me to get ready to go out. You said it was because happy hour was about to end."

"I'm so sorry, Delaney. I really thought with the shots you had that you two would make out and that would be that," Sam says.

"We never thought you two would fall in love and it would blow up your life," Duke says.

I stand up and walk out of the room without a word. Logan stops and says something to Fox, then he's by my side. Neither of us speaks on the way back to the hotel room. It's what I need as I replay all my interactions with Sam and Duke from twelve years ago.

But then I realize I never confronted them about being together and lying to me. It's too much to take. I want to go home, crawl into bed, and cry. I can't because someone is after us. When it comes to Duke, danger follows him. And apparently, me too.

CHAPTER 19

Logan

"What's going on?" Reed asks over the phone.

I left Delaney in the hotel room and walked outside to call Reed. I have to talk to someone about my brother.

"I overheard something my brother said, and—" I swallow, not sure how to say the words. "And I think he may be dirty."

Reed whistles. "Coff, I really hope you're wrong, but I know for you to say that about your brother means you must have overheard something serious."

I've always spoken highly of my brother, and over the years, he's used Reed Hawthorne Security for many cases he's needed help with. And it pains me to even think he could be working with the other side.

"Coff, what did he say?" Reed asks.

"It was more than what he said. We went to Delaney's

house to stop Duke from killing Nelson. But when we got there, we were ambushed by three armed men. They called out to Duke, looking for him. The only people who knew Duke was on his way to that house were you, Ozzie, Delaney, myself, and my brother."

Laughter erupts in the background, and then a door clicks shut. "Sorry about that. Are you saying your brother tipped off these men?"

I take a deep breath. "It's a possibility. One I hope I'm wrong about. But then, he got upset when he recognized one of the men. He then called someone he referred to as Ruiz."

"Ruiz? The man who was coming after Duke and Delaney?"

I lean against the wall of the building. "Yes. And my brother was angry that man had been sent because he was killed, and according to my brother, that guy was the only one the cartel trusts."

Reed groans. "Did you say *cartel*?"

"I did."

Reed sighs. "That's not what we signed up for. I'll ask Trip—"

"Already done that. I'm waiting to hear back from him."

Reed is silent for a moment, and I know he's thinking everything through. "First, I really hope you're wrong about your brother."

I hope I'm wrong, too.

"Second, once Duke is released, the three of you and Ozzie need to fly back to New York."

"There's more."

A couple walks past, laughing about something, and I wait until they are out of earshot.

"We overheard some things Duke said to someone else, and Delaney doesn't want to be around him now."

Reed laughs. "They are essentially running for their lives. She needs to put aside petty grievances."

I sigh. "It's more than that. Trust me. I think it would be best if Duke stayed with Stormy's guy."

"Splitting them up would cost double the manpower since both you and Fox would need backup," Reed says. "I doubt the FBI will foot the bill for that."

He's right. "Then I'll take vacation so no one is paying for my time. And I won't ask for backup."

The familiar pop of a soda can opening comes through the phone, and I can see Reed taking a drink as he does every morning.

"You want to take vacation time?"

"I will. Yes."

He sighs. "You told me you could be objective despite your personal history with Delaney. I have to say I'm not so sure about that right now."

"I can be. Please don't pull me off."

"Why not?"

For the next five minutes, I spew our entire history and how I can't let her go again. I'm sure this is not doing anything to convince him I can be objective, but dammit, he has to know I can't walk away.

He's silent, and I wonder if we were disconnected.

"Reed?"

"Yeah, I'm here. Your brother knew all this when he asked you to watch her?"

"He did. He knew I had eyes on her, and I'd be the best person to keep her safe."

Reed mumbles something. "Coff, were you stalking the woman?"

"No!" I say defensively, but then I think about what I was doing. "I was watching her."

"Jesus. It's a miracle you've been able to stay focused this long. And let me guess, you two have rekindled your relationship?"

"No, not at all." Although, if I'm being honest with myself, part of me wants that. But so many years have passed, and we aren't the same people. What I want is what I had, and nothing will bring that back. Once she learned what her family did, she stayed. How could she stay?

"Let me talk to Stormy, and I'll call you back."

"Thank you."

The more I think about it, the more it bothers me. When I told her about her dad being a criminal, she didn't believe me. But did she really know then? I trusted her, but was I wrong?

I head back up to our room with my head spinning. Delaney is lying on the bed, staring at the ceiling, when I walk in.

"I'm bored out of my mind," she says. "At least if I had a phone, I could read a book or check the news."

I stare at her. In some ways, it's like no time has passed and she's still that girl I picked up in a bar. But in every other way, everything has changed.

She sits up. "How did your call go?"

"Fine."

She laughs. "Well, that tells me a lot. Are we going to New York?"

Yeah, I might have floated that idea by her before talking to Reed. Not my best choice. "I don't know yet."

"Okay, why don't we get lunch?" she asks.

"Why didn't you leave?" I rub my forehead. I should have thought before speaking and eased into this.

Her brow furrows. "You mean twelve years ago?"

I shake my head. "No, why didn't you leave once you learned the truth about your dad?"

Her eyes dart to the window. "Oh. That's not easy to answer."

I cross my arms. "Try."

Her eyes move back to mine as she swallows. "I've asked myself that question many times. The first time I thought something wasn't right was after I overheard my dad on a phone call. I asked him about it, and he had some explanation. I wanted so much to believe him, so I did."

I'm not surprised she'd believe him. "But at some point, you must have seen through his excuses."

She nods. "I did. I called you."

My stomach flips, and I sit down on my bed. I always wondered if she would reach out. But it was something I would never know. "I changed my number about a year after I last saw you."

"Why?"

For a split second, I wonder if I should make something up but then decide the truth is best. "I drove myself crazy checking to see if you'd called or texted. After a year, I figured you wouldn't, so I got a new phone and number, hoping it would help me to stop obsessing over you."

She blinks several times, and her eyes become glassy. She turns away. "Oh."

I sit on the edge of the bed. "If you called, then you were ready to leave?"

She nods.

"Why didn't you?"

When she turns back, her eyes are full of tears. "I was too scared to leave my best friend, family—everything I knew. I didn't have any money saved up."

"Why not?"

She swings her legs off the bed, putting her back to me. "My dad didn't pay me to work at the business. He said my payment was living rent-free and he'd buy me any food or clothing I wanted. He gave me an allowance, but I used most of that on gas. I could never save much. Now I see it was my dad's way of controlling me. A few years later, Duke told me he'd opened a bank account for me. By then, I knew where the money came from, and I refused to touch it."

No, this doesn't make sense. This is not the Delaney I knew. "Did you really know about your dad? You know, back when I asked you to leave?"

She turns back to me. "No. I told you I didn't."

I nod.

"You don't believe me?"

"None of this makes sense, Delaney."

She stands up and faces me, keeping the bed between us. "What do you mean?"

Well, I guess we are really going to get into this. I take a deep breath. "The girl I met was a 'take charge, I'm doing things my way' kind of girl. But the woman I see today just let her dad tell her what to do and she never fought to get her own way. Was the Delaney I knew a lie?"

Her brow shoots up. "A lie? Are you kidding me?"

I shrug. "Explain it to me then."

She grabs a pillow and holds it up to her face, then screams into it. After she tosses the pillow, she turns to me, eyes ablaze with anger. "No, it wasn't a lie. That was me. It is me, dammit! But there is another part of me that, like I said before, was scared to leave my family and friends. And unfortunately, that is the part that got me into this mess. I placed my loyalties with the wrong man."

I've been on my own since I turned eighteen and enlisted. Maybe that skews my judgment a little. But nothing about this woman seemed scared when I met her.

"What were you scared of?" I ask.

She laughs. "Seriously? You, of all people, have to ask?"

I don't respond, and she walks around the bed until she's in front of me. Then she pokes me in the chest rather hard.

"When you left, it hurt. I mean, it hurt like hell. You wanted me to give up everyone I knew and move to Virginia, where I knew no one. Then what? You'd ship out and I would be there all alone. Did you think about that?"

I close my eyes. I hadn't, actually. All I could think about was getting her away from her family.

"I couldn't do that. And you left. I was falling for you. Hard. And you just left like it was nothing. I couldn't lose anyone else like that, so yes, I held on tightly to my family and my friend, Samantha. Did it blind me to my dad? It did."

Tears fall down her cheeks, and I itch to wipe them away for her, but I don't.

"I swore off relationships after you left. But I sure as hell wasn't going to swear off the only people I had left in this world."

"Then why did you call me? You said you called a year later?"

She sniffles. "I missed you so much. I thought maybe we could try again. But when I discovered your phone number didn't work, I knew you really had forgotten about me."

My hands go to her shoulders. "Delaney, I never forgot about you. I have thought about you so much. I tried to date again, but nothing compared to what we had. You ruined me for all women. And I cannot tell you how often I dreamed of finding you again and trying harder to convince you to come with me."

Using her sleeve, she wipes at her eyes. "Yeah?"

"Yeah."

I pull her against me and wrap my arms around her. "I did love you, Delaney. Hell, I'm pretty sure I still do. And even though I've been so angry with you for not believing me that night and coming with me, I see now that I really hadn't thought about it from your perspective. I'm sorry. I'm so sorry."

"No, I'm sorry," she says.

She leans back, and her eyes meet mine. "Sometimes it feels like a lifetime has passed since we were together. Then other times, like now, it feels like no time has passed at all."

She's right. The urge to kiss her is strong, but that would be crossing a line. I'm here to protect her. Although, if I go by that, this entire conversation crossed a line.

Her hand moves up, and she rubs the spot between my eyes. "You're conflicted about what to do. I get it. So, I'll make the decision for you."

Before I can ask what that means, she moves her hand behind my neck and pulls herself onto her toes as her lips meet mine. It's a quick sweet kiss, but the spark is still there. It triggers something in me, and I bend down and crush my mouth to hers. The moment her lips part and her tongue meets mine, I'm more than turned on as my desire for this woman consumes me, heightening every single sensation to a whole new level. In the back of my mind, there's a voice telling me to slow this down. But I don't listen. I can't. I've missed Delaney for far too long.

CHAPTER 20

Delaney

I can't believe this is really happening. I break our kiss and stare at this man.

"What's wrong?" he asks.

My lips curl up into a huge grin. "Nothing. I just can't believe we are here together."

He smiles. "Despite the circumstances, I'm happy we are."

"Me too."

I push up on my toes and resume kissing him. All these years without him, I forced myself to forget how good it could feel if I was in the right man's arms.

His hand moves up my back, under my shirt, and I want more. But when his lips move to that sensitive spot on my neck, my body ignites. I reach for the bottom of his T-shirt and yank it up. He steps back.

"Are you sure about this?" Concern etches his face as he stares at me.

"I'm certain."

He smiles and pulls his shirt off with one hand. My eyes go to his chest, which is much more muscular than it was twelve years ago. I run my hands over his pecs and over his nipple. He moans as my hands roam.

"You're different than you were," I say, letting my hands feel every ridge from his pecs down to his abs.

"Now, it's my turn to see you. Take off your shirt," he demands.

I step back and remove my shirt and pants. His eyes flare as I stand before him.

"You're so fucking beautiful," he says as he reaches behind my neck and pulls me into him. His other hand moves down my back until he grips my ass.

"Take off your pants," I say to him, copying his demanding tone.

He chuckles but shucks them off. Then he backs me up. When my knees hit the bed, I fall onto it. He leans over as he kisses down my neck. I lean my head the other way, giving him access as he trails his mouth behind my ear.

"Right there," I say when he finds my sensitive spot.

His hand moves behind my back, and in one swift move, he unhooks my bra and slips it off my arms. "Delaney, you're so fucking sexy."

He's the only man who has ever said that to me. He's the only man who has made me feel treasured. How the hell did I ever walk away from him?

"Hey, are you with me?" he asks, looking into my eyes.

I nod. "Yeah, sorry. Just remembering you used to say that to me."

He smiles. "You remember that?"

I nod.

"I wonder what else you might remember." He slowly pulls down my underwear, then spreads my legs.

I prop up on my elbows to watch him. He grins as he moves into place. The moment his tongue runs up my slit, I release my arms, falling back as my hips buck up. Then he zeroes in on my clit, licking and sucking.

It's intense and fast, but I don't want him to quit. "Yes!" I hiss out, and my orgasm quickly builds.

He stops, and I find him staring at me.

"What's wrong?"

"I'm savoring all of this. Being here with you. And, of course, this." When his tongue meets my clit again, I'm right there on the edge again. This man always knew exactly how to touch me, and all these years later, it's no different. As I get closer, he inserts his finger inside me, and it's my undoing.

"Logan!" I yell as I come harder than I ever remember coming before.

As I come down, I open my eyes to see he's watching me. Then he kisses his way up my body, stopping at my breast and then moving to my neck.

His phone rings, and he ignores it.

I wrap my arms around his neck as he kisses me. My hands move down his back to his ass. Everywhere I touch is muscle on this man. Then I move my hand around to the front and grip his hard cock.

His moan is deep, and knowing I still have such an effect on him, too, turns me on even more. Despite having just orgasmed, I'm aching with need for this man. I need him inside me now. As I tug at his underwear, his phone rings again.

He breaks our kiss and presses his forehead to mine. "I hate to say this, but I should probably see who is calling."

I nod, wishing whoever it is would leave us alone for just a little while longer. But the phone continues to ring.

He rolls over and grabs it from the nightstand. "It's Brian. The third time he's called." He stares at the phone as he takes a deep breath. Then he answers on speakerphone.

I know I should probably stop, but I can't. My hands roam over his back and around until I graze his nipples. His eyes half close, but he doesn't stop me.

"Hey, Brian, you have news?" he chokes out.

"You all right? Not dead?"

Logan grins at me. "I'm good."

My hand moves down and into his underwear. He leans back just enough for me to get inside and wrap my hand around his cock.

Brian sighs heavily into the phone. "I was worried about you. But I do have news. It turns out we don't need your eyewitness testimony anymore."

I stroke while moving my body up and down his back, mimicking what I want to do but also making sure my breasts rub against him.

He groans. "Why not?"

"Uh, I thought this would be good news. Did you want to testify?" Brian asks.

Logan turns his head and arches a brow at me, but I continue to stroke him. "No, I didn't. What's going on?"

Brian chuckles. "We got lucky. It turns out that parking lot is a park-and-ride. There are a few cameras installed for security purposes. The cameras caught Nelson going in and out of the warehouse. At no time that day was Duke on the video. And Duke also has an alibi. All charges against him have been dropped."

I loosen my grip and remove my hands. The mention of my brother is a bit of a mood killer. But at least it's good news. If the charges are dropped, maybe whoever is coming after us will stop.

"That's great news. What's his alibi?" Logan asks as he watches me retreat off the bed and dig around for my clothes.

"A woman. She came in and said Duke was with her the night before and all of that day. She had some photos they had taken of themselves that the police confirmed match the date and time of the explosion."

A woman just now comes forward? "What's her name?" I ask as I put on my underwear.

"You're on speakerphone," Logan tells Brian.

"Oh, hi, Delaney. The woman's name is Samantha Hatten."

My best friend? She said she was with my brother? They kissed at the hospital. I heard it. Are they in a relationship? I was so angry when I confronted them that I forgot to ask.

Is it possible they have been together since they set Logan and me up? Maybe before then? No, Sam has dated men over the years. She can't be with my brother. She would have told me. Wouldn't she?

"We're making sure all our informants know it wasn't Duke, and they are getting the word out. Hopefully, Duke and Delaney will be safe soon. And then you can go back to New York."

Back to New York. Where he lives. Where his job and friends are. And it's nowhere near me.

"That's great news," Logan says, but he's frowning.

I meet his gaze, wondering if he's thinking the same thing.

"I need to go. Thanks, Brian." He ends the call.

"You're going back to New York." It's not a question. "And I'm staying here. What happened a moment ago can't happen again." Even as those words come out of my mouth, they feel wrong. The idea of this man walking away again makes me ill.

He stares at me for a moment. "Would you consider moving to New York?" he asks.

I stare up at the ceiling. "And do what? Everything I know is in San Diego."

He turns away from me, then walks to the bathroom and slams the door.

Here we are again. I know if I ask him to move here, he'll say no. If I want to give this a try, I'll have to make all the sacrifices, not him.

He storms out of the bathroom. "Why are we here again?"

I jump up. "Because you keep putting us here!" I yell. I'm angry and no longer willing to hold back. "Just like before, you want me to move and give up everything and you sacrifice nothing."

His phone rings again, and I want to throw the damn thing out of the window. He walks toward the phone.

"Ignore it," I say.

His head drops. "I can't. It's Fox."

Fox, the man watching my brother.

He answers the phone and sighs as he sits on the bed. "Okay, I'll let her know."

He turns to face me. "Apparently, Duke is demanding to speak to you."

I know I need to talk to my brother, but I'm still so angry. I've actually been thankful he threw my phone out of the window so I don't have to talk to Sam, either.

"Fine. I'll talk to him."

Logan puts the phone back to his ear. "All right, put him on." Then he hands the phone to me.

"Hello?"

"Delaney! I'm so sorry. You walked out before I could explain," Duke says.

"You explained. Dad ordered you to compromise the FBI investigation. You and Sam used me to do it."

"We didn't *use* you. Sam thought you would have some fun, and I'll be honest, I didn't like the idea of you making out with the guy. Then I found out you slept with him. I was furious at Sam for letting it get that far."

I roll my eyes. "Stop. I don't want to hear anymore." I end the call and hand the phone to Logan.

"You don't want to hear what else he has to say?"

I'm not surprised he heard the conversation since my brother was yelling most of the time.

I shake my head. "My brother is good at twisting words. He's going to keep talking until he's not at fault."

Logan watches me, and I know he wants to continue our conversation, but I just can't right now. In the last twenty-four hours, I've watched my husband die. Even if I didn't love him, I'm still not sure how to process that. I've been shot at. I discovered my brother and best friend have lied to me for years. Then to top it off, the only man I have loved gave me a toe-curling orgasm and then made it clear I needed to do all the sacrificing in this relationship. I've sacrificed for everyone my whole damn life. First my dad, then Nelson, and now Duke. With Manzia as my last name, I'm expected to fall in line.

I need to process everything. "I'm going to take a nap."

"Oh. Okay," Logan says.

I put the rest of my clothes back on and slip under the covers. Somehow, remaining naked doesn't feel right. To my surprise, I drift off to sleep quickly.

I jolt awake to the sound of Logan's phone ringing. "If it's Duke, I'm not talking to him," I say as I yawn.

Logan answers the phone from across the room. "You sure?" he says several times. When he ends the call, he shoves the phone into his pocket but doesn't say anything.

I sit up. "Something wrong?"

He turns to face me. "My brother confirmed it's safe for you and Duke to go home."

"Just like that? It's safe?"

He nods. "Apparently, whatever Brian did to get the

word out that Nelson set up the guys in the warehouse worked. He said they are going after Nelson's family now."

I let that sink in for a moment. "Do you trust that information?"

He sits on his bed. "I do. I may be having some issues with my brother, but I trust him on this."

I want to ask why, but I don't. Knowing we have to part ways again, I need to start distancing myself. And while my life no longer being in danger should be good news, it doesn't feel like it. I avoid his eyes. It's the only way I can keep my emotions in check. It's probably for the best that we get as far as possible from each other. If we can't agree on how to be together, then the sooner we cut our ties, the better.

"Let's go then." I stand and put on my shoes. Then I walk to the door.

He doesn't move for a moment, then the car keys jingle in his hand.

We're silent as we drive to my house. He pulls up and turns off the engine.

"Delaney." He's staring out the windshield, and talking about the inevitable is the last thing I want to do right now.

"Don't make this worse than it already is," I say. I reach for the door, and he grabs my wrist.

"I can't let you go again."

I still. "Logan, you won't move for me. And I can't move for you. We need to say goodbye before we get hurt again." I chance a glance in his direction and am surprised by his glassy eyes.

"It's too late for that."

I blink back the tears that threaten.

"You said you can't move for me. Why can't you? Before, it was your dad, but he's gone. What's stopping you?"

"Everything I know is here. My brother, my friends, my job."

His brows shoot up. "Everything? What exactly would that be? The brother and best friend you aren't speaking to? The job as part of a crime family? Or maybe there's something else you haven't told me?"

I shake my head. "There's nothing else, Logan." Then I turn to face him. "Why can't you move here? That's what you agreed to do twelve years ago. But now it's off the table?"

He shakes his head. "I have a job I love, friends in New York. Friends you would like if you just gave it a chance."

The tears finally break loose and run down my cheek. "I can't."

He huffs out a breath. "From where I sit, it's not that you can't; it's that you won't." He releases my wrist. "Go ahead and leave."

I get out of the car and into my house as fast as I can, and I don't look back. He's wrong. I can't leave everyone.

As I walk past the staircase and toward my dad's office, I notice the bullet holes from the shootout. In the office, papers are all over the floor, as if someone emptied all the files. On the desk, there is a bottle of scotch and a dirty glass. Nelson was at that desk when he asked me for the divorce over the phone.

I run out of the room to the dining room. This has

happier memories, like the time Logan stayed here with us. But then I remember sitting at that table the first time Nelson called me a bitch. My eyes move to the kitchen and the staircase my mom would go up as soon as she finished eating. Instead of parenting us, she would hide out in her room.

I slide down the wall to the floor and cry. I'm almost thirty-four and still feel bound to this house, this family. Why can't I let it go?

Can I live with never seeing Logan again? I've thought about him so many times over the years, and I didn't imagine our connection. It's real, and it's still there.

But can I risk everything again for a man? While this is a different risk than falling in line for my dad or submitting to Nelson, it's still a risk. What happens if it doesn't work out?

I need to talk to Sam. She always helps me think through things. But Sam lied to me. I need to see her and find out why. Since I don't have a phone, I can't call her.

My eyes spot the hook where we keep spare keys. Nelson's car is still parked out front. I grab the spare key.

Wait, what day is it? Sam might not be home. No, it's Saturday, so she won't be at work.

As I walk to the front door, I again notice the bullet holes and shudder. Suddenly, the idea of staying here is the last thing I want. Maybe Sam can help me find somewhere to go. It's the least she owes me for lying all these years.

The Porsche goes faster than I expected. I have to watch my speed so I don't get pulled over. The car smells like

Nelson, and that's not a good thing. He always believed women loved a lot of cologne.

A familiar car is in Sam's driveway. I march up to her door and brace myself to see him. Before I can knock, the door swings open and Duke is standing before me.

"Delaney?" He reaches out and pulls me in for a big hug, pulling me into the house as he does so. "I'm so happy to see you."

Sam walks into the room as Duke sets me down.

I step back. "How long have you two been together?"

Sam sighs. "I think we need a drink for this conversation. Let's go to the kitchen."

I follow her in and hope they have a reasonable explanation for keeping me in the dark.

CHAPTER 21

Logan

It's been two days since Delaney got out of my car and didn't look back. I'm back in New York working on all the paperwork for my last assignment. Since the FBI was involved, it's twice as much as it would normally be.

Despite my great attempt to focus on the task, my mind keeps going back to her. What I don't understand is how she could walk away so easily. It's possible if we tried a relationship that it would crash and burn. Or it would be the best thing.

I go to the kitchen and pour myself a cup of coffee. When I open the fridge to grab my creamer, I know right away something is amiss. The bottle of hazelnut creamer on the top shelf is not the one I bought. How do I know this? Because I used a Sharpie to make a small mark near the bottom, and this one doesn't have that.

Instead of risking it, I close the fridge door and walk my black coffee back to my office. Lightning appears in my door, wearing a grin. Of course, he's behind whatever is going on.

"Can I help you?" I ask.

"Glad you're back," he says.

I know he's waiting for me to drink the coffee and react to whatever he did to the creamer. I take a big gulp and smile at him.

He frowns and steps further in. "No creamer today?"

"Nope. And not to be short, but I've got a lot of paperwork to get through."

Lightning nods. "I understand. I'll let you get to it." He backs out of the office, staring at me.

Once he's gone, I get back to work. But I don't get very far before Ozzie walks in.

"Hey, looks like we have a full day of paperwork."

I lean back. "Yeah. One day at least. Maybe two."

Ozzie frowns. "Are you all right?"

I glance up. "Yeah, why wouldn't I be?"

He shrugs. "You went straight to your room when you got home last night. Now you're drinking your coffee black."

"The coffee is black because of Lightning."

Ozzie nods. "Got it."

Maybe I should talk to someone about what's going on. "But you're right. I'm not all right. It's Delaney."

"I thought I picked up on something between you two. What happened?"

And suddenly, I don't feel like sharing our story again. "Yeah, I thought there was. I was wrong."

Ozzie nods. "Sorry. That sucks."

"Yes, it does."

"Want to grab a beer after work?"

I scratch my beard. "No thanks. I'll probably go home and crash." I'm jet lagged, and despite going to my room last night, I tossed and turned. Sleep tonight would probably be a good thing.

"Okay. I better get back to it." He walks away, and I try again to focus on work.

But after an hour, I've gotten little done, and my mind is going in circles with memories of Delaney driving me crazy.

"Fuck!" I yell as I toss a pen across the room.

Thunder and Lightning walk in and close the door behind them.

"I'm not in the mood for any of your pranks today," I say.

"Clearly," Lightning says. "I overheard what you told Ozzie. And anyone with woman problems should talk to us, not Ozzie."

I cross my arms. "Why is that?"

Lightning grins. "Because we actually have girlfriends." Then he sits in a chair across from me.

Thunder sits in the other chair. "I'm here under duress."

I chuckle. Thunder goes along with a lot of Lightning's antics, to a point. Apparently, if he doesn't, Lightning can get obnoxious. And he already starts out high on the obnoxious scale so that's saying something.

Lightning crosses his legs. "What's going on?"

I sigh. You know what? Fuck it. Lightning knows a little about the woman from my past, and maybe they would be good to talk to. I need to do something.

"You know how I've mentioned a woman from my past?"

Lightning's eyes widen. "Yes, the one you loved, and no one will ever compare."

I frown. "I didn't say that."

He shrugs. "Yeah, you kind of did at the airport. Anyway, what about her?"

Both men watch me, Lightning eagerly awaiting what I have to say. Thunder could be sleeping with his eyes open. He doesn't have many expressions, so it's hard to tell.

"That woman was Delaney, and she was who I was protecting on my last assignment."

Lightning whistles. "Wow, I bet you were shocked when you first saw her."

I shift in my seat. "Not exactly. I'd been watching her."

Thunder cocks his head. "You were stalking your ex?"

I blow out a breath. "No, I wasn't *stalking* her. Why does everyone think that?"

"Cause that's what it sounds like."

Lightning puts his hand up. "We'll get back to that. What happened?"

I lick my lips as I think back on what happened in the hotel room. God, I swear I can still taste her.

Lightning snaps his fingers. "Earth to Coff. Okay, so you're still in love; that we can see."

I lean my head back. "We kissed and more. Then I told

her I wanted to try again. She refuses to come to New York and says she can't leave California. But the thing is, she *can* leave. She just won't."

"Huh," Lighting says.

"What?"

"I get why she doesn't want to drop everything and move here when you haven't seen each other in what, ten years?"

"Twelve."

Lightning nods. "That's a big risk for her if she doesn't know anyone else here. But why does it have to go from nothing to living together?"

Living together? I didn't ask her to do that. I close my eyes. Why would she move all the way across the country if I wasn't willing to do something for her? This is what she was trying to tell me. Why the hell does it take Lightning saying it for me to get it?

"Why don't you two date first?" Thunder asks. "No, it's not going to be convenient with the distance, but it sounds like you two need to get to know each other again."

Lightning points at Thunder. "Exactly. What he said."

Date. That's what normal people do. So why the hell didn't I think of that? Because deep down, I know I want everything with her. But just because I'm ready for it doesn't mean she is. Damn, they're right. I nod. "You're right. All I was thinking about was getting back to what we'd had as if nothing had happened. But a lot has happened."

Thunder stands up. "If you were protecting her, then

I'm guessing a lot has happened in her life. Take it slow. Good luck, man."

"Thanks."

Lightning stands, too. "If you need any more advice, let us know. And sorry about the creamer. I didn't realize you were going through something."

I close my eyes and shake my head. "I knew it. What did you do?"

Lightning's hands go to his hips. "How did you know it? Is that why you didn't use it?"

I stand up and stretch. "Yes. Now, what did you do to it?"

He grins. "I poured out the creamer in there and replaced it with a mixture of sour cream and water. You know, so it would pour."

Huh, it was the same container? Maybe he washed off my mark.

Thunder shakes his head. "Too far, Lightning. Too far. I need to get back to work."

He walks out the door, and Lightning follows.

Thunder's words repeat in my head. A lot has happened to her and in a short time. Her world was turned upside down. And instead of supporting her, I was making demands. Fuck, I'm an idiot.

"Son of a bitch!" Axel yells from the kitchen.

I walk across the hall and spot him at the sink with his head bent over, drinking straight from the faucet.

"What's going on?"

He spits out some water and wipes his mouth with his sleeve. "I used some expired creamer in my coffee."

"If it was hazelnut, it wasn't expired. Lightning swapped it out."

Axel's eyes narrow. "Lightning."

I nod, and Axel storms off. He's not one to participate in the office shenanigans. Hell, he's hardly ever here since he is on assignments more than any of the rest of us. But I have to wonder as he storms down the hall if he might just get Lightning back.

I find myself smiling, and I realize it's because of Thunder's advice. I have no idea if Delaney will consider dating, but I have to try.

Something crashes near the front of the office, and I run toward it. The guys are all standing near Reed's door. I glance in, and on the floor are the pieces of Reed's printer.

"What's going on?" Axel asks.

Reed grabs some papers off his desk and holds them up. "Stacy. Just when you think she can't cause any more problems, she pulls this."

Axel takes the papers from Reed and scans them. "Holy shit. She claims she had another child with Hawthorne and that he is entitled to half of Reed Hawthorne Security."

Lightning steps up to Axel. "Let me see." He quickly scans. "There's no way this is true. It says the son is twenty-two. Hawthorne was married to Alicia's mom then."

Alicia is Lightning's girlfriend and the stepdaughter Stacy tried to kill.

"Well, it's possible, but it would mean he cheated on his first wife," Axel says.

Reed shakes his head. "No, he never would have done

that. Besides, he didn't meet Stacy until after his first wife died."

"Regardless of whether the son is legitimate, why would he get Hawthorne's share of the business? If it's going to kids, then Alicia and her little sister would get a share, too," Lightning says. "There's no logic here."

Reed falls back into his chair. "Exactly. But she's representing herself so she can say whatever the hell she wants, and we still have to defend it. It's bullshit. But by doing this, she's not only wasting our time, but she's also keeping the company in a negative media spotlight."

"Let me guess, she's willing to stop everything for a monetary payout," I say.

Reed points at me. "Exactly. But I refuse to pay. If I do, she'll just keep doing this."

He's right. "Okay, but how do you make her quit?" I ask.

Jerry Reed steps into the office. "Good morning, everyone. I couldn't help but overhear. The way we are going to stop this woman is by asking for attorney fees. A lot of attorney fees. Once she realizes she's losing money, not gaining, she'll stop."

Reed stands up and walks over to his dad and hugs him. Having Reed's dad as the company attorney has been a godsend these past couple of years. We all know we can trust the man. Sadly, trust has been hard to come by with some of our associates.

"Thank you for handling this. When it comes to this woman, I can't see straight. She's taken so much already."

"And that's why we're going to stop her," Jerry says.

CHAPTER 22

Delaney

Last night, after kicking Duke out of the room, Sam finally opened up to me. It turns out she fell in love with Duke the summer I met Logan. She didn't want to tell me unless Duke was serious, too. But then she discovered the truth about my family. Yes, she discovered it before I did. She gave him an ultimatum to leave. He said he couldn't, so she broke it off. And she kept her word, she swears, until she found out he was shot. Apparently, I walked in on their reunion.

Sam has convinced me to stay in her guest room. I'm still angry with Duke for using me, but Sam was adamant that Duke didn't mean for it to go as far as it did, and he's been tormented about it all these years.

He's been tormented? On the one hand, I met the man I've been convinced was the love of my life, but on the other hand, they set us up in an impossible situation where we would both end up hurt. All to keep my dad out of jail.

And after all that, their plan didn't work. Logan's brother continued to investigate the family. So yeah, while I understand what they did, I'm not okay with their manipulation. But until I figure out how to deal with that, I'm trying to be grateful that I can stay here with them and not in that awful mansion I grew up in.

"Rise and shine," Duke says as he knocks on the bedroom door. "We need to get going."

"All right," I shout through the door.

After a shower and a quick breakfast, Duke drives us to the office.

"Nelson's uncle called me yesterday. He wants to take over all arrangements for Nelson's funeral. I figured you wouldn't object," Duke says.

I snort. "Sorry. I know I shouldn't be disrespectful since he's dead. You're right. I have no objection."

Duke glances at me. "There's more."

"Of course, there is."

"He sent over a document he wants you to sign, agreeing you'll forgo any of Nelson's assets. Basically, he wants to keep everything in his family."

I roll my eyes. "I don't want anything of Nelson's."

"That's what I figured. I'll let his uncle know."

We drive the rest of the way in silence. Fortunately, when we reach the office, we find it in good condition. When we ran out of here last week, we didn't bother locking up. Since Duke took all the money from the safe —wait.

"Duke, where's the money you took from the safe?"

"Hidden."

I turn and stare at him, but he doesn't say anymore. "Where?"

He holds his fingers to his lips, indicating I shouldn't speak. Then he grabs a piece of paper and writes something. Then he turns it to me.

There might be bugs in here now.

He's right. We left the front door wide open if the FBI wanted to take advantage of that.

He sighs. "I don't want to run this business anymore." Then he points to the note he wrote.

I nod. "I don't want to be a part of it, either."

"Well then. What are we going to do?"

I shrug. "Maybe just construction?"

He laughs. "I don't think that will make enough money to support us."

"What are you talking about? I do the financial records, and it makes plenty."

He arches a brow.

"That's not from construction?"

He puts an arm around me, then whispers. "I love you, Delaney, but damn, you are naïve sometimes."

"I'm not naïve. Nobody ever told me anything. Shoot me for not thinking the worst of you all."

He chuckles as he loops his arm through mine, then leads me out to the parking lot, where we continue the conversation.

My mind whirls. "I've been doing the books on the illegal side?"

"Yep."

How the hell did I not know that? Well, probably because I don't know what supplies are actually necessary for the projects we do. Or what was really purchased or not. Hell, I never bothered to learn because I have no interest in any of it. It isn't what I wanted to do. I was in design school when my father threatened to cut me off financially if I didn't switch to a different college and take business courses.

Listening to him was my first mistake. It is why I've been trapped here all these years.

"Until we figure out what to do, we will have to carry on with business as usual. The last thing we want is someone thinking they can come in and take over," Duke says. "But we will not have any conversation about it in there. Got it?"

"Got it."

He stares at me.

"What?"

"How are you doing? I mean, really. Nelson was shot and killed in front of you. I was shot in front of you. Hell, you were in the house with all the bullets flying. I know this isn't something you're used to."

I cross my arms. "And you are?"

He shrugs. "Not really. I try to avoid shootouts since they can be deadly and all."

I shove him. "This isn't something to joke about."

He grows serious. "You're right. It's not. But seeing Nelson killed had to have been hard for you."

I take a step back and study him. "Are you serious? You

think I feel sorrow over his death? The man made my life a living hell. Trust me, I'm fine." Maybe I should have talked with him as well as Sam last night so he'd know my mind is not on Nelson. It's on Logan.

We walk back in, and I barely sit down when the bell over our front door dings. In walks a man in a delivery uniform. "Hello, I have a package for Duke Manzia."

Duke steps forward. "That's me."

He takes the package, and the man leaves. Duke carries it to my desk and opens it. He pulls out a box and hands it to me. "Here you are."

It's a new phone.

"Sorry about tossing your old phone out the window. I ordered you a new one with your old number, so hopefully, you can import your contacts."

"Thank you." I tear open the box and follow the set-up instructions. I plug in the charger while it restarts.

As I wait for it to be ready, I grab the first thing in my inbox and get to work.

The phone buzzes and beeps as everything loads. After dealing with my fifth invoice, I'm out of patience and I grab the phone.

I check my messages, and my stomach flutters when I see two texts from an unknown number. Logan. But then I realize they were from a few days ago, and tears well in my eyes. I lean back and wave my hands in front of my face to dry my eyes. Why did I expect any current messages from him? I told him goodbye, and as far as he knows, I don't have a phone anymore.

I wonder what he's doing right now. No, that won't do

me any good. I used to be able to go months without thinking about him. Now, after what happened in that hotel room, I can't go five minutes, and it's driving me crazy.

My phone buzzes, and I grab it.

Unknown: *Hey, I see you got a new phone.*

What the hell?

Me: *Who is this?*

Unknown: *Logan.*

My heart rate picks up. Is it really him?

Me: *How did you know I got a new phone?*

Logan: *This might sound creepy, but it isn't, I swear.*

I laugh as I wait for his next message.

Logan: *I asked Trip to let me know if he got any hits on your phone number. And he just messaged me saying it was reactivated.*

Okay, yes, that is Logan.

Me: *Wow. I literally just got it minutes ago. I don't know whether to be impressed or creeped out.*

Logan: *Told you Trip was good at what he does. And I vote for impressed.*

I'm grinning like a fool just texting this man. But what does this mean?

Me: *So why were you stalking my phone number?*

Logan: *Why does everyone use that word? I was not stalking you.*

Interesting.

Me: *Who's everyone?*

Logan: *It doesn't matter. What matters is I want to talk to you. Can I call?*

My stomach flutters at the idea of hearing his voice.

Me: *Yes.*

I barely have the message sent and my phone is ringing.

"Hello?" I answer.

"Hey," Logan says.

I lean back in my chair, grinning. I feel like a teenager whose crush just called. "What do you want to talk about?"

"I didn't like how things ended with us. I'm sorry I didn't get it. But I understand you don't want to give up everything to move here when we don't know if this will last."

His words surprise me.

"I want to propose something else."

"Okay, I'm curious." I hold my breath, wondering what he came up with.

"Let's date."

I stare out the window as I process what he said. But we live in separate states, so I'm not sure what he's thinking. "How? You're still in New York, and I'm still here."

"That's true. I thought we could talk on the phone and maybe talk over FaceTime and get to know each other again. In a couple of weeks, I can fly out to see you as long as I'm not out on an assignment."

I sit up straight. "I don't really know much about your job. How often do you have assignments, and how long are they?"

"They vary. The longest I've had was a few months, but usually, they are a week at a time."

A few months? That would be hard if we were really together.

"As for how often, sometimes I have assignments with only a day or two in between. Other times I get a week or more."

I guess that makes sense. He was protecting me, and we had no idea how long the threat would last. My mind goes back to the shootout at my house. "The shootout. How often are you in that much danger?"

He sighs. "I'm often in dangerous situations, but you have to understand, I'm trained for it. And I usually have my team or part of it with me. We always have each other's back."

The idea of him out there makes me nervous. "Okay."

"Hey, I've been doing this for years, and before that, I was a Navy SEAL. I got this."

"A SEAL? Like one of those elite soldiers?"

He laughs. "Sailor, not soldier."

"You weren't elite when I met you, were you?"

He laughs harder. "Wow, guess I made a great impression. I'd like to think I was pretty elite. But no, I wasn't a SEAL."

I laugh, too. I never could get that straight when we were together. I think because, in my mind, he said he was leaving the service, so I didn't think of him as a sailor but simply as my boyfriend.

"What do you say? Want to date me?" he asks.

I do, but the last time when he left, it crushed me. "What exactly do you mean by date? Are we dating other people, too?"

"No. I don't want anyone else, and I don't want you with anyone else. Can you live with that?"

I smile. "Yes, I don't think I could handle you with anyone else."

He sighs. "Yeah, the idea of you with Nelson just about did me in. When I first heard you were married, I figured you were in love. There's never been anyone else that has captured my heart, Delaney. All these years, I've missed you. And I hope to hell you will give me another chance."

Tears spring from my eyes. I take a deep breath, hoping I can say the words without crying. This is what I've wanted for so long. "Yes, I want to long-distance date you, Logan."

CHAPTER 23

Logan

I roll into work the next morning, all smiles despite the fact I'm still not sure what side of the law my brother is really on. But I don't want to focus on that right now. I don't recall ever feeling this happy. Yes, Delaney is still in California, and I'm thousands of miles away, but she said yes to giving us a try. And I'm not going to let her go again.

"Wow, you're glowing. What's her name?" Piper asks as I walk past her desk.

"Delaney."

"I'm happy for you," she says, but her smile doesn't reach her eyes.

I lean down so no one else will hear. "You could have something real with him if you get out of your own way."

Her eyes widen, and she opens her mouth but doesn't

say anything. I've noticed more than I'm sure she realizes when she visits my roommate, Ozzie. The guy is so hung up on her but can't do anything about it, or else her cousin—and our coworker, Durango—might kill him. And I'm not exaggerating. That man is so protective of his little cousin. And as far as Piper, I have no idea what is going through her head. It's clear she wants to be with Ozzie, but something is holding her back.

Probably Durango.

I leave her with her thoughts and walk into the kitchen to pour myself some coffee. We instituted a new rule last month: only Piper or Reed can make coffee. It sounds ridiculous, but the food pranks we've been pulling on each other have gotten out of hand. We finally all agreed that messing with the coffee was too low of a blow.

Opening the fridge, I stare at my creamer and remember it's not actually hazelnut. Obviously, Lightning hadn't taken the message as seriously as the rest of us. I slam the fridge door shut and go to my office. Apparently, I take my coffee black now.

Digging in, I decide I'm finishing the paperwork required by the FBI for my last assignment. Once it's done, I submit it, which means it goes to Reed next for review. My phone buzzes on my desk, and I grab it. A text from Trip.

Trip: *I got the results from that search you requested. Call me when you have time to talk.*

My stomach drops. That can't mean good news, and Trip knew the search was in regard to my brother. Am I ready to hear something I can't unhear?

My heart is pounding at the idea that my brother might really be a traitor. I lean back as I remember when we were little. I crashed my bike into another one, and it caused the frame to bend. The owner was this older kid who picked on other kids in the neighborhood. I was scared, but I knew I had to tell him. It would mean I would become his target. But when he ran outside and saw the damage, my brother told him he'd done it.

There were countless other times when my brother stuck up for me like that. He always said loyalty is the most important thing. And as brothers, we always stuck together. I can't imagine how he could go from that to working with the very men he was supposed to be putting away. Knowing I shouldn't put it off, I call Trip.

"Hey, Trip, I got your text."

He sighs. "Yeah. I'm afraid I don't have good news."

I close my eyes. "What did you find?"

"Your brother has an account he opened about a year ago that receives regular deposits. It stands out because those deposits are large. I looked up your brother's salary, and it's more than he makes."

"You know what my brother makes?"

"Approximately. I just looked up the government wages for his likely level. But even if I'm wrong and he's making the top pay grade, these deposits are still too high."

I'm suddenly sick to my stomach. This is not what I wanted to hear. "Someone is paying him off."

"It looks likely. And I wasn't able to trace where the deposits are coming from yet. All I know is it is wired in from an account in Mexico."

Dammit, Brian. Are you receiving money from the cartel? Are you involved with them? He did mention them. But why would he be?

"He's been getting deposits for a year?"

"Yeah. I'm sorry to have to tell you all this. And I would have called you sooner, but I was trying to track down the source of the money."

Nausea washes over me as it all sinks in. I had really hoped I was wrong. But this makes it real.

"Thanks for digging. I need to go." I need to be alone right now. I end the call and grab my jacket. Instead of going to my car, I walk down the road. My head is spinning as I try to figure out what I should do.

If Brian really is involved with the cartel, then my knowing anything could get me killed. Or maybe Brian got himself into a situation and he needs help getting out of it but hasn't felt he can ask. I go over all the possibilities as I walk through Brooklyn. Finally, I stop. Without more information, I'm going to drive myself crazy.

I pull out my phone and stare at it. Once I make this call, there is no going back. I call my brother.

"Logan, you must have read my mind!" Brian answers.

"Why?"

He laughs. "Because I was just about to call you. I have another assignment I need you for."

Already? "What's going on?"

"This isn't something I can explain over the phone. I need you to come back to California."

"I just got back. I'm still jet-lagged."

"I've cleared it with Reed. You and the other guys leave tomorrow."

Other guys? Reed agreed to this, knowing my brother might not be on the up and up? "Okay, I'll talk to Reed then."

"Sounds good. I'll see you tomorrow afternoon."

He ends the call, not giving me a chance to ask any questions. But this is probably a better conversation to have in person anyway.

I jog back to the office, and laughter comes from the kitchen. I cautiously enter and find Thunder, Ozzie, and Durango all wearing T-shirts with cats on them. Lightning is sitting at the table, staring at his phone, ignoring them. Axel is leaning against the counter, sipping coffee, trying to stay out of whatever this is.

"What's going on?" I ask.

Ozzie smiles. "Thunder brought in some shirts for us."

Each shirt is of a different cat. "Why?"

"To torture me," Lightning says.

I glance around the room again. "Hey, we're all here at the same time."

Durango pushes off the counter. "Yeah, but not for long. Reed wants to see you, Ozzie, Axel, and me in his office."

I follow the guys down the hall to Reed's office.

"Close the door," Reed instructs.

As the last one in, I do so, then sit down. Reed's office isn't large, but somehow, he fits us all in here for team meetings. With only half of us here, we can all at least sit down.

"Coff's brother has another assignment for you guys. I just spoke to him about it this morning, and I have concerns."

"What kind of concerns?" Axel asks.

Reed stands up and turns to the window. "This assignment involves the Mexican cartel, and we don't have contacts there you can rely on if things go sideways."

Did I hear him right? "Reed, my brother is asking us to do something involving the cartel?"

Reed turns to me and nods.

"What?"

"Take them down. Well, specifically one man. He's in charge of the cartel's drugs that go in through San Diego."

Durango glances around at us, then Reed. "Why? We all know how this works. If we take out one man, they will have someone to replace him the next day."

Reed leans on his desk. "Apparently, this particular man has put a hit on Agent Folger. He found out Folger was working undercover to take down his operation. How he found out is undetermined at this point."

I stand up, suddenly needing to move. "Wait, he was working undercover?"

"That's what he told me. His superior confirmed it in our call."

I fall back into my chair. Okay, so my brother isn't a traitor. But then, why don't I feel relieved? Something isn't right, but I won't figure anything out until I talk to him privately.

"Who is the man we are looking for?" Durango asks.

Reed stares directly at me. "Ruiz."

The man Brian was talking to on the phone after the shooting. The man who wanted Duke and Delaney dead. Now he's going after my brother. This might be a mission to protect my brother, but if I get the chance, I'll take that son of a bitch, Ruiz, out.

CHAPTER 24

Logan

I spend the next twenty-four hours anxious until I can talk to my brother in person. Thankfully, we have a private flight to California, but even though it's direct, it feels like the longest flight I've been on. The moment we land, Brian is waiting on the tarmac to talk to us.

Before he can even say hello, I take him aside. "Can I talk to you privately?" I ask.

He frowns. "Sure."

I walk him away from the other guys. "What's going on?"

He cocks his head. "Well, I was about to tell all of you the details."

I take a deep breath and ask the question I wish I didn't have to. "Are you working with the cartel?"

He furrows his brow. "I'm not sure what Reed told you, but I was trying to take down their San Diego operation. It's gotten me into some trouble. That's why you're all here."

I'm trained to know when someone is lying, but there is no sign of deception from my brother. But then he's been trained to lie. "If you're having a problem, why isn't the FBI helping you out?"

Brian shakes his head. "McKenzie, my boss, isn't willing to risk exposing the identity of any additional agents on this. That's why we brought you guys in."

He steps away to return to the guys.

"Why are you receiving money from the cartel?"

He turns back to me. "You investigated me?"

I don't break eye contact as anger flares in his eyes. "I had to."

"You had to? Why?" He's turning the tables with his questions. He's using his training on me.

Well, two can play that game. "Answer my question. Are you?"

He sighs, and his head falls back. "Yes, but it's not what you think." This is where he's going to tell me he's been working undercover. "I've been working undercover for over a year. The cartel thinks, well *thought*, I was on their side. I was supposed to get in, get information, and get out. But something went wrong."

The uneasy feeling is still there. "What are you not telling me?"

"What? I'm telling you everything."

I hold his gaze. "No, there's something more."

He closes his eyes. "Fuck, how do you do that? There is something more, and it's why I need your help."

"You kept some of the money, didn't you?" It's what's been bothering me since yesterday.

His hands go to his hips. "What? No, how could you think that? Jesus." He takes a few steps away. "While I was undercover, I met a woman. I love her, Logan. And she's pregnant with my child."

Now, this I didn't expect. "What does this have to do with the cartel?"

"The man who has a hit on me is her father."

Please tell me I heard him wrong. "What did you say?"

"Mr. Ruiz's daughter is the woman I love. And my boss found out." Brian licks his lips. "It's another reason he doesn't want to use FBI agents. He thinks I may have switched sides."

I'll admit, I'm in a bit of shock. I don't know much about my brother's dating life, but I do know if he says he's in love, it's a huge step. But why did he cross the line for a member of the cartel? He had to know that would be a death sentence.

Brian steps closer. "I know how it looks, but I didn't switch sides. We bonded because she feels trapped and wants out. But my boss says I've shown where my allegiance is at. If I survive this, I'm pretty sure he's going to fire me."

I rub my eyes. "Ruiz has a hit on you because you got his daughter pregnant?"

Brian shakes his head. "He doesn't know I've been seeing his daughter. And she doesn't know about the hit."

Well, I should be happy. It appears my brother is not a dirty agent. But of all the women he could have fallen for, it's the daughter of a cartel member. Of course, I fell for the daughter of a crime family myself, so I know how it happens. But dammit, she's pregnant?

"Is she keeping the baby?" I ask.

Brian crosses his arms. "Of course she is."

I hold up my hands. "Hey, I just learned about this. Don't get mad at me for asking questions."

"She is, and I proposed. I want to marry her before the baby is born."

Okay, now I'm wondering if my brother is delusional. "And how do you plan to do that, given who her dad is?"

"I have enough evidence to put him away. Then Sofia will be free to be with me."

I spin around and notice the guys all staring at us, impatiently waiting. I turn back. "Are you serious? The man will continue to come after you, even if he is in prison. I've heard love makes you blind, but damn, Brian, you know how this works."

He nods. "I do. And truth be told, I'm hoping Mr. Ruiz doesn't survive."

"You brought us here to execute your lover's father?" I yell a little too loudly. I'm being an asshole, I know. And a hypocrite since I want the man dead, too.

"What's going on?" Ozzie asks.

Brian glares at me. "No. You have it wrong. Now, I'm going to explain everything to the entire team." He pushes past me and walks back to the guys.

I reluctantly follow.

"Thank you all for coming out today," Brian says. "I know Reed was short on the details of this assignment. There is a man who has put out a hit on me." He pulls his phone out of his pocket and pulls up a photo, then shows each of us. "This is Mr. Ruiz. He is in charge of the cartel's drugs going into San Diego. I've been working to stop him by pretending to be a dirty agent. He found out that I've been undercover this entire time."

"How did he find out?" Axel asks.

Brian puts his phone into his pocket. "I'm not sure of that. We need to detain him and his crew. He has three guys who work closely with him. I'm sure one of them is looking for me. I have photos of all three in my car. It's parked next to your rentals."

"Rentals?" I ask. I'm not going to say the FBI is cheap, but well, they are, so more than one car is surprising. And that, on top of a private flight here.

"Two cars were delivered this morning. Due to the nature of the assignment, it makes sense for you to work in teams of two."

Durango crosses his arms. I don't have to ask to know what he's thinking. We don't like others telling us how to run an operation. And that is what my brother is trying to do. We don't split up unless we have to.

"Explain," Axel says.

Yeah, he's thinking the same thing.

Brian glances around. "Mr. Ruiz will be at a fundraiser tonight. His front is that he's a wealthy businessman." Brian frowns. "Well, his cover. He actually is one, but most of his wealth has come from the cartel; however, the elite of San Diego do not know that."

"Wait," I step forward. "No one suspects he has ties to the cartel? They buy his businessman front?"

Brian licks his lips again, and I'm realizing it's a nervous tick he's developed. "Well, if anyone knows more, they aren't speaking to the FBI about it."

"Is there something you're not telling us?" Durango asks, his arms crossed. "Because you and Coff appeared to have quite a heated discussion over there." He nods to where we were standing.

Brian closes his eyes. When he opens them, he tells the guys everything he told me. They ask the same questions I did.

Ozzie looks at each one of us, then back to Brian. "You want us to go to this fundraiser and kidnap him, then kill him?" Ozzie asks.

I bite back a grin. Ozzie doesn't mince words with Brian. They've worked together enough that Ozzie and Brian have grown close. Like brothers. He already is like one to me as my roommate.

Brian frowns. "The FBI doesn't kidnap; we detain. And no, you do not have an order to kill."

"Of course. That's what I meant," Ozzie says.

Brian shakes his head. "It makes sense for two of you to attend and two to be watching from the outside. Now I managed to get a couple of invitations for you."

Axel steps forward. "With all due respect, you've worked with us enough times to know that we decide how the operation goes. Why are you trying to direct us this time?"

That's exactly what I want to know as well.

"Look, there will be a lot of civilians at this event. And the press will be covering it. You can't go in all rogue, throw a bag over his head, and carry him out. There needs to be some finesse," Brian says, then licks his lips again.

Damn, maybe it's more than a nervous tick. Maybe that's how the cartel figured him out.

"Bag over the head? What the hell are you talking about?" Axel asks.

I arch a brow at my brother. Apparently, he'd been watching me from the moment I arrived at the cemetery that day. And that little dig was for me.

"It doesn't matter," Brian says. "Just try to blend in."

I cross my arms. My gut tells me there's even more. "Brian, what's the real reason you're trying to micromanage us?"

The guys all stare at Brian. He closes his eyes. "Fine. Mr. Ruiz's daughter will be there tonight. I'm concerned she might get caught in the crossfire."

"Jesus," Durango says. "We're not going to go in, shooting the place up. You know we don't do that."

"You're sure Mr. Ruiz doesn't know you're the father?" Axel asks.

"No. He doesn't know she's pregnant. She's not showing yet."

"Okay, give us everything you know, and we'll figure out how to do this," Axel says.

Brian frowns, and I can tell he wants to object, but he glances at me, and I shake my head.

"Fine. Let's go to the cars where I have the photos, and we'll talk."

As we follow him to the rentals, I have a bad feeling about this assignment. My brother is letting his personal feelings get in the way. But then he could say the same thing about me when it comes to Delaney.

CHAPTER 25

Delaney

Sitting across the dinner table from my brother and best friend shouldn't be weird. But the way they keep making eyes at each other is driving me nuts.

I roll my eyes. "Okay, we get it. You two are in love!" I grab my wine glass and take a large gulp.

Sam's eyes widen, and Duke glares at me. Oops. Maybe they haven't said the L-word yet? I just assumed they had based on the way Sam described their relationship.

"We've only recently gotten back together," Sam says.

I stare at them. "What about when we were younger?"

Sam laughs. "Well, Mr. Mature over here responded to my admission of love by grunting, then kissing me."

Duke takes a bite of his potato as he shakes his head. After he swallows, he points at Sam. "I said ditto first. It was a touching moment."

She grins. "Yeah, there was a lot of touching."

"Eww! No," I say as I stand up. "I'm going to go read."

I take my plate to the kitchen. Since I cooked dinner, they agreed to clean up, so I have the rest of the evening free. Once in Sam's guest room that I have now claimed, I check my phone, which I'd left on the bed so I wouldn't look at it every five minutes while preparing dinner. I'm hoping Logan is willing to do a video chat tonight. I want to see his face. I need to.

He sent a text, and I'm grinning until I read it.

Logan: *Sorry, can't talk tonight. I'm on an assignment. I'll text you as soon as I can.*

I moan and flop onto my bed. He told me enough that I know when he's on an assignment, I might not hear from him for days or possibly weeks.

Sam giggles as two sets of footsteps make their way down the hallway. So much for them cleaning up. The door at the end of the hall closes. I'm thankful the guest room is the farthest from them. But then a moan comes through my door, and I realize they aren't far enough away. I turn on music on my phone and turn it up, then stare at the ceiling.

Focusing on Logan made me forget that I'm still stuck living with Duke—even if it is a new place—and working at a job where I apparently have been doing the books for an illegal operation for years.

I sigh. If I'm honest with myself, I figured out years ago that my dad wasn't exactly on the right side of the law. But somehow, I let myself believe the construction business was one of his legal entities. I guess I wanted to believe he wouldn't involve me in his dealings. And for the most part, he didn't. Or so I thought.

Things need to change. If Duke wants to continue to run the business, then he needs to find people he can trust. I'll give him my two weeks' notice.

I smile at the idea. After our dad died, Duke and I received an inheritance. It's enough that I can live off of it for a while until I figure out what I'm going to do. When I first received it, I swore I wouldn't touch it. But the more I thought about it, I realized if I'd worked at any other job all these years, I'd have a savings account. Savings I could spend on pursuing what I want to do. Design is my first love, but I had to drop out of design school because of my dad. Without the proper training, getting a job in that field will be hard.

"Yes!" Sam screams.

Despite my music, I can still hear them.

"Oh, baby!" My brother yells.

I'm nauseated, but then the sound stops. Please let them be done.

I tiptoe out of the guest room and go downstairs. Duke brought a box over from the house for me. I'm curious about what he packed up.

When I open it, I'm surprised to find a couple of blank canvases and my old sketchbooks. After I transferred out of design school, I tried to toss these. But my mom took them and said she'd hold them for me. She understood how important these were to me.

Duke walks down the stairs. Sweat is beaded all over his chest. "Oh, hey." He smiles.

"No. You two are too loud. I can hear it all over my music. If you two have sex, don't make any noise."

He laughs as he walks into the kitchen. "I'll see what I can do." The faucet turns on, and then he steps out of the kitchen a moment later, wiping his mouth. "We'll be down to clean up soon. Don't worry about it, okay?"

I arch a brow. "I'm not."

He nods, then heads back upstairs. I turn my attention back to the box as I continue to unpack it. At the bottom is some old paint. I loved to sketch, and suddenly, the desire to do so again is strong. But as I empty out the box, I discover there are no pencils of any kind.

Painting was never my thing, even though I tried to get into it. But I have this idea I want to get out. Maybe I could paint it.

I set my phone next to me and turn on some pop music as I set up the paint. The blue catches my eye, and I use it first. Slowly, the image in my head comes forth on the canvas. After the last stroke, I sit back.

"Wow," Sam says as she walks into the living room. "I wondered what you were doing down here the past couple of hours."

I frown. "Hours?" I check my phone, and it's later than I thought. "I lost track of time."

"That's really good." Sam continues to study my painting.

"Thanks. I wanted to draw it out, but I couldn't find any pencils."

She turns to me. "I think this is better. You used color."

Wait, she's right. My sketches were always black and white. But the color is what defines this one.

"This reminds me of one of my favorite children's books. It's like a scene from a fairy tale," she says.

I step back and take in the way the blue water meets the vibrant green forest. She's right. The style I used does look like something that should be in a book.

"Have you thought about being an illustrator?" she asks.

"A what?"

She laughs. "You know, the person who does the drawing for kid's books. Or any books that need it. I think you'd be great at it."

The idea of drawing for a living sounds amazing. "I would love to, but I think Duke wants me to keep working at the construction company." I glance up at her to gauge her reaction. Maybe Duke won't take my leaving as hard as I think he will.

Sam's smile drops. "You and Duke both need to get out of that 'construction' business." She uses her finger to put air quotes on construction.

I'm surprised by her words. "Does Duke know you feel this way?"

She nods. "It's why I've been slow to commit. He feels stuck since there is no one else to run things, and he says he can't walk away without a target on his back."

I hadn't thought about that. Duke is the face everyone associates with the family now. He never expressed to me he wanted out. Instead, I thought he was happy to take over.

"I hate to suggest this, but maybe Nelson's family wants to take over."

"Over my dead body," Duke says from the doorway.

I turn and find him leaning against the door frame with his arms crossed.

"Well, it would free both of us," I say.

He steps into the room. "No, it wouldn't. They would take over and have us killed because we know too much. This isn't a business you can walk away from."

"Ever?" Sam asks.

Duke drops his arms and sighs. "I told you I'm searching for a solution. But it might take time."

Sam shakes her head and storms out of the room.

"Well, I was going to give you these, but it might be unnecessary now." He tosses a bag in front of me.

I grab it. Earplugs. The ones the construction guys use. I laugh. "Thanks, I think. But yeah, you better go after her."

"You know, I do love her. I always have," he says. Then he focused on my canvas. "Did you paint that?"

"I did."

"It's really good. I'm sorry Dad cut off paying for art school. But maybe you can go now. Or hell, maybe you don't need school and you can just sell your art."

"Thanks. I'll think about it."

They've both given me a lot to think about.

"Okay, goodnight." He leaves, and I turn back to my painting.

An illustrator. I don't have any idea how I would even pursue such a thing. But I'd like to find out.

I return to the guest room in time to hear Sam moan.

I'm not sure what Duke said to her, but it sounds like they've made up.

Not wanting to hear any of that again, I reverse course and head back downstairs. Instead of sitting in the living room, I grab a coat and step outside. It's not too chilly, so I sit in a chair on the porch.

Staring out at the driveway, it's dark, but there's a frog somewhere nearby croaking. I take a deep breath and think about my future. What do I want to do? I grab my phone to research illustrators.

The deck creaks behind me, and I jump up and turn around. At first, I don't see anything, but then a squirrel runs up to a leaf on the porch, then scampers off. My heart is racing as I laugh. I guess I'll be on edge for a while. Instead of sitting back down, I walk to the railing and stare at the moon, wondering if Logan is looking at it, too. I have no idea where he is or if it is day or night there. Can I get used to this? The not knowing? Then I remember our kiss, and yes, for that, it would be worth it.

I turn my attention back to my phone. The more I read, the more excited I am about pursuing a future that I choose for myself.

Another creak behind me, and I smile, imagining the squirrel. Before I can turn around, a hand is over my mouth, and something hard presses into my side.

"Don't say a word, or it will be your last," a deep voice says. "Let's go."

How the hell did a man sneak up on me?

He pushes me forward off the deck and down the driveway past where it turns. A car I couldn't see from the house is parked off to the side. If he gets me into that car, my odds aren't good. As we get closer, I form a plan to flip him and hope he drops the gun. But then a second man gets out of the car, holding a needle.

"Mmmm!" I yell when I see the needle.

"Relax," the man says. "This will only make you sleepy."

Can I flip the first man onto the second man? I jerk and try to gain some sort of control, but it's useless. I'm panicking and doing it wrong. I try to calm myself, but before I get another chance to fight back, the second man stabs me in the neck.

My eyelids grow heavy. The first man grabs my feet, and they shove me into the backseat of the car. I'm aware of what's happening, but I can't move any part of my body. I try to scream, but nothing comes out.

Duke and Sam might not notice I'm missing until tomorrow. I'm going to have to find my own way out of this mess once this drug wears off. Assuming I can stay alive that long.

CHAPTER 26

Logan

After we talked it through, we ended up going with Brian's plan after all. Since Durango refused to wear a suit, Ozzie and I are attending the fundraiser while he and Axel will be ready for us when we come out with Ruiz.

I'm not sure what Durango's problem is. It didn't take long to get fitted for a suit, and frankly, I'm not going to complain about being served food while we work. Although my gut is telling me something isn't right, I can't put my finger on what it is.

I scan the crowd. It consists mostly of rich people based on the conversations I've overheard. Ozzie catches my attention from across the room. Smiling, I walk through the crowd until I'm standing beside him.

"Something feels off," I say.

He smiles and holds out his hand. "I agree."

I shake it, my eyes now on Ruiz. He's holding a full drink, which is our cue to move.

"Ready?" I ask.

"Always," Ozzie says.

I walk toward Ruiz while staring at my phone. I bump into him, causing him to spill some of his drink.

"I'm so sorry!" I say as I lead him to a nearby table.

He sets down his drink, and I hand him a napkin, causing him to turn from his drink.

Ozzie is there instantly and appears to reach over the drink to grab a different napkin. He's good; I'll give him that. I was watching for it and didn't see Ozzie dump the powder in.

"Here, let me help you." I try to dab at his suit.

"Stop." He tosses the napkin onto the table, grabs his drink, and walks away.

I keep my eyes on him for twenty minutes, waiting for him to take a sip, but he doesn't. It appears the drink is only for show.

"Mocktail?" a waiter says as he walks by with a tray.

"Sure, thanks." I take one. I need to do something to blend in.

Ozzie is already standing in a group of men, laughing. I take a drink of the red liquid as I walk over. It's strawberry flavored.

"Then he rang the bell!" a round man yells. The rest of the group, including Ozzie, laugh loudly.

Ozzie takes a sip of his mocktail, then spots me. "Oh, hey, everyone, this is Walter," Ozzie introduces me with the fake name we agreed on. "I just met him earlier tonight."

"Welcome, Walter," the round man says. He pulls on his collar. "I think maybe these mocktails aren't really mock, if you know what I mean." He sets his empty glass on a table and pulls off his tie.

I stare at my drink which is halfway gone. "Shit."

We set down the glasses and walk as fast as we can to the exit.

Once we're clear of the crowd, Ozzie slows down. "I don't feel right. There was something in that drink."

I grab my phone and try to type out a message to the guys to let them know something has gone wrong. But the screen is blurry. I type something and hit send. I hope to hell it makes sense.

Someone grabs my left arm. "This way."

I shove my phone into my right pocket, then try to free myself from whoever has a hold of me, but I can't shake him. Then another man grabs my right arm. Where is Ozzie?

They drag me for what feels like a mile and then toss me onto a hard floor. Someone moans near me, and I recognize the voice.

"Ozzie?"

"Yeah."

"Where are we?"

"I think a van."

How the hell were we made?

"Hey, can you sit up?" Ozzie asks.

I try but fail. "No, you?"

"No."

The van moves, and we roll around on the floor each

time it turns. Finally, it stops moving, and the back door opens.

"How much time before it wears off?" a man asks.

"Not much for this one," another man says.

I turn toward the voices as my vision seems to be clearing up. One man is tall with tattoos on his face. The other man is shorter and wearing a suit. I'd guess he was at the fundraiser.

"Let's get them tied up," Suit says.

Tattoo gets in the van, holding a rope, and ties my hands behind my back. Then he stares at me. "Can you walk on your own?"

I shrug.

"Try."

He jumps out of the van, and I scoot toward the open door and then get out. I'm standing, not steady, but I'm up.

"Get the other one," Suit says.

Tattoo jumps back into the van and ties Ozzie's hands in the same way. But when Ozzie gets out of the van, he falls to the ground.

"He had more," Suit says.

Tattoo lifts Ozzie, which can't be easy since the man is over six feet tall and all muscle. They take us inside what appears to be an office building. Inside are several men with guns. My bad feeling is getting worse.

We are taken into the same room and tied to chairs. By the time the men leave us alone, whatever they gave us has worn off.

"Hey, boss," a man says outside the door. "That man at the fundraiser died."

"Shit!" Suit says. "Asshole was sucking down those drinks." He sighs. "It should be fine. They will determine he had a heart attack."

A few moments later, Tattoo walks in, dragging someone behind him. He throws the guy in a chair, and that's when I see it's my brother. He has a black eye and likely a broken nose. Tattoo ties him in a chair, just like us.

Ruiz walks in smiling. "Well, well. I'm so happy you could join me here." He turns to Ozzie. "Sorry about this. It looks like you were just in the wrong place at the wrong time."

I'm not sure what to make of that. Were we made or not?

"Why are we here?" I ask.

Ruiz leans against the wall. "The other day, I overheard my daughter talking to a friend. She was quite upset, so I listened. She mentioned Agent Folger. I was surprised to hear his name come from her lips. But I was more surprised by what she said next."

Ah, this can't be good. Dammit, Brian, of all the people to get involved with.

Ruiz takes a few steps and leans over Brian. "She was upset because you canceled your date with her last night."

The man straightens up and shoves his hands in his pockets. "I thought I must have misheard, so I asked her what she meant. The expression on her face, it was like a child caught with a hand in the cookie jar." He paces in front of us. "She told me you two were dating. But that couldn't be because my daughter is young, and frankly, you couldn't be that stupid. But it turns out you are because my daughter kept pulling up her collar. I yanked it down, and you know what I found?"

I close my eyes. My brother had this thing about marking women he slept with back when we were in high school and college. The only reason I know about it is that girls would ask me if I did it, too.

"She had a hickey. A goddamned hickey. I asked if it was from Agent Folger, and she said yes." He walks over to Brian and smacks him across the face, causing the blood pooling under his nose to fly onto the nearby wall. "You put your hands on my daughter!"

Enough time has passed that I know without a doubt Ruiz didn't drink any of his tainted drink. He'd be out if he had. And we really need him to pass out, but luck is not on our side.

"I told her I would kill you," he continues. "But then she told me I couldn't." He stares at the ceiling, then his gaze returns to my brother. "Because she's pregnant, and you are the father."

"Oh shit," Ozzie says under his breath.

I glance over at Ozzie, and based on the subtle movement of his hands, I know he's doing what I'm doing, working our way out of the ropes. We need time alone in this room so we can work faster without being caught.

I don't know what is going through Ruiz's head, but it's probably worse than if we had been caught drugging him.

Brian finally looks up. "Your issue is with me. Why are they here?" He nods in our direction.

Ruiz laughs. "Well, since you fucked with my family, I figured I'd fuck with yours."

Well, this really isn't good.

Ruiz goes to the door and opens it. "Bring her in."

He's going to make his daughter watch him torture Brian? That's cold.

But it isn't his daughter who enters the room next. It's Delaney. Her hands are tied, and she's stumbling as Tattoo brings her into the room.

"What's she got to do with anything?" Brian asks.

Ruiz smiles. "My daughter told me this two weeks ago. For two weeks, I've been trying to figure out how to make you pay for what you've done. I had my guys follow you. I was pleased to learn your brother was in town. But simply killing him really wouldn't be enough. No, you need to see the pain on his face so that lives in your memory for the rest of your life."

I brace my legs in case I need to move fast if he pulls out a gun. Thankfully, they didn't bind our feet.

"And after I saw these photos, I knew what I had to do." Ruiz pulls up a picture on his screen and turns it so Brian can see it.

From where I sit, I can tell they are photos of Delaney and me. In one, we are holding hands. He flips, and in another one, my arm is around her. We appear to be a couple.

"Now I will kill the girl in front of your brother and then your brother in front of you." He turns to Ozzie. "Unfortunately, you just have to die."

Ruiz turns back to Brian. "All because, apparently, I can't kill you. But I can torture you and make your life hell."

Ruiz walks to the door but then turns back. "Folger, it's bad enough you played me, you double-crossing liar. But my daughter? You took what is most precious to me. Now I'm doing the same."

He leaves the room, and Tattoo comes in. We don't have much time, and I haven't been able to get the ropes off my wrists yet. I glance at Ozzie, and he shakes his head.

"Well, sorry about all of this. My boss is a little crazy," the guy says. He pulls a gun out of his waistband and aims it at Delaney.

"No!" I yell.

The man winces. Delaney is crying.

He turns to me. "I'm sorry. You do seem like nice people. Well, not you," he says as he glares at Brian.

His henchman has a conscious? Maybe we can use this to our advantage.

"Hey," I say to the guy.

Then gunshots erupt outside the room.

"What the hell?" He runs out of the room, leaving the door open.

"Get down!" I yell as we all force our chairs to the floor.

Delaney runs to my side and gets beside me.

Footsteps come toward us, and we are sitting ducks. But then I heard a familiar voice.

"Ozzie? Coff?" Axel yells.

"In here!" Ozzie yells.

Axel steps into the room and assesses the situation.

"I'm so happy to see you," Ozzie says. "But talk about cutting it close."

Axel unties Ozzie, who then runs to me to untie me while Axel stands guard at the door.

"It took us a few minutes to realize that message from Coff was you guys needing help. I thought you butt texted."

I untie Delaney as Ozzie unties my brother.

"How did you find us?" Brian asks.

"Durango made us all have a tracking app on our phones," I say as I untie him.

Brian stands up and rubs his wrists. "They didn't take your phones?"

"Not mine," I say.

"Nor mine," Ozzie says.

"That's odd," Brian says.

Tattoo was the one who tied us up. It would have been him to grab the phones. Maybe he really does have a conscious.

CHAPTER 27

Delaney

WE HEAR SOMEONE COMING, and Logan steps in front of me as a woman walks into the room holding a gun. I step back.

"Harding?" Coff asks. "What the hell are you doing here?"

The woman shakes her head. "I can ask the same about you guys. But let's save the conversation for later. You need to get out of here. Ruiz has another team on the way, and I'd like to avoid more bodies."

Logan takes my hand and follows the guys out of the room. I'm still wondering who the hell this woman is, but she seems to be in charge, and the guys are following her instructions.

"Is Ruiz dead?" Brian asks.

Harding shakes her head. "He's in custody."

She leads us out of the building to two black SUVs parked across the street. "Get in," she tells us.

I get in the back with Logan and Axel. Ozzie, Durango, and Brian go in the car with Harding.

"Who is she?" I ask once we are on the road.

Logan squeezes my hand. "I'll tell you once we're out of here."

"Can I use your phone to call Duke?" The sun is rising, and when they wake up and find I'm gone and my cell phone is on the front deck, they'll worry. Plus, they need to know that Ruiz is aware of where I was staying, so he likely knows Duke is there, too. Although if he wanted Duke, he would have grabbed him.

He hands it to me, and I call, but it goes to voicemail. I leave him a message, explaining what happened as briefly as I can.

The driver takes us across town and pulls into a parking garage, where he parks next to the other SUV. We all get out and follow the woman into an elevator. No one says a word.

The air is thick, and I'm so uncomfortable that I have to stifle a giggle. It's not an appropriate reaction, but sometimes I laugh when I'm nervous. I manage to control myself for the rest of the way as she leads us to a conference room.

Once the door is closed, Brian turns to Harding. "What the hell is going on, and who the hell are you?"

Durango steps forward. "Easy tiger."

Harding puts her hand on Durango's arm. "It's fine."

She moves her gaze to Brian. "I'm CIA. Agent Harding. Please, everyone, take a seat."

CIA? What the hell? It's bad enough the FBI is involved. Why would the CIA be involved, too? We all sit in the chairs surrounding the table.

"Why the hell does the CIA care about anything involving Ruiz?" Brian asks.

The conference door opens, and the man with tattoos who injected me with a needle walks in. Axel stands and draws his gun, but Harding steps in between them.

"He's with me," she says.

"He was about to kill us before Axel and Durango showed up," Ozzie says.

"Agent Walker," he grins and waves at all of us. "No, I had been tipped off that someone was coming. I had to make it look like that was what I was going to do. That's why I was slow about it." The man's persona has completely changed from when we were in that room. He's grinning and seems way too excited to be here.

"That's why you didn't take our phones," Logan says.

Walker nods. "I knew it was going to get ugly quick, and I hoped you had someone tracking you who would arrive before Harding."

"Two CIA agents were going after Ruiz?" Brian asks. Despite the fact he's clearly angry, he sits in one of the chairs. Based on his heavy breathing, I wonder how badly he's injured.

"Are you all right?" Logan asks.

Brian leans back. "Yeah, pretty sure I have a broken rib, though."

"Okay, what's going on?" Durango asks. "Why are the FBI and CIA going after the same target? Don't you communicate with each other?"

"Apparently not," Brian says.

Harding sits at the head of the table. "We do. We were aware of your involvement, Agent Folger."

Brian glances up. "You were?"

Harding nods. "And what I'm going to tell you will be hard to hear. I'm sorry. Your superior brought us on board because he's concerned you've flipped."

Brian stands up and throws his hands in the air. "My assignment was to play a dirty agent, not actually be one."

Harding shakes her head. "No, he says his concerns started years ago. Apparently, your brother, Coff, had a relationship with your target's daughter, and there was concern that you pushed them together."

I laugh, and all eyes are on me. "Sorry, it's just this is all so ridiculous."

Harding's brow furrows. "Please explain."

I take a deep breath and explain how I overheard my brother and best friend talking and how they were why Logan and I dated all those years ago. "It had nothing to do with Brian."

Logan puts an arm around my shoulder. "That's true. Once my brother found out who I was dating, he told me I had to end it immediately."

"What choice did I have?" Brian says defensively. "She was the daughter of a man I'd been pursuing for a couple of years. I couldn't continue to work the case if my brother was dating her. And I'm sorry, Logan, I had no idea you'd never find love again. Hell, you were so young. I figured it was just a fling."

He never found love again? He's mentioned he hasn't found anyone, but I didn't know it was really *no one*. Although I never loved again, then, I swore off love. It hurt too damn bad when he left.

Brian slams his fist on the table, and I jump. "I gave McKenzie no reason ever to doubt me. His claim I could be a dirty agent is bullshit."

"Who's McKenzie?" I ask.

"My boss," Brian says. "The CIA was involved to see if I was dirty? That was it?"

Harding stares at Brian and nods. "I said it would be hard to hear. But we determined your boss was wrong. And fortunately, today, we were in the right place at the right time."

"Ruiz is going to keep coming after me," Brian says. "It's personal for him now."

"I thought Harding said he was in custody," I say.

Harding nods. "He is, but that won't stop him from ordering his men to go after Agent Folger. Brian, you need to stay here until we figure out our next move."

Brian laughs. "Next move? Unless that man is dead, I'll always be looking over my shoulder. Not sure how I'm supposed to live with Sofia and raise our child. I can't put them in danger of a stray bullet."

Walker frowns but doesn't say a word. It appears Harding is the one in charge here and that everyone in this room knows her.

Brian shifts in his seat and grunts in pain.

"We need to get you checked out by a doctor," Harding says.

Brian nods. "First, tell me why you are telling me this? If McKenzie called you, I'm certain he told you to keep me in the dark."

Harding leans back in her chair. "He did. But you can't simply walk out of here and go back to your regular life. You will be dead by sundown."

I glance at Logan. He's staring at Harding and showing no emotion. Maybe what she said hasn't sunk in. I squeeze his arm to let him know I'm there for him. He doesn't react but continues to stare at Harding.

"What will it take to get my brother safe? Ruiz dead?"

Harding's eyes dart to Walker. "Coff, we're going to pretend you never said that. But to answer your question, even if Ruiz were to die, your brother would still be in danger. While Ruiz wants him dead for his poor judgment in getting involved with his daughter," she says while arching a brow at Brian, "his second in command would be forced to step up and make an example of the dirty agent they believe got Ruiz taken down."

Logan mumbles something under his breath, and Brian stares at the table, shaking his head.

"Can't he transfer to another office?" I ask. "Maybe somewhere on the East Coast."

Harding stands up. "No, I'm afraid that wouldn't work. As long as he is going by Brian Folger, he can be found."

"So, he changes his name," I say. I don't know why I keep talking since this is so out of my depth, but I swear I can feel the hurt and anger rolling off of Brian, and I want to help.

Harding steps up to me. "I'm afraid it isn't that easy." She turns to the rest of the room. "I need to speak to a colleague. I'll be back."

"Wait," Walker says as he glances nervously at me. "There's something more you need to know."

Harding turns her attention to him. "What's going on?"

He sighs. "When I was bringing her in," he points at me, "I purposely brought her into the wrong room so she would see the man in there. I knew we needed another witness."

When Walker carried me into the office building, whatever he'd given me was wearing off, but I didn't let it show. He barged us through a door, and a man in a suit got up and yelled at him. Then he placed me in the office next door, where I could hear their entire conversation. What I heard concerned me, but I haven't brought it up because we are dealing with a bigger issue here.

"Who was it?" Harding asks.

"Mayor Sinclair," Walker says.

My mouth drops open. "That was the mayor?" Now that I think about it, he did resemble his sister, Janet, from the library.

Walker nods.

"Fuck, Walker!" Harding yells. "You know better than to do that."

Walker throws his hands into the air. "We needed more than I could get, and we both know it."

"The things he said to that other man..." I replay it in my mind. "He shouldn't be mayor."

"What other man?" Harding asks, turning her attention away from Walker.

"Clark," Walker says.

Harding blows out a breath. "Ruiz's number two guy?" She shakes her head at Walker but then turns back to me. "How did you hear them? Did Walker leave you in that room?"

"No, I placed her next door."

"I had no idea that man was Janet's brother."

Harding leans against the table. "Who is Janet?"

I explain how Janet essentially runs the library and all the rumors about how her family runs the town.

"Small town?" Harding asks.

I shrug. "Sort of. Although being a suburb of San Diego means it isn't too small."

"What did you hear him say?" Harding asks.

I meet her gaze. "He was asking that other guy, Clark, to kill someone for him. Why would a mayor do that?" I ask.

Harding runs her hand through her hair. "Shit. You heard the mayor setting up a hit on someone? Do you remember who?"

"He kept saying Summer. 'Can you take out Summer? I need him gone by tomorrow.' I wasn't sure if that was a real name or a codename."

"Summer?" Walker confirms.

I nod.

"I'll be back. Wait here," Harding says as she runs out of the room, and Walker follows.

"This is bullshit!" Brian says. "I know what she's going to suggest, and I'm not leaving Sofia and the baby!"

"So, you'll stay here and die instead?" Ozzie asks. "This is bigger than just you, you know."

Brian frowns.

"Hey, did you not just hear what Delaney overheard? We might have several huge issues here," Logan says.

Ozzie kicks his feet up onto the table. "Well, the fact they are going after Brian and they know he has a brother and his name, is pretty serious to me." He turns to Brian. "They'll come after him to get to you. Just as Ruiz did today. And they'll go after Delaney to get to Coff to get to you. They've already shown they will."

I stand and pace in the small space at the end of the table, focusing on this problem because I can only handle one at a time. "Then we have to take out Ruiz and his second in command," I say as I stop and face the group.

Durango's brow shoots up. "I thought you worked in an office. Is there something more about you I should know?"

I glance at Logan, and he shakes his head.

"She may be onto something, though," Axel says. "If we take out Ruiz and those three men Brian showed us photos of, maybe someone else will come in and take over who doesn't have a beef with Brian."

Logan leans forward, closer to Brian. "What do you think? You know the organization better than us. Would that work?"

Brian wrings his hands together on the table. "It might, but there's something we haven't considered."

"What's that?" Logan asks.

Brian sighs. "If Ruiz told the cartel about me."

All the men appear crestfallen.

"Who's the cartel?" I ask. "Can't you just take them out, too?"

Ozzie stands up and walks to the end of the table. "The Mexican cartel. And no, you don't just take them out."

I lean against the wall and sink to the floor. Ruiz worked for that cartel? While I'd never met the man before, I heard my dad mention his name over the years.

While I had learned my dad was involved in illegal dealings, he was careful to make sure I didn't know too much. And frankly, I didn't want to know. But even in my wildest thoughts, I never connected my dad to the Mexican cartel. Why would I? This isn't an area I'm an expert in. All I know about them is what I've read in the news. And frankly, it hasn't been good.

But Duke. He would likely know how connected my family is. Although there's no point in my asking him about it. There's no way he would have any pull with the cartel after just taking over Dad's business.

Ozzie rubs his temples. "There has to be something we can do. Maybe Delaney is right, and we just need to bomb the hell out of the cartel."

Logan stands up and puts his hands on Ozzie's shoulders. "We are not doing that."

Ozzie slumps his shoulders. "I know, but we have to do something."

"We will. Let's wait for Harding to come back, and we can discuss all our options."

Ozzie nods. "I really don't want to have to get a new roommate."

Logan laughs. "Yeah, that would suck."

The door opens, and Harding walks in without Walker. "I have good news and bad news."

"Bad news first," Axel says.

Harding nods. "We have a couple of agents who have been monitoring the cartel for some time, and Ruiz did tell them about Agent Folger."

"And the good?" Brian asks.

"It appears they only know you were working for Ruiz and not that you worked for the FBI."

"Can we trust that?" Logan asks.

Harding nods.

"How is that good news?" I ask. "What does it matter if they know he was with the FBI? They know his name."

Harding leans on the table. "The good part is that Ruiz never told them that Brian was a dirty agent. As far as they know, he was a loyal worker."

Logan sighs. "Which means the cartel shouldn't be going after Brian if your information is accurate."

"Correct," Harding says. "But just in case, we need to keep you three hidden until we are sure." She points at Brian, Logan, and me. "And I know just the place."

CHAPTER 28

Logan

Well, it isn't what I expected, but as long as we're safe, that's what matters. When Harding said she had a place for us to hide out, I assumed it would be a safe house or apartment.

Nope. We are staying in the bunkhouse of a rancher friend of hers in Northern California. An unused bunkhouse and I can see why. There are four sets of bunk beds, all in one room, one bathroom, and a kitchenette. I guess the good thing is we don't have to fight for who gets top or bottom bunk.

I'm curious how she knows of this place since she's based out of Seattle, and this appears so far in the middle of nowhere that I can't imagine she had an assignment near here.

Ozzie volunteered to stay with us, and Reed agreed.

And as much as I wish I had some private time with Delaney, I know that won't happen with Brian and Ozzie here, too.

Hell, sleep might be hard to come by if last night is any indication. My brother snored so loud, but then it could be due to the fact that his nose was broken by Ruiz.

After getting checked out by a doctor in that building Harding had us in, it was confirmed he had one broken rib, a broken nose, and was lucky not to have internal bleeding. I'm not sure how they determined the last one, but hell, maybe they have an MRI stashed in their offices somewhere.

Ozzie's bed creaks as he gets up. "Holy shit, it's cold in here." He goes to the wood-burning stove and shoves in a log.

That's another thing. That stove is our only heat source, and since no one woke in the middle of the night to fuel it, we're now freezing our asses off. We've only been here one night, and I shouldn't complain since I've stayed in worse.

"Why is it so cold?" Delaney asks, the shivering coming through her voice.

I grab my blanket and go to her bed. She scoots over and allows me to crawl in with her. I wrap my arms around her and pull her up against me. I would have shared a bed with her last night, but these are twin beds, and the odds of one of us getting pushed off the bed were high.

"Because no one put wood in here last night," Ozzie says as he puts in another log. Then he runs back to his bed and wraps himself in his blanket. "Give it a few minutes and it will be toasty in here again.

Brian snores through our entire conversation. The guy probably needs his sleep to heal.

"You think we'll hear something today?" Ozzie asks.

"It hasn't even been twenty-four hours," I respond.

Ozzie sighs. "I wonder if they have any games here."

We arrived here late last night and went straight to bed after we got the heat going. I glance around the small space from Delaney's bed.

"I don't see any, but maybe they have a deck of cards in a drawer."

Ozzie holds up his phone. "The guys want to FaceTime. You up for it?"

"It's early."

He laughs. "Not in New York."

I don't want to move from this spot next to Delaney. "We never FaceTime on assignments unless it's important."

Ozzie laughs. "Guess you're forgetting about that time in Texas."

I groan. I had forgotten about it. We got trapped in a small office building for a week. The place was closed for the holidays, thankfully. But we got so bored we finally began chatting with the guys just for entertainment.

"Fine, but tell them in five minutes. We need heat first."

"Will do."

I pull Delaney closer, and she wraps her leg around mine. "If we get out of here—"

"When," I correct her.

She nods. "*When* we get out of here, I don't want to work for Manzia Construction anymore. After Nelson died, Duke said we needed to keep up appearances for a while, but I can't go back. Not to that house or that job."

I sit up and look her in the eyes. "What are you saying? Are you willing to move to New York?"

I shrug. "I'm not sure I'm ready for that yet." Her hands go to my chest. "I'm just trying to figure out what to do next."

I lean down and kiss her forehead. "It's okay if you don't know what you want to do. You've been through a lot. Let's get through this, and then you take time to think it all through. All right?"

She kisses me lightly on the lips. "Thank you."

"Warm enough yet?" Ozzie asks.

I roll my eyes. "Yeah, fine. Let's do this."

Ozzie wraps his blanket around his shoulders and sits in a chair by the wood stove. I grab a chair and join him. He holds up his phone, and as the screen comes on, we discover—to our horror—we are looking up Thunder's nose.

"What the hell, dude?" Ozzie asks. "Why?"

The phone flips around and finally moves out. Thunder grins. "Sorry. Didn't realize it was on yet."

"Liar!" Lightning says from behind him. "He thought it would be funny to give you an up-close and personal view."

"How are you all doing?" Durango asks as he reaches out and moves the camera to him.

"We're doing all right," I say.

Ozzie shakes his head. "It's so cold here. All of California and Harding put us in the damn mountains."

"It's cold, but we have a wood stove, beds, and a kitchenette," I say.

"Well, don't make it too awkward for Ozzie, Coff. I heard you have your girlfriend there," Lightning says.

I grab Ozzie's phone and show them the cabin. "We are all in bunk beds in the same room. Nothing's happening." I circle so they can see the kitchenette, then I return the phone to Ozzie and sit back down.

"Wow, close quarters. Just like the barracks," Axel says.

"What's the plan?" Durango asks. "Harding isn't telling us anything."

I glance at Ozzie and then back at the phone. "Same here. We're waiting to find out if the cartel was told anything more about my brother."

"Hey, anything new there?" Ozzie asks.

Durango frowns. "You haven't been gone very long. What could be new?"

Ozzie shrugs. "Any news on Stacy's lawsuit?"

They all shake their heads. "Reed hasn't mentioned it, and none of us want to bring it up," Lightning says.

Well, that's understandable. Even saying her name puts everyone in a bad mood. That woman has put Reed and the rest of us through hell.

Thunder smiles. "Oh, there is some news! I almost forgot."

Lightning's hand suddenly comes up and covers the camera lens. "No, don't tell them that."

"Why not? You know I have to."

I glance at Ozzie, and he rolls his eyes.

"Guys, covering the camera does not mute you. We can hear every word," Ozzie says.

Delaney laughs at their antics as she steps up next to me.

"Fine," Lightning says. Then he steps back and crosses his arms.

"Is Lightning pouting?" Ozzie asks.

"Yeah," Thunder says, still grinning. "You remember that assignment Lightning had where he had to wear a fox costume?"

Remember? Hell, we'll never let him forget.

"Well, the guy is coming to town again and has requested Lightning for protection."

"Please tell us he has to wear the costume again," Ozzie says.

Thunder laughs. "He does! Can you believe Reed okayed that?"

Frankly, no, I can't. "Wow, Lightning, what did you do to piss off Reed?"

Lightning grabs the phone and steps away. "It wasn't my fault."

"Yes, it was!" Thunder yells from behind him.

"I thought it was Ozzie's mustard. I didn't realize Reed had brought in his own bottle."

Ozzie shakes his head. "Why do you always come after me? You know what, never mind. I'm glad you got caught and have to pay the price. I'll let Reed know we need photos from this assignment."

Durango grabs the phone and appears to be running. A door slams shut. "Hey, I'm in my office. I have to tell you the best part. They don't know." He grins. It isn't often we see Durango smile. He's a fairly serious guy. "I removed Ozzie's label from his and put it on Reeds. I knew Lightning was going to do something while you were gone. Before Reed's lunch break, I switched the label back."

"Damn. You guys really get into this, don't you?" Delaney asks, as she readjusts the blanket she has wrapped around herself.

"You have no idea," Ozzie says.

Durango holds a finger to his mouth, telling us to keep quiet. Then he exits his office and blinks a few times. He turns the phone to show us Lightning standing there with his arms crossed.

"I heard every word, asshole."

"You heard nothing," Durango says.

"You're on my list now," Lightning says.

Durango holds the phone up to his face, and Lightning is following behind him down the hall. "It was worth it."

"Give me that." The phone shuffles around, and it's back to Thunder. "As you can see, you aren't missing anything. Stay safe. If you need anything, let us know. You know we'll hop on a plane right away."

"Thanks," I say. "Hopefully, we'll see you soon."

"Sounds good."

Thunder ends the call, and I stand up to stretch. Finally, the place is warming up.

"Well, I guess we should see what food Harding packed for us." I walk to the cupboards and find a couple of boxes of protein bars. After checking all the drawers, that's all I find.

"Well, I hope you like protein bars." I toss one to Delaney, Ozzie, and Brian, who finally opens his eyes.

No real food, no games, and we can't go outside. I shouldn't complain since I've had much worse. But I really doubt Delaney has any experience roughing it. I guess I'll find out what my girl is like when she gets hangry.

My girl. I smile as I watch her. She's finally my girl again.

CHAPTER 29

Delaney

I WAKE the next morning when Logan gets out of bed. Despite the fact the beds are small, he stayed with me because I couldn't get warm. It's so cold here, and I can't seem to warm up even when I stand next to the stove.

Instead of going to the bathroom, Logan puts on his shoes.

"What's going on?" I ask.

"Thought I heard something. I'm going to check it out," he says.

I glance toward the front window. It's still dark out.

Ozzie sits up. "What's going on?"

"Thought I heard something," Logan says. He goes to the back door and carefully opens it.

Muffled voices come through, but I can't make out

what is being said. There is the official bunkhouse, but it's far enough away we shouldn't hear voices from there.

With an uneasy feeling, I get up and put on my shoes, too.

Logan comes back, leaving the door open. "We have to go. Now. Don't turn on any lights."

Brian gets out of bed, already fully dressed and ready to go. Logan motions for us to follow him. We go out the back door, and the moon is partially covered by clouds, so it's hard to see, but we make our way into a field of tall grass.

Logan stops and turns to us.

"What did you hear?" Ozzie asks.

"Three men were talking. They said the phone pinged near here. It sounded like they were going into each building, and I'm pretty sure ours was next."

"They are tracking your phones?" I ask.

Ozzie and Logan look at Brian. "Most likely Brian's."

Brian frowns. "Why mine?"

"Let me see your phone," Logan says.

"The government can track it, right? Since they issued it?" I ask. "Is that who is out there?" I point back to where we came from. "Does Ruiz have someone in the FBI helping him?"

The guys all turn their gaze to me. Brian frowns. "Wow, that's a lot of conclusions you just jumped to. It's not the government," Brian says as he grabs his phone out of his pocket. "And sadly, there are plenty of people out there who have figured out how to track a phone. It could be any of our phones."

"Doubtful," Logan says as he takes Brian's phone from him. "Ozzie and I shut ours down and removed the battery."

"With the exception of checking in and that FaceTime call yesterday," Ozzie says.

Logan turns off Brian's phone and then removes the battery. It makes a crunching sound.

"Hey!" Brian says.

"Sorry. But what the hell, Brian? You didn't even turn it off."

"What about hers?" Brian points at me.

"Took care of it before we got here," Logan says.

Brian looks at all three of us. "Well, why the hell didn't you tell me to do the same?"

Ozzie shakes his head. "Kind of figured an FBI agent would know the basics. Let's go."

We silently make our way through the field to the other side, where the main house and a barn stand. I shiver as the guys take in our surroundings. Logan rubs my arms with his.

"Hey," Ozzie steps up next to us. "We either steal a car or some horses."

"I vote for a car," Brian says.

Logan nods. "Car it is." Then he takes off toward the house.

Ozzie grabs my arm, and we get to the car as Logan opens the door. Ozzie and I get into the backseat, and Brian takes the passenger seat. The engine starts.

"Get down," Logan says.

Ozzie pushes me to the floorboard, and Logan peels out at high speed.

"Stay down," Ozzie says.

I nod.

"Shit, there's more of them than we thought," Logan yells.

A gush of air hits me as Brian opens his window. Several gunshots go off, and then several close by. That's when I realize Brian is shooting out the window at whoever is shooting at us.

"Hold on!" Logan yells.

The car spins in a circle, and I stay curled up in a ball. Logan straightens out, and we are moving fast again.

"This might hurt," he yells.

We hit something, and I'm slammed against the back of the passenger seat. Then the ride smooths out.

"You can sit up now," Logan says. "Anybody hit?"

I crawl up onto the back seat. Ozzie is already sitting upright.

"I'm fine," Ozzie says.

"Me too," Brian says.

Logan glances back. "Delaney?"

I sit in the seat and glance down. "No bullet holes." But I'm shaking. "Can you roll up your window?" I ask Brian. Although I know the shaking isn't from the cold.

"What if shutting off our phones isn't enough?" I ask.

"Then they'll find us again," Ozzie says.

I blink at him. "Well, that's not reassuring."

He turns to me. "Sorry, it's not."

"We're going to have to ditch this car," Logan says.

Ozzie nods.

"Why would you do that?" I ask.

Logan glances at me in the rearview mirror. "Because the owner will report it stolen if he hasn't already."

Which means we could get arrested. Wait. Maybe we should. "Wouldn't we be safer in jail?" I ask.

All three men say no in unison.

"Ruiz has men paid off throughout San Diego, including the police department. If we get arrested, our names will go into the statewide database. We'd be sitting ducks," Brian says.

Logan pulls down a long, dark driveway into a clearing. "We'll leave the car here and stay in the trees as we walk."

We get out of the car, and Ozzie checks the trunk. "Nothing," he says.

I shiver.

"You'll warm up as we walk," Logan says as he takes my hand.

I stumble on the tree roots as we move. "How are you guys seeing so well?" The little bit of moonlight is blocked by the trees.

"You'll get used to it," Ozzie says.

And he's right. A few more minutes and my eyes have adjusted better. And thankfully, I've warmed up, too.

Thunder crashes overhead.

"Dammit!" Brian says. "We better take cover."

Lightning flashes, and rain begins to fall. We pick up our pace as Logan directs us deeper into the trees. There is a light ahead of us that he seems to be heading toward. He stops and turns.

"There is a house ahead with a shed next to it. We can hide out there, but we need to be silent. Got it?"

We all nod. Fortunately, the thunder and rain cover the sound of our footsteps. We get to the building, and there is a large padlock on it.

"So much for that plan," Brian says.

"Over here," Ozzie whisper yells. He's pointing to a van with a flat tire.

"At least we know no one will try to use it anytime soon," Logan says. He tries the door, and it opens. "Well, that's lucky, at least."

Lightning illuminates the sky again as we all get into the van. Logan rolls the door slowly so it doesn't fully close. Fortunately, inside, it doesn't smell, and the seats are all reasonably clean. There are three rows and the driver and passenger seats.

"Why don't you all try to sleep, and I'll keep first watch," Ozzie offers.

My adrenaline has fully kicked in, and the idea of sleeping seems impossible.

"Sounds good. Wake me in a few, and I'll take over," Logan says.

Brian is already in the back seat, snoring. He's just like Duke, I guess. Logan lies down and motions for me to join him. I snuggle close.

"How can you go to sleep after we were just running for our lives?"

He chuckles. "Because we know we might not get much sleep, so we grab some here and there when we can.

Besides, until this storm passes, there isn't much else we can do. It isn't safe to stay out in the open."

"But what if they find us?"

He strokes my hair. "That's why Ozzie is keeping watch. If he sees movement, we'll go out the back or side and run to the path beside the house."

I sit up. "What path?"

He grins. "There's a dirt path. As we were walking over here, Ozzie and I scanned the area for all our escape routes."

I snuggle back into his arms. "Were you always like this?"

"Like what?"

"On guard. Prepared. Alert."

He sighs. "For as long as I can remember." He strokes my back until I fall asleep.

"We should get going. You want to wake her?" Ozzie asks.

I sit up, and the cold hits me. I don't know how long ago Logan had left the seat, but I miss his warmth now. My entire body shivers. "I'm up."

"Let's go," Logan says as he takes my hand and leads me out of the van.

Birds chirp as we make our way around the house to the dirt path he'd mentioned earlier. We walk fast, and I'm thankful as I begin to warm up. The sky is slowly lighting up as the sun rises.

Once we're a distance from the house, Ozzie stops and turns to us. "When I put the battery back and tried to turn on my phone, I discovered it was dead, so I wasn't able to send Harding a message. Logan, is your phone working?"

He puts in his battery and then turns it on. A moment later, he frowns. "It has ten percent left." He types out a message to Harding explaining our situation.

"Harding said there was a town northeast of where we were staying. We've been going north, and I think we need to head a little more east now," Ozzie says. "Looks like the sun is rising there, which confirms our direction."

I glance over, and the sky is brighter where he pointed, but the sun is still too low to see.

"Agreed," Logan says.

Brian nods, and Ozzie turns and begins walking again.

CHAPTER 30

LOGAN

A SMALL TOWN is visible about a mile ahead in a valley. Based on the terrain, I don't have high hopes that I'll get a cell signal for my phone. But maybe we can find a landline if that's the case.

"Is this typical for your assignments?" Delaney asks as we walk along a dirt path leading us down and out of the trees.

"Do you mean all this walking or the running for our lives part?" I grin.

"Both."

I glance at her, and she's watching me, concern etched in her eyes. I take her hand. "Usually, we don't end up walking as much because we have cars." Then I squeeze her hand. "And if we do the assignment right, we usually aren't running for our lives."

We make our way down a switch back into the valley.

"Have you ever been shot?" she asks. "I mean, besides my dad shooting you."

Ozzie glances back with an arched brow.

"The warehouse shootout in California," I remind him.

He gives a knowing nod and turns back.

Then I turn my attention back to Delaney. "To answer your question, yes." I don't think going into any of these details will benefit us right now, so I rack my brain to come up with a new topic.

Brian, who is leading us, stops and turns around. "Any chance you have a signal?" he asks me.

I check, and I'm shocked, but I do. "I do. I'm calling Harding."

Everyone sits while I make the call. She confirms what I suspected. The town we are headed to is remote, and it will be several hours before anyone can get here to pick us up.

"Well, we don't need to rush then," Brian says in response to my news.

"The men chasing us are likely still out there. If they are familiar with this area, it's logical that they would think we are walking this way," Ozzie says.

"Or they can just track our phones again," Delaney says. "Why aren't you guys worried about that?"

"They don't need to track our phones to figure out where we are going. There's nothing else around here but this town," Ozzie says.

He's right. I take in the area. The edge of town is visible in the distance, but there are almost no trees there. Certainly, no forest to hide in.

"What's wrong?" Ozzie asks as he walks up next to me.

I nod to the town. "We're sitting ducks if we go down there."

He takes in the town and the forest we left. "I agree. If those men are still looking for us, they'll come here, and we have no idea where they might come out of the forest."

"Harding said we are to meet our ride at the water tower on the other side of town, but it will be a few hours, at least, before anyone arrives."

Brian scratches the back of his neck as he stares down at the town. "That's really all out in the open."

"Yeah, we need a place to hide. Let's get closer. Maybe we'll find a vacant house," I say.

Brian winces and rubs his chest.

"Hey, how are you doing?" I nod to his ribs.

He grunts. "As good as can be expected. I'll be happy when we can rest."

We find a road and walk along the side, which makes me very uncomfortable. There's nowhere to hide if someone were to come along. Fortunately, we've only seen one man on a tractor so far.

"Hey, that might work," Ozzie says, pointing at an old barn.

It's about two hundred yards from what appears to be a new barn. Maybe it's not in use anymore.

"It's worth a look," I say.

Once we enter the property, we run to the barn, and Ozzie and I slip inside to check it out. The only thing we find is some old hay.

I pop my head outside and signal Brian and Delaney to

join us. They run to the barn, but Delaney trips and falls a few feet away. I go to her as she tries to stand but falls again.

A car engine grows louder, so I pick her up and get her inside the barn before a car passes. The last thing we need is someone to see us sneaking in here.

"At least we can hide in here for a while," Ozzie says.

Brian stares at the ceiling. "This thing looks like it could collapse at any moment."

I set Delaney on the ground. "Way to think positive."

He grumbles, "Just being realistic."

Delaney rubs her ankle.

"Did you sprain it?" I ask.

Her eyes meet mine. "I think so. When we were running, there was a hole I stepped in just outside the barn."

Her ankle is already swelling, and there is no way she will be able to walk on it. I turn to Ozzie. "How far would you say the water tower is?"

Ozzie thinks for a moment. "Probably about a mile of walking."

That's what I thought, too.

Ozzie bends down and assesses her ankle. "We could take turns carrying her, but that will draw attention to us."

"Ozzie and I will go to the water tower and then direct the driver here to get you two," Brian says.

I hate separating from them, but it's a better plan than carrying her out in the open. "All right," I say.

We sit in silence for a couple of hours, each watching out a different side of the barn. Several cars drive by on the road, but fortunately, no one turns down the driveway toward us.

Ozzie stretches. "We should head out."

"Okay," Brian says. "It might be a couple of hours, but we'll be back."

I nod. "Good luck."

They leave, and I turn my attention to Delaney. She's leaning against the wall of the barn.

"Are you in a lot of pain?" I ask.

She shakes her head. "No. I'm sorry. If we get caught because of my clumsiness…" She turns her face away from me.

Tucking my finger under her chin, I turn her back to me. "You have nothing to be sorry for. Shit happens."

"Well, a lot of shit has been happening lately. You know I never saw you in action before."

I tilt my head. "In action?"

Her hand goes to my chest, and just the slightest touch from her sets me on fire.

"All soldiery."

I raise my brow. "We've been over this. Sailor, not soldier. And I don't think that's a word."

Her gaze turns heated. "Let me rephrase. All sexy and strong." She grabs my shirt and pulls me to her.

Our lips meet, and it goes from a soft kiss to an inferno in seconds. Her hand moves up my back under my shirt, and without thinking, I pull it off. Her eyes widen, and she smiles.

"Damn, Logan," she says as she traces the lines of my abs. "I could stare at you all day."

I chuckle as I lay my shirt on the ground, then she leans back on it. I climb over her as she spreads her legs. As I kiss her, I press into her center. Even with both of us wearing pants, I can feel her heat. Her nails run down my back, and I moan. Damn, I forgot how good this woman feels.

"Logan, I want you now."

"I want you, too, but…" I look up toward where I was keeping watch.

"No one will think we're hiding in this random barn," she says.

She does have a point. I turn my attention back to her as I reach into my back pocket and realize I don't have a wallet or condom because we are in a barn running from someone who is trying to kill us. I rock back onto my knees.

"Don't," she says as she props herself up on her elbows.

"Don't what?"

"Get in your head."

I sigh. "I don't have a condom, and someone could walk in."

She reaches for my belt. "First, I'm on birth control and I'm safe. Second, we might not survive this day, and I will regret it if I'm not with you right now."

I'm stunned by her words. "You sure about not using anything?"

"Very. Not get these damn pants off!"

I stand and remove them. She disrobes from a sitting position, then lies back on my shirt.

"That can't be comfortable," I say, staring at the hay beneath her.

She grabs me and pulls me down. "Stop overthinking. Just feel," she says as she directs me to her entrance. She's already so wet.

One thrust and I'm fully seated. We both moan because, damn, this is the best feeling ever. Then I start moving. She does something with her hips that brings me back to when we were together all those years ago.

"Ah fuck, I'm not going to last long if you keep doing that," I say.

She does it again. "Me either."

I reach a hand down between us and find her clit. I circle it with my finger as I thrust harder.

"Oh, yes!" she yells. "Right there!"

Her core tightens around me as her orgasm hits her. I thrust in and out, watching this woman come apart beneath me, and that's all it takes to set me off. I push in hard as I come, and I swear I see stars.

I collapse next to her, not caring about the scratchy hay. I pull her into my arms, and we lie there, recovering for a couple of minutes.

We are going to survive getting out of here, and I will do everything in my power to make this woman happy. She's it for me, and I want to make sure she knows that.

"Do you think anyone heard us?" she asks, pulling me from my thoughts.

It's then I realize we weren't exactly quiet. "I'm going to check."

I pull out and look out each side of the barn. "There's no one around. And we were quick."

She laughs. "Just shows you how much we both needed that." She sits up as I walk back to her.

"You're right. We needed that. I'm sorry, I don't have anything for you to clean up with."

"That's all right. It was worth it."

I sit down and wrap my arm around her. She leans into my shoulder, and I hold her for a little while.

"As for what you said before, we will survive this day. And we will also be doing this again," I say.

She lets out a long breath. "I hope so. I went twelve years without having good sex. There's a lot I want to make up for."

I squeeze her tight. "Me too."

CHAPTER 31

Delaney

THANKFULLY, we were fully dressed by the time Ozzie and Brian returned with another man. We were all flown back to San Diego, and despite Logan's concerns, Harding said my house was clear if I wanted to pack some things.

I have no idea how long I might be gone, so I fill up my largest suitcase with clothes and toiletries. Logan is sitting on the bed, patiently watching me pack. Once I close the suitcase and zip it, he stands up.

"All done?"

"Yes."

He leans over and gives me a quick kiss, then grabs my suitcase. "Let's go."

His phone buzzes, and he checks it. "Wait here."

"What's going on?"

He goes to my window and glances out. "Someone is here."

I walk up beside him and glance outside. My mom gets out of the unfamiliar car. "That's my mom."

Then a man gets out of the driver's side.

I blink several times. "Uncle Leo?" I run to the stairs.

"Delaney! Wait!" Logan says, chasing after me.

As I bound down the stairs, the front door opens, and they walk in.

"Uncle Leo?" I ask.

The man grins, and my mom steps up behind him.

Two armed men are instantly on our porch with guns pointed at my mom and uncle.

"It's okay," Logan says. "She knows them."

The men retreat, and Leo closes the door. "Delaney!" my uncle says. "It's great to see you again! But who were the armed men?"

"They're here to protect Delaney," Logan says. Then he holds out his hand. "I'm Logan."

My uncle shakes his hand. "Leo Manzia."

"Hello, again, Mrs. Manzia."

My mom steps in, frowning as she takes in Logan. I spot the moment she recognizes him. "You're the boy who broke her heart when she was in college." My mom glances at me. "Why is he here?"

I stare at my uncle in disbelief. "I thought you were dead."

He laughs. "Dead? Why would you think that?"

"Duke told me our father killed you."

Leo's brows shoot up. "Wow. And you believed him?"

He pats me on the shoulder, then turns to my mom. "She's a bit gullible, then?"

My mom doesn't respond because she's still focused on Logan. "Delaney, you haven't answered me. Why is he here?"

I take a deep breath before I dive in. "He's here to protect me. It's a long story, but there are some bad people after me."

My uncle puts his arm around me. "Well, it's a good thing I'm here then. Obviously, your brother has been doing a piss-poor job of taking care of you. Where is Duke anyway?" he asks, glancing around.

"I don't know." That's partly the truth. If I were to guess, he's at Sam's house. "Why are you back?"

"I'm here to reclaim what's mine. The business, this house, this woman." He pulls my mom into his arms.

"Reclaim? I don't understand," I say.

My mom steps forward and gives me a hug. She smiles, which I can't say I've seen her do in years. "There's a lot you don't know about your dad. Let's have some tea, and I can tell you."

She loops her arm through mine, leading me into the kitchen. My uncle and Logan follow.

"We really should be leaving," Logan says.

"Nonsense," my uncle says. "We need to talk first."

My mom fills a kettle and puts it on the stove. Leo and Logan sit at the kitchen table. My mom takes a seat, and I stand there, wondering if I'm dreaming. Leo isn't dead. Why would Duke lie to me?

"Take a seat, honey," my mom says.

I do. "Why would Duke tell me you're dead?"

Leo shrugs. "I guess he figured I was never coming back. Hopefully, he'll understand that I'll be taking over."

I lean back. "I don't think he'll have any complaints."

Leo smiles. "That's wonderful to hear. What about you?"

"Have at it. As long as you understand, I'm not going to work there anymore."

"Trust me, he understands. He's not like your father," my mom says.

I turn to my mom. "You're smiling. I don't remember seeing you smile before. What's going on?"

She rubs my shoulder. "Because life is good now. Years ago, Leo and I dated. We were serious. But then Leo ended up going to prison," my mom says.

"And Rocky told your mom lies and tricked her into marrying him," Leo says.

My mom reaches across the table and places her hand on Leo's. "Rocky led me to believe that Leo had been unfaithful." Her smile drops, and she frowns. "He tricked me into marrying him."

"Why are you telling me this?" As much as I'm not a fan of my father's, no kid wants to hear how he tricked your mother into marrying him.

"Because you need to know that before Leo went to prison, he ran the family business. This house was meant to go to him after your grandparents died. Rocky knew that."

"Maureen, don't waste another thought on that man," Leo says as he squeezes her hand.

My mom leans back. "You're right. He's gone now, thanks to you, and it's time for us to appreciate our freedom."

They smile at each other as I'm caught up in her words. "What do you mean thanks to Leo he's gone?"

Logan frowns.

"It's nothing for you to worry about," Leo says.

I glance at Logan, who is watching Leo.

"You were the one who tipped off the FBI about the stash of drugs in that barn," Logan says.

Leo smiles. "Maybe I was, maybe I wasn't." He shrugs. "Maybe I had someone tell Rocky someone was going to rob his stash." He sighs. "If they all happened to arrive at the same time, well, who knew what might happen?"

I stand up. "You killed my father?"

Leo arches a brow. "You're angry?"

"Yes, I'm angry! He wasn't perfect, but he was still my dad!"

My mom stands and puts her hand on my shoulder. "Delaney, this was the same man who controlled you and me. He made you marry that horrible man and work at his business instead of pursuing your true passion, all while he did whatever the hell he wanted. He may have been your father but in name only."

Deep down, I know she's right. He never supported me in anything I wanted to do. It always had to be what he wanted. My dad was more concerned with his business than his own daughter.

"Why now?" Logan asks.

My mom and Leo turn their attention to him.

"Why did you decide to set up Rocky now? Why not years ago?"

Leo clasps his hands on the table. "It was time."

Well, that's not really an answer.

"And we want you to know, Delaney, that you will always have a home here. If you want." He's looking directly at me.

The tea kettle whistles, and my mom gets up.

She brings the kettle over, then a tray with four cups and a few types of tea.

"If you weren't dead, where have you been?" I ask.

Leo grabs a cup and tea bag. "It's a long story, but I've been living in Barcelona."

Logan clears his throat and then stands up. "Thank you for the tea, but we really do need to get going."

My uncle stops mid-pour of the hot water into his teacup. "Nonsense, you haven't even had any tea yet."

"Sorry, but we can't stay," Logan says.

Leo glances at me as I stand up. "Well, you both must come for dinner soon."

"Yes," my mom says. "Let's do Sunday dinners. But Delaney, I'm not so sure you should bring him." She nods to Logan.

"Sunday dinners, what a fantastic idea, Maureen!" Leo says.

I ignore my mom's comment as Logan walks toward my chair. Now is not the time to get into anything with her. "Thank you for the tea," I say, even though we didn't have any.

"Oh, if you speak to your brother, tell him to call me," my mom says.

"Will do!" I yell as we reach the foyer.

Logan grabs my suitcase and leads me out.

Once we are in his car and pulling out of the driveway, I turn to him. "What the hell was that?"

He shakes his head. "I don't know, but it was weird."

"Weird is an understatement. My uncle is not dead. Apparently, he set my dad up to be killed, and now he and my mom are a couple?"

"Yep," Logan says.

"This isn't real life. This is a soap opera." I lean back in my seat. If I really think about it, though, my mom has been depressed for as long as I've known her. This is the first time I can say she seemed happy. "If she's happy, then I really don't care if she's with my uncle or not."

Logan glances at me. "I'm surprised."

"Why?"

"I remember you being protective of your dad all those years ago. I'm surprised you didn't jump across the table when your uncle admitted what he'd done."

I turn my attention out the window. "Initially, that was my first reaction, but then, as my mom pointed out, my dad wasn't exactly a dad with the things he made me do."

"What all did he make you do?"

"You know about it all. He made me quit design and marry Nelson. After Nelson and I were officially wed, I realized my dad always put the business before me. Before his family."

Logan grabs my hand. "I'm sorry."

I shrug. "It's in the past." Although the strong urge I have to cry tells me, it's not for me.

"Are you still on board with getting away from the business? You know, now that your uncle is here?"

I turn to him, but he's staring straight ahead. "Of course I am."

He blows out a breath. "That's good because I can't be a part of what your family does. You understand that, right?"

"I do."

We pull into the garage of the federal building.

"What are we doing here?" I ask.

"Harding asked us to meet at my brother's office."

"Where is your brother?"

Logan frowns as he parks. "He was supposed to stay with Harding until we could all meet back up here."

As we walk to the elevator, he takes my hand again.

"I guess I don't understand why we wouldn't drive straight to whatever safe house they decide to put us in."

Logan shrugs as he presses the button for Brian's floor. "We will probably switch cars here before we go."

When we step into the FBI's lobby, Harding is there talking with Brian.

Brian walks to Logan and gives him a hug. "Harding confirmed it's safe for me to return to my place and to work here. McKenzie apologized for doubting me."

"It's good to see both of you alive and well," Harding says.

I shiver, thinking about how close we've come to dying.

"Let's go to my office," Brian says.

He leads the way, and once inside, he shuts the door. "Please have a seat."

We all sit in the area off from his desk, which includes a couch and several chairs.

"How were you able to confirm Brian is safe so fast?" Logan asks.

Harding takes a deep breath. "We have hours of taped conversations between Ruiz and the cartel. Once everything went down, we assigned several more agents to the case, and they were able to get through the tapes quickly." Harding leans forward. "Agent Folger has been able to work out a good deal for you, Ms. Manzia. I'll let him explain the details."

I don't really know Harding that well, but her abruptness has me concerned.

"A deal? For what?" I ask.

Brian leans forward. "The case against the mayor is going forward, but that does raise a problem." He looks at Logan. "Apparently, the mayor is very much aware of who you are, Delaney."

I wrap my arms around myself. "That's not good, is it?"

Brian shakes his head. "I received intel last night that there's a reward that will go to whoever kills you."

Logan clenches his fists. "How many people know about this reward?"

Brian sighs. "A lot."

Logan glances up. "All of Manzia's enemies?"

Brian nods.

"Okay, so there are a higher number of people coming

after me now. Does that change the plan? I'm still hiding out, right?" I ask.

Brian doesn't meet my gaze. "It changes everything," he says. "Your father's enemies have connections everywhere. There is nowhere you can go that will be safe."

A chill spreads up my body. "Are you saying it's a foregone conclusion that I'll die? Should I just walk out into the street now?"

Brian's brow shoots up. "No, that's not what I'm saying." He sighs. "I'm saying that our original plan to have you and Logan stay in a safe house won't work. Even if the mayor is convicted, there will be people coming after you for the cash."

"Isn't the reward to prevent me from testifying? Once I do, wouldn't it be revoked?" I ask. I don't know how this works, but that seems logical. Why would the mayor pay for something once it's too late?

"He's not the only one offering a bounty. Once word spread that someone was going after the Manzias, well, others jumped in on it, too."

Manzias? "That means my family isn't safe. You have to protect them!"

Brian nods. "I've sent a couple of agents to locate your brother and discuss the situation with him."

I wring my hands together. "My mom and uncle are at the mansion."

Brian nods. "I'll send someone there as well."

"I have a couple of agents watching the house who can share this information," Harding says.

If we all have to hide for a while, what will happen to

the business? Not that I care about it, but if we can't run it, someone will take it over. Or will my uncle fight for it?

"Delaney."

My eyes go to Brian.

"There is only one way for you to survive this."

Logan is staring at the floor, avoiding my eyes. "Brian, you better not be suggesting what I think you are."

"I'm sorry, Logan. It's the only way." Brian turns to me. "You will enter the witness protection program. You will be given a new name and place to live. They will ask you to change your appearance, likely cutting and dying your hair."

Brian keeps talking, but I don't hear anything more. My heart is beating so loudly. Witness protection? I look at Logan. Would I get to see him? Based on the hurt emanating from his eyes, the answer is no.

Someone taps my leg. "Delaney, did you hear me?"

Brian is next to me. "You'll need to leave today."

"What about her testimony?" Logan asks.

"We'll do a video deposition before she leaves. I've already worked it out with the mayor's attorney," Brian says.

I don't hear the rest of their conversation as my stomach rolls. I run toward Brian's desk and find his trashcan. I grab it just in time for the contents of my stomach to come pouring out as I vomit.

Then I lean against his desk. Logan is there handing me a tissue. I wipe my mouth and toss it into the trashcan. I leave tonight.

"What about my family?" I ask. "Can I talk to them?"

Brian walks into my view. "You can call them this afternoon. But after tonight, no."

I meet Logan's eyes. "If I do this, I'll never see you again, will I?"

His eyes grow glassy as he shakes his head.

"How can I leave you when we finally found each other again?" I ask.

He pulls me into his arms, and I cry. I hold on tight as I let it all out.

CHAPTER 32

Logan

"Hey, you coming with us tonight?" Ozzie asks as he stands at my office door at RHS.

I shake my head.

He walks in and sits in a chair. "Come on. It's better than moping around the apartment all night. That's all you've been doing for the past couple of months."

I appreciate Ozzie trying to help, but I'm not up for putting on a smile.

"Maybe next time," I say.

He sighs. "That's what you say every time."

"Well, one day, it will be true, right?"

He stands up. "I hope so."

I stare at my screen. I've been bound to desk duty since my last assignment. The one where I had to say goodbye to Delaney. It's been two months. I replay that last day with her over and over in my head. She refused to go, and I had to insist. It was the only way to keep her alive. I told her maybe we could see each other again after the mayor's trial. I knew it was a lie, but it was the only way to convince her to save herself.

Here at the office, the guys all know what happened. And it's no secret my mind isn't right, and I have no idea how long it will take until it is again.

Reed says there is plenty of paperwork, and he wasn't lying. At first, the guys were happy I was helping them with theirs. But then it switched to worry that I might not ever snap out of this. And I get it. Deep down, I feel the same way.

Durango pops his head in. "You coming?"

"Not tonight."

He frowns. "No. Reed's office. He called a meeting."

I stand up. "Thanks for letting me know."

Durango steps aside as I walk out my door. I don't miss the look of concern on his face. Not something you often see from him, which tells me I really am a mess.

We are the last two to step into Reed's office.

"I wanted you all to hear this from me. It's good news. The judge dismissed all of Stacy's claims."

Several of the guys cheer.

"That's great. Did she finally admit she was lying about the kid?" Thunder asks.

Reed shakes his head. "No. But the DNA test came back, showing he was not Hawthorne's son. After that, she had no further evidence."

"It's finally over!" Lightning says.

Reed frowns. "I hope it is, but she can appeal. And based on the fact this is Stacy we are talking about, she probably will. But for today, it's a win."

"That's good. Let's hope she comes to her senses," Lightning says.

"That's all I had for you today. Coff, can you stay?" Reed asks.

As the guys filter out, I take a seat closer to Reed's desk. "What's going on?"

"I wanted to check in with you," Reed says.

I nod and stare out his window. "I guess I'm about the same as the last time you asked." I run my hand through my hair. "I know I need to just get over it, but I can't."

Reed walks over and closes his door, then leans against the front of his desk. "No, you aren't supposed to just get over it. It's clear you love her. I'm sorry things went down the way they did."

"Yeah, me too. Oh, I finally finished the full report about what happened."

Reed nods.

"Sorry it took so long, but since my brother had to sign off on what I said…"

He pats my shoulder. "I know. That's why I didn't rush you." He walks back around his desk and sits in his chair. "Do you know if the mayor has been sentenced yet?"

I shake my head. "He never made it to the hearing. He was killed."

Reed arches a brow.

"No, it wasn't me. Brian told me they believe it was Leo Manzia as revenge for putting a reward out for his family."

"Well, for what it's worth, it's good that Delaney was able to get free of that family."

I nod. I could have freed her from that life if she'd only come with me to New York when I first asked her to.

"Hey, I hear the guys are going out tonight. You should go with them."

"I'll think about it," I lie.

Reed is looking out for me like the other guys, but I'm not in the headspace to go out and have fun.

Instead of going back to my office, I head to the front door to get some air. But I stop short as I see Ozzie and Piper in a liplock.

"What the fuck?" I ask.

They jump apart.

"Are you two official?"

Ozzie looks at Piper, who stares at her shoes. "No."

I shake my head. They are both aware that her cousin, Durango, is in his office down the hall, and it could have been him walking through here.

This isn't a conversation I want to have with them, so I walk past them and out the door. I've actually discussed this with Ozzie a few times. I don't like keeping something from Durango. He's my teammate, and we are supposed to have each other's backs, not lie to each other.

Thunder runs out of the office, laughing.

Lightning is right behind him, holding a stuffed animal. "No foxes!" he yells.

"I couldn't help it! It called your name!" Thunder yells over his shoulder. "Squeeze its belly!"

Lightning stops running and squeezes the thing's stomach. "Lightning!" He squeezes it again, and again, it says his name.

"Huh, actually, I like this one."

Thunder stops running and turns back. "You do?"

Lightning grins. "Yeah, tonight when Alicia is calling out Paxton, I can squeeze this and hear Lightning, too."

Thunder frowns, and I can't help but laugh. "That's sick even for you," I say.

Lightning spins. "Coff? Are you laughing?"

I am, but I stop.

"No!" Lightning says. "Don't stop. It's good to see you smile again."

"Sorry, I've been a downer."

"Don't apologize for how you feel," Thunder says. "What happened really sucks."

That's an understatement.

"Logan?"

I must be hearing things because that sounded like Delaney. I turn to find a blonde staring at me. But I'd recognize her anywhere.

She sticks her hand out. "My name is Anna. Nice to meet you."

I take her hand and fight the urge to pull her into my arms and kiss her hard. "Anna."

"I drove a long way to see you."

I nod. "Thunder, can you tell Reed I need to take the rest of the day off?"

Thunder glances at the woman standing next to me. "Okay. Is this—"

"Yes," I say, cutting him off. I'm still holding her hand. "Let's go somewhere we can talk."

She nods, and I lead her to my car. Once inside, I turn and stare at her.

"You look good as a blonde," I say.

Her hair is also shorter, and she's wearing a denim skirt and a white button-up shirt. It looks good but not like something she would have chosen herself.

"Thank you," she says. "I missed you, Logan. I couldn't stay away. I hope you're not mad."

I shake my head. "I missed you so much, too." Then I start the car and drive us to my apartment.

It requires using a key card to get to the elevator and up to our floor. I lead Delaney into the apartment and toss the keys on the counter. Then I turn my attention to her.

I stare at this woman, amazed. "I can't believe you're here."

"I couldn't go another day without seeing you. Without touching you," she says as she places her hand on my chest.

I grab her fingers and stare at her. I have so many questions. I'm angry she compromised herself to come here, but on the other hand, I get it. I need her like I need water.

She lifts up on her tiptoes and kisses me. I don't even try to stop. I return her kiss, walking her backward toward my bedroom. Once inside, I kick the door closed even though Ozzie won't be home for hours.

I break our kiss long enough to unbutton her shirt. "There are a lot of buttons," I say as I realize this could take a while.

She steps back and pulls the shirt over her head. Well,

that works. Then she removes her bra while staring at me. "Take off all your clothes," she says.

I've got everything off before she even unzips her skirt.

She smiles, then laughs. "That was really fast." Finally, her skirt falls to her ankles, and she removes her underwear.

"You have no idea how much I've missed you and want you." I kiss my way from her neck toward her breast.

"Logan, I haven't been with anyone since you," she says nervously.

I pull back and look her in the eyes. "I haven't, either. I don't want anyone else."

She smiles. "I'm still on the pill."

That's all I need to hear. I lift her up, and she wraps her legs around my waist, pressing her heat against my cock.

I growl as I spin us so her back is against the wall. While holding her in place with one hand, I move my other hand between us. "Fuck, you're so wet." I kiss her hard. Then I pull back to watch as I line up my cock.

"All I do is think about you, and I'm wet. Logan, after being with you again in the barn, it's all I can think about."

I tease the tip of my cock at her entrance. She tries to thrust toward me but can't with the way I'm holding her. "All you can think about?" I ask, then I rub the head over her clit and watch how I'm glistening in her juices.

"I masturbate every night, thinking of you," she pants out.

I meet her eyes. "You do?" I keep rubbing her clit, working her up.

She nods. "Sometimes more than once a night."

"Fuck, that's hot." I line myself up and thrust inside her.

She squeezes me, and I hold still, trying hard not to come too fast. While it was great last time, I want her to know I can last when I want to. And she feels like heaven, and I want to stay inside as long as I can.

I continue to pump as I kiss her neck, finding that sensitive spot she has just behind her ear. When I reach it, she moans, and her hands move down my back to my ass as she presses me in farther.

"Harder!" she demands.

I push in and out harder, causing a clock hanging on the wall to fall to the floor. Her hands move to my shoulders, and she finds a way to push herself up and down, changing the angle against my cock. It also causes her breasts to bounce up and down. God, she is the sexiest woman I've ever known.

"Right there, Logan. Oh God, yes!"

The familiar tingle begins in my lower back. "Oh, fuck. Delaney, I'm not going to last."

She moves faster against me. "Harder!" she demands again.

I pump harder, causing some items on the top of my dresser to topple over.

"Yes!" she screams as she tightens around my cock, squeezing it.

I pull out and thrust to the hilt one more time as my orgasm hits hard. I brace one hand against the wall to hold us steady as my vision blurs as I come harder than I think I ever have before.

As soon as I feel stable enough to move, I carry us both

to my bed and lay us down. I kiss her forehead, her cheek, then her lips.

She smiles up at me. "Logan?"

"Hmm?"

"I want to do that with you for the rest of my life."

I chuckle. "It was amazing, but I think we might need to eat sometimes."

"Uh-uh," she says as her breathing evens out. "I'm tired. I drove straight here without resting."

I want to ask her where she came from, but she falls asleep before I can. I pull a blanket up and over us and let myself fall asleep, too.

CHAPTER 33

Delaney aka Anna

I YAWN as I wake up in Logan's arms. I can't believe I'm really here in his apartment, in his embrace. These last couple of months have been miserable. I appreciate what Brian did for me, but it's lonely as hell, and Missoula is so cold.

"I want to stay here and never leave," I say.

He twirls my hair around his fingers. "Me too."

My head is resting on his chest, and I snuggle into him.

"Where did you drive from? You said it was long," he asks.

I sit up a little so I can see his eyes. "Missoula."

"Oh, wow. That's not close."

I settle back onto his chest. "I wasn't sure about coming. I was worried I'd find out you had a new girlfriend."

He moves his hand and runs it down my back. "I haven't so much as looked at another woman since you. I can't stop thinking about you."

"It's the same for me, too." I trace the ridges of his stomach. "Do you think they'd let me move to New York?

His heart rate picks up at my question.

"I don't know. We could always ask Brian." He sighs.

"What's wrong?"

He leans up and kisses my forehead. "I'm pretty sure I was being followed shortly after I got back. That concerns me. But maybe with the time that's passed, whoever was watching me gave up."

"I don't like Missoula. I'm not sure why your brother would think a Southern California girl would fit in there."

He laughs. "Well, that's probably why it was chosen. Who would expect you to live somewhere cold?"

I shrug and then settle in, enjoying his touch.

A phone ringing startles me, and I realize I fell asleep again. I sit up, and Logan is rubbing his eyes. Then he gets up and grabs his pants. He pulls his phone from his pocket.

"It's my brother." He puts the phone to his ear. "Brian, what's going on?"

Brian is talking loud and fast, and I can almost make out the words from several feet away.

"Slow down. No, they didn't find her." He looks at me. "Because I'm with her now."

Then he holds the phone away from his ear as his brother yells. I do catch a few choice names.

Logan puts the phone back to his ear. "Are you calm

now?" He grins at me. "Good. Now, she came to me." He pauses as Brian yells something more. "Why do you think?" Logan asks, then holds the phone away again as Brian yells.

Once the line goes silent, Logan puts it back to his ear. "Why not have her move to New York?" he asks.

While he's focused on the phone call, I take the opportunity to stare at him. He's standing in the middle of the room naked, holding a phone. He's the sexiest man I've ever known, with a body sculpted to perfection. And he has a full beard, unlike when we first met. I was never a fan of beards, but somehow, it looks right on him.

"Okay, I'll call you back." Logan ends the call. "You know, it's really hard talking to my brother with you ogling me like that."

I stand up and walk to him. "Is that so?"

"It is." He bends down and kisses me, then stands straight again. "But we have to go. Apparently, the FBI has an informant who alerted Brian that someone was watching for you in New York, and they reported that we left RHS together."

He grabs his shirt and pants and puts them on. I do the same.

"You think we were followed here?"

He sighs. "Not that I noticed, but I'll be honest, I let myself get a bit distracted."

"Okay, but if we were followed, someone could be waiting outside your door."

He nods. "It's possible. That's why I need you to follow my instructions, all right?"

"Okay."

He draws his gun and slowly opens his door. After he steps out of it, he motions for me to follow. We bypass the elevator and head down the stairs. Before we exit to the garage, he puts his finger over his lips, indicating we need to be quiet. Then he takes my hand, and we run out the door toward his car. It beeps when he uses the fob to unlock it.

He opens the back door. "Get in the back."

I jump in.

"Stay down."

He drives fast through the garage and out onto the street. His eyes go to the rearview mirror and then back to the windshield several times. "We're being followed."

"I'm so sorry. I put you at risk."

"Don't be sorry. Just hold on."

He takes a turn hard, and I'm tossed to the other side of the back seat. He speeds up, slows down, takes another turn. I want to look up because I'm getting motion sickness. Then the car stops.

"What's going on?" I ask.

"I lost him. Stay down." Logan pulls his phone out of his pocket and types a message. "I have to warn Ozzie not to go back to the apartment."

He sends the message, then meets my eyes. "When I pull out of here, we'll likely be followed again. But I have an idea. Go ahead and sit up and put on your seat belt."

I do this as he exits the garage we are in and accelerates. I glance back, and there is a car following us, going just as fast. It moves to the next lane.

"Logan, it's coming up beside us."

"I know. That's the plan."

The car gets closer, and the passenger window goes down. All I see is a gun aimed at our car. Just as the gun is almost aimed at me, Logan turns hard to the right, exiting whatever highway we were on. The other car can't get over in time.

"That will buy us a little time," he says. "But we can't go back to RHS."

I lean back. "This never will end, will it?"

"It will. I'll find a way," he says as he stares at me in the rearview mirror.

In that moment, I believe him. I know he'll try. But if anything happened to him because of me, I could never forgive myself. "I'm sorry I came here and put you at risk."

He doesn't respond, and we drive in silence. I have no idea where we are heading, but it's away from the city. Logan grabs his phone and hits a button.

"Hey, can you do me a favor? I need a burner."

A burner phone? What is he thinking?

"Yeah, I'm heading to Lightning's cabin. Can you meet me there? Thanks." He tosses his phone in the passenger seat.

"What's going on?" I ask.

He stares at me for a beat in the mirror. "I'm working on a plan."

He doesn't elaborate, so I lean back and close my eyes. There is no point in arguing with him now. I'll wait until I hear his plan.

"We're here," he says.

I jolt awake, surprised I fell asleep again but happy to get out of the car.

"This is Lightning's cabin. A couple of the guys will meet us here, and we'll work out our next steps."

"Okay."

He gets out of the car and punches numbers into a keypad, which then opens the garage door. He gets back into the car, and we drive in.

I follow him into the house. The first thing I notice is the view of the lake.

"Yeah, that never gets old," he says as he walks up behind me, wrapping me in his arms. "I need to set something straight."

I turn in his arms. "What?"

"Your coming here was not a mistake. I've been miserable without you. And I have no idea how we can be together, but I'll do everything I can to make it happen."

All the emotions I've been trying to keep contained bubble to the surface as I sink into his arms. What he says is what I want, but now I see it's too dangerous. I know my dad had many enemies, and if they are all truly out to get me, it's just a matter of time before they find me. The fact someone was watching where Logan works for two months tells me they aren't giving up. It's not fair to force him to jeopardize everything in his life for me.

Dammit! Why couldn't I see before that coming here like this is selfish?

His phone rings from the counter, and he steps away from me to check it. "It's my brother again."

"Can I talk to him?"

His brows go up. "You want to? He's pretty pissed."

I nod, and he hands me the phone. "Brian, it's me."

"What the hell were you thinking?" he yells through the phone.

"I'm going to see if there is any food here," Logan says, then walks into the kitchen.

I wander down the hall into a back bedroom. It's better if Logan doesn't hear what I need to ask. "I'm sorry. I was going crazy without Logan, but I see now the danger I've put him in. Is there any way I can go back to Missoula tonight?"

"Delaney, no. You rented a car in your new name. It won't take much for someone to figure that out and then find your address in Montana."

"Oh." I sink onto the bed. For some reason, I thought I'd just be able to go back and maybe visit Logan now and again until this was over. Clearly, I hadn't thought this through.

"I might be able to get you relocated with a new name again. But if I can pull this off, you have to let my brother go. Understand?"

I swallow back the sob that tries to escape, but I sniffle. "I understand." And this time, I really do understand.

Brian sighs. "Okay, I'll see what I can do. Where are you?"

"Logan says it's Lightning's cabin."

"Okay, I'll see if I can pull this off. But it might be a day or two."

"Okay, thank you."

He ends the call. And I sit there on the bed, staring at

the wall. Start over. Again. Without Logan. Again. I wipe away the tears.

It's not just Logan I have to leave forever. Duke and my mom. I miss them. When I was told I had only hours to leave with my new identity, somewhere in the back of my mind, I thought it was temporary. But now I realize it's not.

While I have the phone, I call Duke.

"Hello?"

"Duke, it's me."

"Delaney? Is that really you?"

"It is. I've missed you guys so much."

"We've missed you."

I wipe away the tears from under my eyes. I hadn't expected Duke's voice to make me so emotional. "Are you safe?"

"I'm fine. Sam and I are in Hawaii on vacation. Leo and I have been working on clearing everything up so you can come home."

"What do you mean?"

He chuckles. "The less you know, the better. Once it's safe, can I call you back at this number?"

"No. You won't be able to reach me."

He sighs. "Okay, then call me in a few days. Promise?"

I won't be able to call him, but he won't hang up until I do. "I promise."

Then I end the call before he can hear me crying and knows I'm lying. I try to stop crying, but I can't. I lie back on the bed and take several deep breaths to calm myself. If

I only have a small amount of time left with Logan, I don't want to spend it crying in a bedroom.

I take several more deep breaths, and I get my emotions under control. But then the front door opens. Logan is in the kitchen, so who the hell is coming in the front door?

CHAPTER 34

Logan

"Thank you for bringing this up." I take the burner phone from Ozzie. "How'd you get here so fast?"

"I wasn't too far from here when you called."

My friend is avoiding my eyes.

"What's going on?" I ask.

He shrugs. "I needed a drive to think, and I always enjoy the drive out this way."

"Anything you want to talk about?"

Ozzie chuckles. "No, you got enough going on. Speaking of, are you going to tell me what you have planned? Because if it is what I think it is, one of you two is going to get caught."

Delaney walks out of the back bedroom, her eyes red-rimmed. I walk to her.

"What's going on?"

"I called Duke. I miss my family despite everything."

I wrap my arms around her. Although I can't understand why anyone would miss Duke, I do get being separated from your family. It's hard not being near Brian sometimes.

"Hey, I have something for you." I take her hand and lead her to the kitchen counter where I left the phone.

"It's a burner phone that has a set number of minutes. If you really want to call Duke or me, you can. It's not traceable, well, not easily," I explain.

"Thank you," she says.

"So, what's the plan?" Ozzie says. "Are we driving her back to wherever she lives now?"

Delaney shakes her head. "No, I spoke to Brian, and he says that my new identity has been compromised, and I can't go back."

She can't go back, and she can't stay here forever.

"We need to find out who is after her and take them down," I say.

Ozzie nods.

"I don't think that's possible." I take a deep breath. "Brian said this is bringing out all my dad's old enemies. I don't know how many he had, but I'm guessing it's a large number."

Ozzie holds up his hand. "I want to help you out, but Coff, we don't have the resources or manpower to take on what could be every criminal in California."

"Nor are you going to do that," Delaney says. "Brian is working on another plan."

When she doesn't elaborate, I take her hands in mine. "What plan?"

She avoids my eyes. "He says he might be able to get me another identity and location. He's not sure, though."

My heart sinks as I realize I will lose her again. The next few hours or days might be our last. That isn't enough time for me to figure out another way out of this.

"I'll be right back." I manage to step outside and around the side of the cabin. I want to punch something, but there's nothing to punch. Why did she come back into my life if she's going to be ripped out again?

I stare at my phone. I want to call my brother and find out the odds of him getting her back into witness protection. But if he says they're good, I'll lose it. Instead, I send a message.

Me: *Is she going back into witness protection?*

I close my eyes and lean against the wall. If Brian would tell me the names of everyone who is after her, I could take care of them myself. Maybe he will.

I go to send another message as his reply comes up.

Brian: *Yes. Working out the details now.*

Me: *Give me the names of the men after her.*

Brian: *You know I can't do that. Besides, I don't have a complete list.*

I sink down to the ground. This can't be how it ends.

"Hey."

I turn and spot Ozzie standing a few feet away.

"You okay?"

I shake my head.

He sits down next to me. "Yeah, the situation is pretty shitty."

"I asked my brother for the names of the men going after her. He said no."

Ozzie nods. "You want to take them out?"

"Of course I do."

Ozzie tilts his head. "Okay, let's say you do that. What's to stop their friends from coming after you or to blame her for it, and then you have more people going after her?"

I turn and stare at him. "So, what? I'm supposed to do nothing?"

Ozzie sighs. "Maybe for now. At some point, these guys will give up and move on to someone else."

I rub my eyes. "We don't know they will."

"Maybe not all of them, but enough of them that maybe you two can work something out."

Leaning my head back, I stare at the sky. "You said a hell of a lot of maybes."

He chuckles. "Nothing in life is certain. But don't give up all hope. I'll help you figure out something."

"Yeah?"

He pats my arm. "Of course. What are best friends for?" He stands up and holds out his hand. "Now, let's get back inside."

I take it and stand up. He's right; I can't give up hope. Or at least I can't be all moody and sad around her when I don't know if I'll ever see her again.

Once we're back inside, Ozzie claps his hands together. "It looks like we have some time to kill. Who wants to play cards?" He opens a few drawers.

"Don't you need to get back to the office?" I ask.

He smiles. "Nope. Reed asked me to stay up here and keep an eye on things."

Reed asked him to stay? He must think I'd be unfocused. Well, if Ozzie left, he'd probably be right. I'd love nothing more than to spend the time I have left with Delaney in bed.

"Found some!" Ozzie shouts from the kitchen. He walks to the dining room table and sits down. "Rummy sound good?"

Delaney glances at me, then Ozzie, and shrugs. "Works for me."

I sit and join them as Ozzie shuffles the cards.

Three hours later, I'm staring at Ozzie's knowing smirk. "How the hell did you win every game?"

Ozzie shrugs. "I'm that good." He stands up and stretches. "And I'm also hungry. Let's see what's in the kitchen."

Delaney stands and stretches, too. "I've never played cards for that long."

"We've had many nights of playing cards," I say, referring to Ozzie and me.

She grins. "Many nights of cards? I figured you would be going out to bars and picking up women."

"Danger!" Ozzie says as he walks back into the room. "Don't answer that."

Delaney laughs.

I debate if I should say something. I mean, I've been with women over the years but not that many. Before I speak up, headlights flash into the room.

I grab Delaney's hand and get us out of sight of the window.

"Unknown car. Two men," Ozzie says. His body is behind the hallway wall. "Wait, three men. And a second car." His eyes meet mine.

He doesn't have to say it. This is going to get ugly fast.

I pull Delaney into the kitchen and move a rug. Then I pull up the latch door. She stares down.

"There is a short ladder. It's a cellar for storing potatoes."

She glances down again. "At a lake cabin?"

I shrug. "Lightning's parents were into storing food just in case. There's probably some powdered corn from the nineties down there, too."

The front door bursts open.

"Go!"

She goes down into the dark cellar. I close the door and put the rug back, then duck behind the kitchen island.

"Just give up the girl. We don't have a beef with any of you," a deep voice yells out from the living room.

It's silent for a moment.

"No?" the same voice asks. "All right. We'll do it your way."

Bullets spray the living room, many making their way through the kitchen wall.

"Stop!" the man yells. "Go find them," he orders.

I grab the knife block that's on the counter near me. Two men walk into the kitchen with their guns drawn. I throw a knife at the first man, striking him. Then I reach for my gun as the second man turns in my direction. I fire before he can. They are both down.

Ozzie said the first car had three men, but we don't know how many were in the second car. Three shots go off near the bedrooms.

Knowing one man is likely waiting for me to walk out of the kitchen and into his trap, I go out the back door and make my way to the front of the house. The two cars are parked in the driveway, and no one is in either.

As I come around to the front door, I spot a man standing there, aiming a gun at the kitchen.

"You have to come out of there at some point!" he yells. It's the same guy who has done all the yelling.

"You're right," I say.

He whips around, and I shoot.

Instead of going inside, I walk around the other side of the house to one of the bedroom windows. A man is crouched behind the door. I tap on the glass to get his attention. He jumps up and shoots out the window. I hop out of the way in time, but it did what I intended, alerting Ozzie of his location.

Another gunshot and I glance back through the window. Ozzie took the man out. He sees me and holds up one finger.

One left. I nod.

Then I slowly make my way toward the back of the house until I hear a sound near the front. I change course in time to hear one of the car engines starting.

By the time I get around the front, one of the cars is backing up. I shoot out a tire and then a second one. At least we will have one man to question. But then I see the gun in his hand. I shoot straight through the windshield.

Ozzie steps out and joins me in front of the house. "The cellar?"

"Yep. Was that all of them?"

Ozzie nods. "Guess I'll call Reed, and you take care of her."

I help Delaney step out of the cellar. She's shaking, and I pull her close.

"They're all dead," I say.

She pushes away from me and walks to the two dead men in the kitchen. Then she notices the man in the living room and goes to him. "I recognize him."

"Who is he?" I ask.

"He worked with my dad for several years, then he was gone. I thought he was dead."

I bend down and pull his wallet from his pants. "Walter Collins."

She nods. "Yes, he used to always ask Dad to fix him a Collins, the drink. He thought it was funny. My dad thought it was obnoxious. Then I would be asked to go upstairs."

Ozzie returns to the room. "Reed is on his way, along with an FBI agent Brian had sent to help us.

~

IT WAS one hell of a long night explaining everything that happened to the FBI agent. Fortunately, we were allowed to leave, and Ozzie drove the three of us to a hotel. The moment we were in bed, we were all out.

I wake the next morning surprised to find Ozzie sitting up in bed, wide awake, staring at his phone.

"Good morning," he says. "You should check your phone."

I grab my phone from the nightstand. "It's dead."

"Here," Ozzie unhooks his from a charge. "Use this."

"Thanks. You carry chargers on you now?" I plug my phone in.

"No, I asked if they had one I could use when I checked us in last night." He nods at my phone. "That's going to be a while. Reed sent us a message this morning." He turns his phone around so I can read it.

I read it again as it sinks in. "Holy shit. We took out Manzia's biggest enemy?"

Ozzie nods.

Maybe there is hope. "If we can take out other enemies, then she can be free."

Ozzie smiles. "That's what I was thinking, but based on what I've dug up, there are a lot of enemies."

My phone rings. "Guess it's partly charged now. It's Reed," I say, then answer it. "Reed?"

"I'm about five minutes away. Just wanted to give you a warning so you didn't get spooked when I knock on the door."

I laugh. "All right. I'll let everyone know."

I end the call and tell Ozzie Reed's on his way. Then I turn to Delaney and kiss her cheek to wake her up.

She smiles as she slowly wakes up. "Good morning."

"Good morning. Reed is going to be here in about four minutes."

Her eyes widen, and she jumps up and runs to the bathroom. She's still in there when Reed knocks on the door. Ozzie checks through the peephole and then opens the door.

Reed walks in carrying what appears to be a grocery bag on top of a pizza box.

"I figured you guys might be hungry."

"Pizza for breakfast?" I ask.

Reed frowns and then glances at Ozzie, who is grinning.

"Late lunch. Check the time."

I do, and it's almost one in the afternoon. "Late lunch? You mean normal lunch?"

Ozzie takes the pizza from Reed. "I don't care what we're calling it. I really appreciate it. Thank you." Ozzie sets the box on his bed and opens it up. "Pepperoni. Perfect." He takes a slice and has it half eaten by the time he finally looks up. "What? I'm hungry."

Reed shakes his head. "Anyway, I have something for Delaney."

"I'm here," she says as she steps out of the bathroom. Her hair is wet from a quick shower.

Reed pulls a white envelope out of the bag and hands it to her. She opens it up and spills the contents onto our bed. Then her glassy eyes meet mine. "Brian did it. He got me a new identity. But he said it could take days."

This is really happening.

"Due to the urgency, he was able to push it through faster than normal," Reed says.

"Urgency?" I ask. "We just took out one of Manzia's biggest enemies last night. We take out a few more and she can stay."

Reed glances at Ozzie, then back to me. "Coff, can I talk to you privately?"

The last thing I want is to get a lecture, but if it gets me some breathing room right now, I'll take it.

"Sure," I say.

He nods for me to follow him, and we step outside the room into the hallway. Once the room door closes, he stares at me. I swear his eyes are getting glassy.

"What's going on?" I ask.

His brow furrows. "Your brother did something more. And I want to talk to you about it."

I turn my back to him. "He's sending her to another country, isn't he?"

"No, it's about you."

Well, that has my attention. I spin back around. "Me?"

Reed nods. "Brian said you're a wreck without Delaney in your life. And I can't say I disagree after what I've seen these last two months."

My heart is pounding loudly. Did my brother get me fired?

"When he put in the request for Delaney, he put in a request for you as well." He takes another white envelope out of the bag and holds it up. "If you want it."

I'm not sure I heard him right. "What? He can do that?"

Reed shrugs. "He knows the right people. If you want

to, you can go with Delaney."

"Go with her? You mean change my identity?"

Reed nods.

Give up everything for her. Hell, that's what I was asking her to do for me, wasn't it? When I asked her to move to Virginia, then years later to New York?

"But what would I do? For work."

Reed smiles. "Well, you're in luck because if you choose this route, I have a job lined up for you."

I run my hands through my hair. If I choose it. I have to choose it. She's everything to me. But then I wouldn't see the guys again. Ozzie. Reed.

"Look at the details before you decide." Reed hands me the envelope, then leaves me alone outside.

I open it and read through everything twice. It says my name is Matthew Hill. My residence is east of Seattle, and I'm employed by Morgan Thompson Security. What? I can transfer to Stormy's other team? Yes, I would be leaving my current job behind, but the two groups work together from time to time, so it's not like I would never see them again.

I run into the room to Reed. "Morgan Thompson? How?"

Reed smiles. "I talked to Stormy and Cowboy about it. We all agreed that it could work. The guys would all be discreet."

"What's he talking about? Are you leaving RHS?" Ozzie asks.

Delaney glances up from the bed.

"Seattle?" I ask her.

She nods as she stands up.

"Brian had a similar envelope for me," I say. "What do you say? Want to go to Seattle with me?"

Her entire face lights up as she runs into my arms. I pick her up and spin her around.

"Is this real?"

I nod. "It is."

"Wait," Ozzie says. "You're transferring?"

I set Delaney down. "Yes, but it's more. I'm changing my name, too."

"Wow. When do you go? We need to throw you a going away party or something," Ozzie says.

Reed turns to him. "I'm afraid that's not an option. They need to leave tonight. I'm supposed to drive them to the airport."

Ozzie blinks several times. "Oh wow. That's fast. You already have a passport?"

I pull one out of the envelope.

"Okay. Should I try to convince you to stay?" he asks. "We were going to take them all out, remember?"

I nod. "I still plan to. But this gives me more time to do it and be with her."

"I get it," Ozzie says. Then he pulls me in for a hug.

"I'll see you again," I say. "When you work with MTS."

He pulls back. "Yeah, but it won't be the same."

And he's right. Not having my best friend as my roommate or even on the same coast will be hard. "I know. But when it's right, you have to go for it."

He nods.

"That applies to you, too. Whatever is holding you two back, don't let it."

Ozzie's brow jumps. "If Durango heard that, he'd disagree."

"Something tells me I don't want to hear whatever this is about," Reed says.

I laugh. "Probably not." I turn back to my friend. "Look, I get that he's protective, but he's taking it too far. You're a good guy, and if you need me to tell him that, I will."

"Thanks, Coff." He steps back. "Wait, what do I call you now?"

I glance at Reed.

"Coff works. But just so you know, this is Morgan Thompson's newest employee, Matthew Hill," Reed says.

Ozzie smirks. "Matthew?" Then he turns to Delaney. "How about you?"

She smiles. "Jolene."

Ozzie nods.

"Now, you are still going to see these guys, but you all should probably hold off on socializing in any way for a while. At least until Brian gives the all-clear," Reed says.

Brian. My older brother always looking out for me.

"What about my family?" Delaney asks. "Will I ever see them again?"

Reed shoves his hands into his pockets. "I don't know. That's something Brian will have to answer. But you have to assume the answer is no."

Delaney takes a deep breath and turns to me. "I can't believe we get to leave here together. I thought this was it."

"I thought you were going to leave without me, but there was no way this was going to be it. I'm never leaving you again."

CHAPTER 35

Delaney aka Jolene

Three months later

I'm nervous as I step into the Morgan Thompson Security building. It's the first time I've been here. Logan, or Coff, as I now call him to prevent saying the wrong thing, has been working here for a few months, and today is the first day all the guys are in town at the same time. Apparently, on those rare occasions, they have some sort of huge paintball competition here. And since we still aren't going out in public very much, they decided that was another reason it was time for paintball.

All I know is I'm happy to be included. The guys' girlfriends, Sarina, Connie, and Lucy, have invited me to a weekly happy hour at Lucy's house. That is the highlight of my week. But this is the first time I'm meeting some of the other guys.

"We're ready to kick some ass," Coff says as we walk out the back door.

"Now that's funny," Rover says as he pulls on coveralls.

Another man walks up behind Rover. "It will be funny after he does it."

Rover's hands go to his hips. "Hey, whose side are you on?"

The man grins. "Not yours."

Coff laughs. "Jolene, this is CT. CT, this is my girlfriend, Jolene."

I'm still trying to get used to being called Jolene.

CT nods in my direction. "Nice to meet you. You two need coveralls. They are over there." He points to a bin.

Coff walks over and comes back with two.

"Yes, that's what I was saying!" Connie says as she walks out of the woods with Lucy and Sarina.

"What were you all doing back there?" Rover asks.

"Plotting to take you out," Connie says, then she kisses Rover.

He steps back. "Put them on different teams!"

"Already done," CT says. He's now holding a clipboard.

I lean closer to Coff. "They take this very seriously, don't they?"

Fox laughs behind us. I turn, and he's zipping his coverall up. "You have no idea."

"It doesn't matter because I always win," another man sitting on the stairs says.

"Bullshit," Sarina says.

"*Ooohhh!*" several guys respond.

The man stands up. "One time I lost to you. *One* time."

Sarina smiles. "It will be two after today, Trax." She steps away, then turns back. "Maybe you guys should call me Trax from now on."

The man doesn't even smile.

"Does he have a sense of humor?" I ask Coff quietly.

"Not that I've seen yet."

"Okay, listen up!" CT yells. "The teams are as follows: on the blue team are Sarina, Cody, Connie, Coff, Jolene, and myself. On the red team are Rover, Lucy, Maverick, Trax, and Fox."

"Wait, no! You can't put Coff and his girlfriend together!" Rover says.

CT rolls his eyes. "Fine. Jolene, you get to be with that polite man there. Everyone, make sure you grab the right color paintballs."

"Here," Lucy says as she hands me a container. "Teammate."

"Thanks."

"Don't let anything Rover says bother you. He speaks before he thinks sometimes."

I nod. "No, I'm more concerned with the fact that I have no idea what I'm doing. I've never played."

She steps back. "Have you ever been shot with a paintball?"

I shake my head.

"Dammit, Coff. Well, you should know it hurts, so be ready for that. I can't believe he didn't take you out for target practice."

I laugh. "I'm not worried about that. I can hit a target."

"Oh, you've shot a real gun, then?"

I nod.

"Hey, they started," Fox says as he runs by us.

Lucy follows him, then yells over her shoulder. "Hide. We have ten seconds, and then it's game on."

Coff may not have prepared me for this game, but he did take me for a walk through this forest last week. And I distinctly remember a tree down on the edge of it that I will fit behind. I run to it and jump over. There is a bush covering part of the tree from view, and I hide behind that. If anyone comes around the corner, I have an unobstructed view and can take them out before they see me. I hope anyway.

"Go!" CT yells from somewhere.

Then I hear several shots go off.

"Dammit!" Lucy yells. "First one out again?"

Several more shots go off, and there is a lot of yelling. By the time it settles down, I'm unsure who is left. Then someone slowly rounds the corner. It's Cody. I shoot. His head droops. "Dang it!"

He turns and walks back to the building. It's silent for some time, so I decide to make my way closer to the center, where most of the shots were fired. As soon as I'm over the log, I'm hit. I turn and look up to find Trax smiling at me from up in the tree. He waves.

You can climb the trees? Well, that would have been good to know. I walk out, looking for Coff, but he's not on the deck.

"Your man's still in there," Lucy says.

"Who's left?" I ask.

"Coff, Sarina, Fox, and Trax," she says.

"No!" Coff yells, and more shots go off.

"Not cool!" Trax yells.

Coff and Trax walk out of the forest, and Sarina is behind them, all smiles.

"I won again!" she says. Then her body jerks. "Ouch!" she yells.

Fox steps out from the trees. "Nope, I won."

"What?" Sarina glances at everyone on the deck. "Dammit, I counted wrong."

We all take off our coveralls and place them in a bin.

"Hey, don't think I've forgotten about that welcome party," Rover says to Coff. "As soon as it's safe to do so, I'm on it."

"Thanks," Coff says.

Coff is all smiles around these guys. I tried calling him Matthew, but I couldn't do it. It doesn't suit him. But Coff does. I'm happy this has all worked out. And yes, he's been here three months, but we held off on doing anything in public, like a welcome party at a bar, until we are certain no one is searching for us.

"Huh. My brother sent a text telling me to call him right away," Coff says, staring at his phone.

He takes a few steps off the back deck as he makes the call. "Yeah, she's here." He turns to look at me. "All right." He pulls the phone from his ear and turns on the speakerphone. "It's my brother."

"Jolene?"

I walk closer. "I'm here."

"Good. I have news I want to share with both of you."

I glance at Coff, and he's frowning at the phone. "What's going on?" he asks.

"There was an explosion last night at a warehouse just south of San Diego. I'm not sure how, but Ruiz was inside, along with all of his top men. And there were quite a few members of one of the Mexican cartels. In total, thirty-three men died."

My mind is racing. Were they murdered? Was it an accident?

"Why were they all in the same building?" Coff asks.

Brian sighs. "That's a very good question. Unfortunately, we don't have the answer, and we probably never will."

"Was it an accident?" I ask. There's no way it could be with so many top players in there.

"No. It's still early, but it appears a truck loaded with explosives was inside the warehouse, and it blew up. Harding says her agency picked up on communication that indicated a rival cartel is responsible."

I sit down on the steps of the deck as I process what he is saying.

"Another cartel is taking over what Ruiz covered?" Coff asks.

"It appears that way."

Coff sits next to me and puts an arm around my shoulders. "Okay, thank you for letting us know." He ends the call.

I wipe my eyes. Over the past three months, several of my dad's enemies have died. According to the FBI, each one was a drug deal gone wrong. While I want to believe that, I can't. All those men lived for years, and then, in the span of a few months, they died. And now this.

"You okay?" Coff asks.

I shake my head. "Are you behind all this?"

How could he be? He was with me all last night.

"All of this?" he asks.

"They are all dying."

He takes my hand. "I'm not the one behind it."

I whip my eyes to his. "But you know who is?"

He shrugs. "I have a suspicion."

Then another thought hits me. "Wait, if the cartel that worked with Ruiz and my dad is gone, someone else will take over. What will happen to my brother? Or my uncle?"

I wish Duke would leave the business. Uncle Leo seemed happy taking it over, so I don't understand why Duke is still there.

"I don't know."

I stand up. "Can we go home? I want to call Duke on the burner phone you got me."

It's been hard, but I haven't used it. Brian assured Coff he was keeping an eye on Duke and my family.

We say our goodbyes, and Coff drives us home. Home. The moment I first stepped into the apartment arranged for us, it felt like home. Maybe it's because I knew we'd be together here.

Once we get inside, I go into the bathroom and retrieve the phone. I keep it taped up under the bathroom sink at the back of the cabinet.

It powers on, and I call Duke. It goes to voicemail. I hang up and call back.

"Hello?" he answers cautiously.

"It's me."

"Delaney?"

I walk out of the bathroom toward the living room. "Yes."

"I'm so happy you called! It took longer than I'd expected, but we did it! You can come home now," he says.

I stop in my tracks. "Why do you say that?"

He sighs.

"Duke?" I walk to the sofa and sit down next to Coff.

"You know I want to tell someone, and I can't tell Sam. I pulled it off. After Dad was killed, I thought my chance was gone."

"Slow down. What are you talking about?" I glance at Coff, and he's frowning, but Duke is talking loudly enough for him to hear.

"Wait, Brian didn't tell you about me, did he?" Duke asks.

Now I'm really confused. "He told me there was an explosion."

"Just a minute." A door slams shut, then birds tweeting comes through the phone. "I had to step outside. I'm going to walk out toward the street."

"Is there a listening device in the house?"

He chuckles. "No, I don't want Leo to hear any of this. And what I'm about to tell you is for your ears only."

"And Coff. I don't keep any secrets from him."

"He's fine. I'm still surprised Brian hasn't told either of you."

I lean back, impatient with my brother. "Told us what?"

"Well, I've been working with Brian for over a year now."

"You're an agent?" Coff asks.

"Uh, Delaney?" Duke asks.

I arch a brow at Coff, and he shrugs. "I'm on the couch, and he's beside me so he can hear."

Duke sighs. "Well, thanks for letting me know. And to answer his question, no, I'm not an agent. I'm an informant. Or I was until Dad was killed. That screwed up everything. That's why I was so angry with Logan."

I close my eyes as I try to process what he's telling me. "Duke, this makes no sense. You were all about the business. How could you be an informant?"

"You were miserable with Nelson, and it was my fault. I had to do something. But really, I blamed our father for all of it, too. After what they'd done to you, I wanted to make them both pay."

I don't remind him again that it was his actions that got me into that mess with Nelson.

"I approached Brian and told him I'd give him information as long as he could guarantee our father and Nelson would go down."

"He guaranteed that?" Coff asks.

"He did."

Coff shakes his head.

"But when Dad died, I had no choice but to take over everything. Brian told me he couldn't keep up our deal if I was running things. Before I had a chance to do anything about it, Nelson set me up."

My mind goes back to a few times I'd walk in while Duke was on the phone, and he'd react strangely. The morning of my dad's funeral stands out the most.

Coff stands up. "This is why Brian was intent on keeping you safe, too?"

I turn on the speakerphone and set my phone on the coffee table.

"Yes," Duke says.

Coff's hands go to his hips. "I thought it was because you were Delaney's brother, and Brian was doing it as a favor to me."

Duke laughs. "It's the government. You think he can justify the expense of security for me as a favor?"

Duke doesn't know that Brian somehow got Coff a new identity as a favor. But he doesn't need to know.

Coff sits back down. "Then tell me once you had security, why did you risk it all to fly back to try to kill Nelson?"

"That asshole was trying to destroy our lives. I couldn't let him get away with it. Besides, I knew if I went there, you guys would follow, and between all of us, someone would take him out."

"You left in the middle of the night. What if we'd all slept in?"

He laughs again. "Why do you think I chose a connecting flight with a four-hour layover?"

I'd just assumed it was the earliest flight he could get. But he's saying he planned it that way?

"You used us," Coff says.

"I'm sorry, but it had to be done. You should be thanking me. I released Delaney from the prison he had her in."

My hands go to my temples as I try to massage away the headache coming on. He's right. Nelson was never going to let me go alive. "Duke, what does any of this have to do with the explosion?"

Duke doesn't answer.

"Duke, are you still there?"

"Yeah. You aren't going to like this, but it had to be done."

"Tell me."

He blows out a breath. "The mayor couldn't get away with trying to have you killed, Delaney. I talked to Leo about it, and he suggested we take out all of our problems at once. It was brilliant, really. He called a guy in Mexico who can make things happen. Then he invited everyone to the warehouse to talk business. Then boom."

"Uncle Leo took out everyone trying to take over the family business?"

"He's an impressive man, and he works faster than I've been."

"Duke, what does that mean?"

He sighs into his phone. "I know you've been following the news and watching the headlines in his area."

I have, and that's how I know about all the men being killed. "Are you the one making the drug deals go bad?"

"Maybe. But Leo found a better way. And he wants to run the business. I can't tell you what a relief that is."

"So, you're out then?"

"Not completely, but enough that Sam is happy. For now. But she misses you. When can you come home? Leo has the guest room saved for you."

"Doesn't my brother want you as an informant still?" Coff asks.

Duke laughs. "No, after the explosion, he wants nothing to do with me. Now, Delaney, you can have your old job back."

Is he crazy? I finally got away from the business and everything about it. Why would I want to go back to that?

Coff is watching me closely.

"Duke, I'm not coming back."

"Well, where are you? At least let me bring Sam to visit you. We both want to see you."

"I'll think about it. I need to go. Bye, Duke." I end the call and curl up on the sofa.

Coff opens his arms, and I lean into him. "Are you all right?' he asks.

I shake my head. "My brother set up over thirty people to be killed."

He sighs. "Yeah, but does it help to know they were bad people?"

"I don't know. Maybe?"

Coff rubs my arm. "You know, just because your brother said it was safe to go back doesn't mean it is. It might never be."

"I know. But I'm hoping I can see Duke and Sam again someday. While I'm still angry at Sam and probably will be for a while, I can't cut out someone like that. She's been my best friend since we were in high school."

He cups my face. "I get it. We'll figure out something. I still can't grasp why Duke would walk away from pursuing your family's business, but he must have his reasons."

I straddle his lap, and he leans back against the couch. "I think it's all for Sam. Which I'm happy about because I don't want to think about or hear about that business ever again."

He grins. "And what do you want to think about?"

"You." I lean down and kiss him.

When I pull back, he stares at me. "I'm sorry you had to walk away from everything you knew, but I'm happy you did. I'm so happy to be here with you. I love you, Delaney, Anna, Jolene."

I cup his face with my hands. "I'm so thankful for having you back in my life. I love you, too, Logan, Matthew, Coff."

He grins, and I lean forward and kiss him.

CHAPTER 36

Fox

"Hey! Glad you made it!" Peaches says as I walk into the bar.

"Yeah, I might not stick around long if Julia brings her boyfriend."

Detective Julia McNamara. She's someone we rely on quite a bit in our security business and also the woman I've been fawning after for as long as I can remember. Last year, I finally got the courage to ask her out, but right before I did, she introduced me to her boyfriend.

I was too late. And she's been dating the asshole ever since. I shouldn't say asshole. Honestly, I don't really know him. And I don't want to.

"Well, she's here by herself right now." Peaches nods toward the back of the room where Julia stands with Rover and Coff.

My eyes catch hers, and she waves. I wave back.

"Here." Peaches hands me a shot. "I'm buying a round of shots."

I take it and frown. "Are you trying to get everyone drunk?"

He laughs. "One shot? No. This is just my way of welcoming Coff to MTS."

Even though Coff has been working at Morgan Thompson Security for several months, we couldn't have a welcome party for him due to his circumstances until now.

"Thanks." I drink it and set the empty glass on the bar. Then I follow Peaches as he walks to where some of our guys are.

He gives each a shot. "Welcome aboard, Coff."

Coff's eyes dart around. "Thanks."

He's still nervous despite getting the all-clear from his brother. I don't blame him. It's in our nature.

Rover slaps his back. "Don't worry, we won't get too rowdy and draw attention."

Coff's focus goes to Rover.

"We all know you're still nervous. It's understandable."

Julia laughs. "If you don't want rowdy, I better warn Dan when he shows up then."

"Who's Dan?" Coff asks.

"My boyfriend."

If I have to watch the two of them all lovey-dovey, I'm going to need another drink. I head back to the bar and order a beer and a shot. As I down the shot, someone sits on the stool next to me.

"Hey, it's Fox, right?"

I turn and look right into Dan's eyes. So much for avoiding him. "Yeah. Dan, right?"

We met at the police station once, and despite being good friends with Julia, I've not run into him since, not that I've spent as much time with her since he came into the picture.

"What can I get you?" the bartender asks him.

He points at me. "Whatever beer he has is fine."

The bartender nods, then leaves to get his drink.

"Which one of you guys knows Julia the best?"

I study him, wondering why he's asking. "Depends on what you mean, I guess?"

The bartender sets down his beer, and Dan takes a few gulps.

"I'm wondering how she feels about public displays." He turns to me. "Is she for them or against them?"

I laugh. "Public displays? Do you mean like billboards? Because I have no idea where she stands on those."

He laughs. "You're funny. No, I mean public displays of affection."

I grab my beer only to discover it's empty. Guess I drank it fast once Dan sat down. "Are you asking if she'll slap you if you kiss her in front of everyone?"

He frowns. "I'm not being very clear, am I?"

I shake my head.

He leans closer. "I'm going to propose to her, and I plan to do it at the station."

Propose? So soon? "You haven't been dating long. Isn't that a bit fast?"

His eyes find Julia as he smiles. "When you know, you

know." Then he turns back to me. "What do you think of my station idea?"

It sucks. It's not romantic, and she'll hate it. "I don't know. Maybe you should ask Rover's girlfriend, Connie."

He slaps my arm. "That's a great idea! Thank you." He leaves and walks toward the group. When he reaches Julia, he picks her up and twirls her around.

"Hey, can I get three shots?" I ask the bartender.

"Sure." He lines them up, and I drink them down.

I'm sure I'll regret this tomorrow, but right now, I don't want to think about how I waited too long and now she's going to marry that douche.

Since I rarely drink, the alcohol hits me fast. But I like it; it's numbing the pain.

"Fox?"

I turn to find Julia standing next to me.

"Are you all right?"

I nod.

She stares at me. "Did Dan say something to upset you?"

I laugh because she's perceptive, but I can't tell her the truth. "Why would you think that?"

She glances back in his direction. He's talking to Connie. "You looked angry when he was talking. Then he left, and you ordered shots."

I turn to her and lean a little closer than necessary. "You keeping an eye on me?"

She shivers, and I can't help but want it to be because she has some feelings for me. I lean back up. What the hell am I doing? I don't hit on women with boyfriends.

"I happen to be looking over, and I noticed. That's all. So, what did he say?"

I keep my eyes on the bartender, willing him to walk back to this side of the bar. "We just talked about the weather."

She crosses her arms. "The weather?"

I nod. "Yeah, I'm not happy that it's supposed to rain for the next three days."

She rolls her eyes. "Fox, it always rains here."

"Julia!" Dan calls out.

I glance over, and he's waving his hand, signaling her to return.

"I better go. Hope you can get over that rain."

I sigh. "Doubt it."

She opens her mouth, but whatever she was going to say, she decides against it. She taps the bar, then walks back to her boyfriend.

The bartender finally returns.

"Three more shots, please."

He stares at me for a moment, and since I appear sober enough, he doesn't question it. Once they are on the bar, I drink them down. Then I walk over to the guys.

"Coff, welcome to the team."

He smiles. "Thanks. Glad this all worked out."

"One thing I want to know," Cody says. "When I started, I got the smallest office and was told it was because I was the newest. But Coff here has an office that's double the size of mine. What gives?"

CT whispers something into his ear. "Oh, that makes sense. I guess."

I turn and catch the moment Dan leans down and kisses Julia. All I see is red, and I want to pull them apart. Instead, I turn without saying a word and walk out of the bar.

Or more like I stumble out of it. I can't believe he's going to propose so soon. While I don't hang out with Julia as much as I used to, we still go to the gun range every few weeks. She never mentions Dan, so I didn't think they were that serious. I want to punch something, but instead, once I'm a block away, I yell. "Fuck!"

"Hey, I've been looking for you," a familiar voice says.

I turn and am staring into the face of a man I tried to kill. He kidnapped Julia last year. Fortunately, I was able to stop his plane before he flew her out of the country.

"Doogan. How did you get out of jail?" I'm slurring, and based on the man's smile, he knows I'm drunk.

That's when I notice two other men standing off to the side.

"It doesn't matter. What matters is I found you."

The two guys step closer, and I brace myself, ready to take them.

"Why were you looking for me?" I ask.

Doogan sneers. "That plane you destroyed wasn't mine."

Okay, so when I said I stopped his plane, what I really meant was I blew it up. Unfortunately, Doogan wasn't standing close enough to the plane when it happened.

"And now I owe a very powerful man a lot of money. That makes me very angry."

The alcohol is kicking in fast now, and I'm pretty sure

I'm swaying. The two men are starting to look more like four men.

"You should be angry with yourself," I say. "You put yourself in that situation."

"Just as you have put yourself here," he responds.

The two men move fast. Even though I see the first guy's fist coming, I move too slowly to block it in time, and he hits my face. I jerk back and hit the second guy in the stomach, but not before another fist comes at my face. Dammit, it's like I'm moving in slow motion.

"Finish him!" Doogan demands.

Then a sharp pain erupts in my stomach. I glance down, and my shirt is covered in blood. Dropping to my knees, I look up at the guys. One is holding a knife. I press on my stomach as I go down, face first, into a puddle.

I reach into my pocket for my phone. It's not there. It's in my jacket. I reach for it, but I'm not wearing my jacket. It must be at the bar.

My lids grow heavy. I need to get up and get back to the bar. But I can't move. I'm too heavy. Finally, I close my eyes and hope one of the guys realizes I'm missing before it's too late.

***

Want to find out what happens to Fox? Check out *Securing Julia*.

OTHER BOOKS BY DANIELLE PAYS

Reed Hawthorne Security series
Thunder (Lars and Madison)
Lightning (Paxton and Alicia)
Coff (Logan and Delaney)
Ozzie (Ozzie and Piper)

∼

Morgan Thompson Security series
Defending Sarina (Maverick and Sarina)
Shielding Connie (Dax and Connie)
Rescuing Cara (Grayson and Cara)
Securing Julia (Fox and Julia) Coming September 2023

∼

The *Dare to Surrender* series
Chasing Her Trust
Taking Her Chase
Saving Her Target
Trusting Her Hero
Captivated

Embracing Her One

∽

The *Dare to Risk* series

Deceived

Pursued

Played

Consumed (Josh Morgan and Shaw)

Tangled

ABOUT THE AUTHOR

Danielle Pays writes steamy romantic suspense with twists you won't see coming. She enjoys romance as well as mystery and suspense and blends them both using her beloved Pacific Northwest for inspiration with its mix of small towns and cities.

When she's not writing her characters into some kind of trouble, she can be found binging Netflix shows, trying to convince her children to eat her cooking, or playing with her puppy.

Follow her at www.daniellepays.com or on Facebook at https://www.facebook.com/daniellepays/

Printed in Great Britain
by Amazon